WHEN THE HARVEST COMES

WHEN THE HARVEST COMES

A Novel

DENNE MICHELE NORRIS

RANDOM HOUSE

NEW YORK

Random House
An imprint and division of Penguin Random House LLC
1745 Broadway, New York, NY 10019
randomhousebooks.com
penguinrandomhouse.com

Published in the United States by Random House, an imprint and division of Penguin Random House LLC, New York.

RANDOM HOUSE and the HOUSE colophon are registered trademarks of Penguin Random House LLC.

Parts of Book One appeared originally in *Apogee Journal,* issue 7, titled "The Reverend," and in *American Short Fiction,* issue 72, titled "Audition."

Hardback ISBN 9780593729601
Ebook ISBN 9780593729618

Printed in the United States of America on acid-free paper

9 8 7 6 5 4 3 2 1

First Edition

Book design by Caroline Cunningham

The authorized representative in the EU for product
safety and compliance is Penguin Random House Ireland,
Morrison Chambers, 32 Nassau Street, Dublin D02 YH68, Ireland,
https://eu-contact.penguin.ie.

For my father, Rev. Dr. Dennis Earl Norris

The end of the road is so far ahead
it is already behind us.

Don't worry. Your father is only your father
until one of you forgets.

—Ocean Vuong, "Someday I'll Love Ocean Vuong"

I needed to be alone so that he could come back.

—Joan Didion, *The Year of Magical Thinking*

BOOK ONE

ONE

Davis Josiah Freeman is perfectly safe.

He lies flat on his back, legs spread, ankles in the air, sweating from the heat of Everett's body on top of his. He revels in Everett's power—the strength of his arms, the hardness of his chest, and the tuft of dark hair that fans out from his navel. Davis loves the softness of that hair against the hardness of Everett's body, like a window through which he could almost touch Everett's soul.

Davis aches when Everett pushes deeper; he whimpers, then opens. He would be willingly consumed by Everett, swallowed whole, if it were possible. He places one hand on Everett's chest, the other gently on his neck, and pulls him down. Eyes meeting eyes, lips parting for lips. When Everett is inside him, Davis becomes another thing, a being both powerful and delicate, animal yet celestial. Everett is uncomplicated in his manliness: the depth of his voice, his penchant for bourbon and stout, the sheer size of him—both height and broadness. He becomes beastly during sex, and with any other man, it would scare Davis. But with Everett, he need not be fearful. Davis looks up at the way Everett's eyes have gone slack, almost milky white—his pupils having rolled to the back of his head.

In some ways Davis envies Everett this existence: moving through the world with the easy confidence of a man who is always in charge, always sure of himself. He is passionate and unafraid of a fight. Davis knows that with Everett by his side, he gets to live a particular kind of freedom. He can be silly. He can be naïve. He can have a tank full of sugar, as he'd once heard the Reverend say.

Davis can do this because he is loved and desired, which means he is protected.

His breath catches when Everett takes his wrists, pulls them up over his head, and brings them together, binding him to the bed. Everett lowers his chest until their torsos meet. He buries his lips in Davis's neck, breathing in the perfume with which Davis carefully dabbed himself that evening. He nibbles, Davis moans, and Everett thrusts deeper, rougher, his body now slapping hard against Davis, who shudders, then whimpers again, his voice turning up on the final syllable as though the name—Everett—is a discovery, both question and answer. He arches his back, opening himself more fully. Everett peers into his eyes, then spits into his mouth. Davis feels his flesh come alive; the tips of his fingers burn—trees turned to ash. Everett is anywhere, everywhere, his presence heard and felt with the matter-of-factness of air, trees, and water.

He fills Davis, and he fills the room.

With every movement more frenzied than the last, he drives Davis to bite his bottom lip, to clench the sheets. Davis convulses, and when he comes, fingernails digging into Everett's back, he considers this: He could not escape this man if he needed to. He is not strong enough to fight Everett off, not quick enough to move from underneath him. He loves the vulnerability of this, the theoretical danger in their union. He thinks, all the time, of that vulnerability—in a way it turns him on. It's an illusion, of course. Everett would never harm him. But he loves it nonetheless, and he knows Everett loves it, too.

IN TWENTY-FOUR HOURS, they will be married.

Davis wants to stay right where he is; he wants to remain under Everett, held by Everett for as long as possible. He wants to revolve around this beastly man like he is the sun. After Everett comes—groaning, panting, the hair on his body slick with sweat—he lowers himself down to the bed, arms encircling Davis, lips breathing warm air along Davis's neck, where he rests.

"Stay inside me," Davis whispers. His voice is shaky, his body still trembling. He closes his eyes and turns to his side. Everett nods and continues kissing his neck and shoulder. He loves the way Davis fits so easily in his arms—body short and slight, golden skin soft and clean, and so damn pretty. He runs a hand up and down Davis's leg.

"You were tossing and turning in your sleep." Everett looks down at Davis. He knows not to ask too explicitly. Davis has a lot of pride. He lets Everett in when he's ready, and not a moment sooner.

"I'm sorry. Did I wake you?" Davis runs his fingertips along Everett's arm, his breath silent. Everett kisses him again, then shakes his head.

"I'm used to it." He pauses, listening as waves lap the shore. "But you kept saying something I've never heard you say. 'Sunny Boy. Sunny Boy.'"

Davis brings Everett's hand to his mouth. "He called me that." He kisses the pads of Everett's fingers.

"Who?" Everett holds Davis tighter.

"He used to say I slipped out easy like I was covered in Crisco on the sunniest day of the year."

"Your father," Everett says.

"The Reverend." Davis rolls his eyes. "It was a lie, you know."

Everett feels a chill move between them.

Davis gazes through the open window, the curtain blowing in the paltry autumn breeze. "I hated him calling me that. My mom almost died because of me."

"It wasn't because of you," Everett says.

Davis shrugs, then turns over, facing Everett. "I should call you Sunny Boy." He sits up, planting both hands on Everett's cheeks. "You're like a planet. My gravitational pull. I couldn't get away if I tried." He lays down again, resettling into Everett's arms.

"Do you wish he was coming to the wedding?" Everett holds Davis tighter, their bodies fully flush against each other.

What Davis wishes for is the ability to make himself even smaller, daintier. "If I'd wanted him to come to the wedding, I would've invited him."

Everett brushes his nose along Davis's neck, his voice a whisper. "It seems like you were dreaming about him, Davis."

"Well, I don't remember it. You're the one who brought it up."

Davis looks out through the window upon the Montauk beach as earthbound snowflakes, glittering pink and white, slowly make their way. They won't last; most won't even reach the ground, merely dancing in the sparkling moonlit sky. Davis wraps Everett's hand in both of his, holding it tight to his body. He tries to match his breathing to the rise and fall of Everett's chest.

Two

Someone will come. Sirens will sound in the distance. Lights will rise from darkness like seraphs, dancing red and blue. Salvation will be brought by men sent from God. These men will come from the east. There is a campus not too far in that direction, a satellite of the state university. They will move as quickly as possible along the highway, over black ice, close to the barrier that divides east and west.

Tread marks will lead them to an indentation in the guardrail, scratched with white paint. The men will jump down from their trucks, rubber boots clomping to the pavement. One of them will wonder aloud how that white car got all the way down the hill by the quarry. "You can hardly see it," he will say, his hand at attention. His eyes will strain under the swirling clouds that block the moon, that mute the stars. Another, braver man will lead them over the guardrail. They'll follow the path cut by the car as it flipped, landing on its caved-in roof.

The Reverend remains strapped in his seat, upside down, his nose inches from the ground, unable to move. His Toyota crashed into a tree with such might that several elderly branches, heaving from the weight of the snow, sought relief. They broke from the trunk, tumbled through the air, and landed on the overturned car. Periodically it creaks, warning him. At some point the car will give under the excess weight. But by then the Reverend will be saved. The men will have come and gone and in between, ripped him free.

They will come shouting into their walkie-talkies, demanding backup, cursing, not caring if their words offend him. The glare from their flashlights will find him, then blind him. Someone will shout for the men at the top of the hill to aim their headlights at the quarry, give them some light. The Toyota's lights will be extinguished by then, the battery having died. Once there is light, the Reverend will see how the snow has frozen beneath him, how the windows have shattered, how the car he gave his sixteen-year-old son nine years ago crumpled around him as though it were nothing more than a toy, a Matchbox model like the ones Davis used to play with.

The youngest, newest trooper will kneel as close to the car as possible. He will extend his arm through the broken window, shining his flashlight into the Reverend's face, then up and down his body.

"Are you hurt?" he will ask.

"Davis?" the Reverend will ask the man. "Is that you?"

"Sir, are you hurt? Can you move?" The trooper's voice will ring with easy authority over more sirens sounding in the distance, coming their way. Over the chatter of the Reverend's teeth, for by this time he will be delirious and so cold that his words will be nearly unintelligible.

The Reverend will try to turn his head until he can see the trooper's eyes. He will try, but he will fail. He will know that the trooper's voice is not his son's voice, the trooper's hands—large, pale, and strong—are not his son's hands. He will wonder if these are the hands that will keep him alive, bring him to safety. He will wonder if safety is what Davis sees in That Man, the white man, the one he plans to marry. He will wonder if Davis ever saw this thing in him.

"Sir, don't worry. We're going to get you out of here."

"I need to see my son," he will say.

"Everything is going to be fine."

"Sunny Boy," he will say.

"Your son isn't here. He's safe. It's only you in the car." The trooper will consider the fact that he, too, would be thinking of his son if it were him trapped in that seat, hanging upside down, waiting for help to come. With his free arm he will slowly reach his hand through the broken window until he can gently press his palm against the driver's shoulder. He will do his best to look the driver in the eye. "Sir, we're going to get you out of here."

THREE

Between the comforter and Everett's body wrapped around his, Davis is plenty warm. He pushes himself up, watching Everett's arm fall from around him. He shifts from his side, rises, and tiptoes to the window. He looks out at the water. The house is well insulated, but if he tilts his chin and turns his head just so, he can hear the ocean: waves washing up, washing down, the tide lingering at its crest before rolling lazily back. The world—still dark, still quiet—belongs to him, and all the feelings he carries into their wedding day.

Davis moves through the master suite, opening the door to the hallway, where despite his best effort, he wakes Bam-Bam, Everett's golden retriever, who follows him to the kitchen. He opens the freezer, pulls out a stainless steel tumbler, and fills it with ice, then water. Standing by the counter, he starts chugging. He is overwhelmed by his joy, his body shaky, his breath shallow and quick. But there's something about drinking an excruciatingly cold glass of water that fortifies Davis; it seems to bring him back to earth. He can't believe this day is here! He grips the edge of the counter, tries to flatten the soles of his feet against the tile floor. Anything to keep his body in the moment, which he suspects will help tether his mind.

Davis is wildly, indescribably, incandescently in love. Certainly, Everett is the kind of man Davis dreamed of—charming, success-ful, and passionate amid any number of additional easy-to-spot qualities. But those traits, Davis thinks, are not the reason for the love. Davis loves Everett because he *knows* Everett. Everett is a knowable man, perhaps the first he's encountered. Everett is the exact opposite of the Reverend, and the most vital thing Davis knows about Everett is his innate goodness.

It felt like a dream come true when Everett's parents offered the Montauk house as a wedding venue. Davis knows the Caldwells are fond of him, but despite Everett's insistence that they love him, Davis has never quite believed it. Getting married in their beach-side Hamptons house, a home filled with decades of memories, is a welcome that Davis never expected, and can never repay. All he can think, as he looks around the kitchen, as he peers through the sliding glass doors toward the beach, as he refills the tumbler with water, is that now he is part of this family. He gets to make memo-ries here, too.

"Come on, boy!" Davis says, gesturing for Bam-Bam to follow him back upstairs. He's so excited he can't sleep, but what he can do is run scales and arpeggios while he has some time before Everett wakes up. He runs them every day, and even though he'd promised Everett he wouldn't practice the viola this week, he's done them every morning. When they arrived, he commandeered one of the smaller guest bedrooms so he could slip away, unnoticed, for short bouts of practice. When he opens the door, he pauses as Bam-Bam looks between him and the master suite. Davis smiles, bends down, pets Bam-Bam, and gestures for the dog to follow him inside, but Bam-Bam trots back to his post at the door to the master suite, plops down, and wags his tail before closing his eyes.

"Smart. You've got a big day ahead of you," he says to Bam-Bam, winking, before he quietly shuts the door.

He opens the case, pulls out the viola, and places his ebony practice mute on the bridge.

After he tunes, he begins with open strings, taking the opportunity to feel the knuckles on his right—his bowing hand—contract and extend. There's tension in his shoulders, so he breathes deep, letting them sit where they fall naturally. He pulls the bow along the C string, fully extending his arm until the bow comes to a stop at the tip. He brings the bow back to the frog, and then he repeats the same two long strokes on the other strings. Although the volume is muted, there's still richness, fullness, in the tone. Next is a round of three-octave major and minor scales, to get his left hand warmed up. Davis was trained in the Galamian method—the beginning of each scale has an extra turn for intonation and finger precision. With each scale, he uses a different bow stroke, tries a new rhythm—from legato to staccato, from quarter notes to triplets.

For Davis, scales and arpeggios are like daily meditation. He can quiet his mind, turn his attention to observing, which is different from thinking. The stillness of his body, contrasted with the quick dexterity of his fingers, has a way of calming him, bringing steadiness. Davis had tried explaining this on their second date. Everett, who'd worn a deep blue button-down, tucked neatly into gray flatfront slacks, had laughed at the thought of playing scales every day. "Don't you get bored of them?"

A question that normally might've hurt or offended Davis, instead, amused him.

He doesn't know the way his eyes glinted, having caught an errant ray from the restaurant's lighting. He doesn't know how his sudden smile, joyful yet slightly condescending, managed to capture the most tender sort of happiness that Everett had ever seen. What Davis does know, what he remembers, is how quickly he shook his head, how he leaned forward and really looked Everett in the eye. His boldness in that moment still delights him. He almost knocked his fork to the ground as he tried to explain the joy of scales, the beauty in setting aside time every day to go back to the beginning, to lose yourself in rote practice.

"Think of it like this. On a playground you've got your slide, your tire swing, your seesaw, your jungle gym. They're bolted to the ground; they never move. One day, I slide down the slide, then I run over to the tire swing, sit on top of it, and swing around in big lopsided circles. Then I climb into the jungle gym where I crawl through the yellow plastic tube, but not the red plastic tube with the right angle, because I want to climb down the mini ropes course, and the red tube doesn't lead to that. Then I'll run over to the see-saw and ride that with my friend. The next day I'll start with the tire swing, but I'll turn it sideways so I can slide my legs through the hole in the middle and spin round and round like a top, rather than sitting on top of it swinging in lopsided circles. And then I'll go to the seesaw, but this time I'll sit on the other side so I can face the street instead of the school parking lot. I'll chase my friend up the giant slide, because I'm not feeling gravity that day, and when I end at the jungle gym, I'll climb up the ropes course and walk the plank backward until I end up in the pirate's quarters. That's where I can steer the ship and look out over the rest of the playground. Do you see what I'm getting at?"

Before Everett could respond, Davis kept going. "Every day, I have to play on that playground because it's the only playground my school has. That's the equipment; that's what I've got. But am I running around solo or is it a giant game of TV tag? Am I running up the slide or sliding down it? Everything about how I use the playground is completely up to me. Nobody gets to tell me what to do! In the constraints, in the limitations of the playground, I find my freedom. Scales and arpeggios are the same way. I know the notes and they never change, so I have to get creative. Do I slur my F-minor three-octave scale in triplets going up, and staccato in square eighth notes going down? Am I solo pianissimo in my A-minor arpeggio today, or am I mezzo forte? Do I spiccato the bow in G-major because it's a joyful key, and then go legato and molto adagio in F-minor because it's dramatic and I'm playing Brahms in a recital that night?" Davis sat back then, noticing that Everett's eyes had never strayed from his. "It's very different from when I'm learning a piece, Everett. Scales and arpeggios? That's the playground. That's where I get to run and play and jump and be free."

"Wow," Everett said. "You really took that metaphor and ran with it."

Davis smiled and shrugged, suddenly bashful. "Did I?"

Everett narrowed his eyes, but he smiled, too, as he did it. "You've said all that before."

Davis laughed. "Swear to God, I came up with that on the spot!"

Davis watched Everett watching him as he crossed his legs, sat back, and brought his martini to his lips. They nearly closed the restaurant, and when the check came, and Davis reached for it, and Everett reached faster, Davis said, "But I asked you out." And Everett, with his big green eyes, glanced up as he pulled a credit card from his wallet and said nothing. When Davis started to pull his own credit card from his satchel, Everett, still staring—the movement barely perceptible—shook his head. Davis felt compelled to set the satchel down, and when he did, Everett smiled.

Only then did Davis glance at his dessert plate, which still held a few bites of cinnamon apple pie. "I don't even like pie, but this is so, so good." He sliced himself a small bite, speared it with his fork, and ate it. Then he looked at Everett again. "You seem like a man of few words." He sliced another bite.

"Why do you say that?" There was something mysterious in Everett's voice.

"You've been so quiet tonight."

The waiter came and silently collected the check and the credit card. All the while, Everett's gaze went uninterrupted. "That's more about you than it is about me."

"Are you saying I talk too much?" Davis narrowed his eyes.

Everett grinned. "No, not at all."

When Davis said nothing, Everett continued. "I like how much

you talk. I like your voice." He tilted his head to the side. "So I listen. But I promise I'm not"—he made air quotes—"'a man of few
words.'" He blinked. "I'm just a man." And then, after another few
moments of silence: "Why? What are you thinking about?"

"Huh." Davis closed his eyes and bit his lip. "I was just . . ." He
paused, pensive. "I don't think I know what that feels like."

"What what feels like?"

The waiter returned, handing Everett the receipt and his credit
card, smiling at them both, thanking one, then the other. Through
all of this, Everett never moved his gaze from Davis.

Davis leaned in close as Everett picked up the pen. "To be like
'I'm just a man.' What does that feel like?"

Everett shrugged and furrowed his brow. He glanced down to
sign the check. "It doesn't feel like anything, really. It's just . . . I
don't know, it just is."

FOUR

Most mornings Everett rises first. Everett is the one who paces through the apartment, making coffee, opening the blinds, turning on the TV for a bit of news before grabbing his gym bag or heading out for a run. Most mornings Everett does this while Davis sleeps; waking and rising, watching as Davis immediately curls into a ball, as if on cue, hugging his knees to his chest and burrowing deeper into the blankets. He loves this about Davis—the way in which he sleeps, small and heavy, his body never wanting to be without Everett's body beside it. Every day, even in slumber, Davis lets Everett know how much he is needed.

He wakes now, opens his eyes. The bed feels light beside him. He turns; Davis isn't there. He coughs, sits up, scratches his head. There it is—the slow, mournful strain of the viola, wafting through the house, down the hall, into his ears. He smiles—of course Davis is going to practice. Everett rises and pulls on a pair of sweatpants. He wants to see Davis, but Davis has asked that they stay apart until that afternoon. He's excited for their First Look, having enthusiastically thrown himself into the traditions of their big day. Davis probably hasn't made himself coffee, so Everett will make a pot. He glances down at his watch on the bedside table: They have an hour, maybe two, before the house bustles with vendors and family— Everett's family, anyway.

Anticipation surges through him. Today is a big day, certainly— Davis's excitement for their wedding is palpable. But for Everett, it's not about today. There was a time when Everett thought he'd never marry again, but those years feel distant, a husk of a memory. He's been around the block enough to know that it's not about the wedding day. It's about tomorrow, and the next day, and the day after that. It's about the privilege of having Davis by his side for all the tomorrows coming down the line. Everett knows that everyone takes it for granted that he is strong, the rock in this relationship; but they don't see how calm, how steady, how self-assured Davis is. How his mere presence is enough to quell any rumble of self-doubt that lingers in Everett's subconscious.

He opens the bedroom door, moving quickly, almost tripping over Bam-Bam, who, not allowed to sleep in the master bedroom of his family's beach house, is splayed against the door in the hallway. Everett stops for a moment, bends down to pet the golden retriever, looks into his eyes, bright as they were twelve years ago when he was a pup. Bam-Bam, awake, ears perked at the music coming from down the hall, lifts his pupils, wags his tail, and blinks.

"I'm getting married today, buddy!" At the sound of Everett's voice, then his bare feet moving down the hall, Bam-Bam starts, rises, scampering behind his master.

The house is too warm for Everett, but he keeps the heat high for Davis, who generally runs cold. In the kitchen, Everett pours himself a glass of water and starts the coffee maker. He listens to the machine heat the water, sputter and drip the dark liquid, the noise an approximation for his excitement, which he feels like a quiet, persistent thrum. Beyond the kitchen is a small back patio made of stone. It's been cleared for later, for the bar, but there is plenty of room. He opens the glass door, impeccably clean, and waves at Bam-Bam to join him outside, where he runs in circles in the sand, while Everett crouches to his knees. Push-ups—one hundred of them. Quick, efficient: all the way down, elbows bent at ninety degrees, then up just as quickly, elbows straight, fingers balled into fists. After twenty-five he crosses his legs; at fifty he uncrosses them and lifts his left arm, bending it behind his back; at seventy-five he switches, lifting and bending his right. His eyes focus on the stone underneath him; they watch as the tiny golden cross at the bottom of his thin golden chain falls flat against the stone with each descent before he pushes up again. Rising to his feet, standing at his full height, barely breathing any harder than he was before, he feels himself settle into his body, into his legs, into his stance as he gulps down the water, watching as the tide falls high onto the shore, then slowly recedes, in and out, in and out, the sound washing over him. In minutes the world brightens, and by the time he walks back inside, just as the coffee maker has released a full pot, the kitchen feels drenched in sunlight.

He opens a cabinet, intending to pull down two mugs, when Davis bounds into the kitchen.

"Everett!"

Before he can think, his arms are encircling Davis, who has jumped into them. Legs around Everett's waist, arms around Everett's neck, Davis kisses Everett, his lips tender, soft, sweet. Oh, how he loves this boy!

Everett smiles first. "I thought you wanted to wait until the First Look."

Davis shrugs. "I had to see you."

Davis brings his nose to Everett's nose. His eyes, brown, are wide and generous, and filled with love. He kisses Everett again. "Thank you."

Everett peers straight into Davis's eyes. "For what?" His arms are under Davis, supporting him. He brushes his thumbs against Davis's thighs.

"For being there last night. For being here now." Davis's voice breaks. He laughs, suddenly shy. "This is so stupid. I'm sorry."

"It's not stupid." Everett shakes his head.

"You were right last night. I was thinking about the Reverend, and Olivia, and how I don't have any family here today." He pauses, sniffling. "And my mom. I was thinking about how much I miss my mom."

"Of course you were. Why wouldn't you be thinking about all of that?"

"I wish she could meet you. I think she would like you." As Davis smiles, his eyes begin to water. It surprises Everett, this rare, bald-faced display of emotion. With his right hand, he moves his thumb to Davis's cheek.

"Hey," he says, his voice gentle. "She would be so proud of you. She wouldn't want you crying on your wedding day." He wipes away a single fallen tear and brings his forehead close to Davis's. "Only happy tears, okay?"

Davis nods, kisses him again. When he jumps down, all smiles and brightness, he runs his hands up Everett's chest, his eyes serious, his voice barely more than a whisper. "I can't wait to marry you." In an instant, he's gone, back upstairs and preparing for the day. In time, the house will flurry with family members, friends, and vendors, all there to make sure the wedding is successful. But for a few more minutes, it's only for them.

As Everett sips his coffee, as he turns to face the shore, he thinks back to a year ago. The memory is sticky, not all of it easily returning to him. Davis, onstage in Seattle, the two of them had been flown out last minute so he could substitute for a world-famous soloist, stricken with a sudden flu in San Francisco. The performance was a roaring success; a standing ovation, a satisfied smile and a few tears dotting his cheeks as Davis stood and bowed, then acknowledged the orchestra, then hugged the guest conductor, a woman with whom he'd gone to music camp in high school. Then the high-donor reception, Everett wearing Hugo Boss and standing by Davis's side, prosecco in one hand, the other lightly but steadily placed against the small of Davis's back—nothing more than extra assurance, a touch of protection and possession—as patrons lined up to shake this new star's hand, to ask him about the concerto, his teachers, his years at Juilliard. To gift him their well-wishes for the bright and prosperous career that was surely ahead of him. To tell him how important he was, how he was reshaping the face of classical music and, as one audience member put it, "shocking these old opera queens so far out of their chairs they land outside the closet they didn't know they were in."

Then there was the middle-aged white woman who almost tried to touch his hair, her eyes roving over his body and only once meeting his. "Have you always known?"

Davis blinked, his expression blank for a moment. The smile came after his words. "That I wanted to be a musician? Yes, absolutely."

She could've left it at that, should've left it at that, but of course that wasn't the choice she made. "No, that you were . . . that you . . ." She gestured at his sparkly, blush-colored, backless jumpsuit.

Davis never stopped looking her in the eyes. He lightly touched her forearm, then leaned back. "Oh, you mean have I always known that I was meant to wear couture?" He laughed, curtsied, and then said with a perfectly straight face, "Of course! Always."

The woman laughed, then hugged him, patted him on the arm, and said, "Well, you've certainly chosen the right career!"

Then later that night, together in their hotel room, the fire dying, the curtains open, the view overlooking Puget Sound as Everett turned Davis to face him, spread Davis's legs over his, and entered him. They had been going at it for a while now, at this point moving with the grace of one body. Their eyes met, then their lips, Everett fucking him slowly, each stroke moving deeper until he touched Davis's core, until Davis could mute himself no longer. Everett kissed Davis just below his earlobe, then nibbled, then uttered two simple words. "Marry me." No thought, no planning, no pretense, something he'd been wanting to say, to do, but in this moment, his words—these words—a spontaneous whisper. His face was somber, his intent genuine, eyes like bullets that pierced Davis all over. Everett was not a man to play games, not ever, and Davis knew this.

Davis bit his lip, tightened the arm that was draped across Everett's shoulders. He tensed his fingers against Everett's back. He moaned as Everett went deeper. He threw his head back as he bounced his buttocks on top of Everett's thighs. Then Everett went slower, deeper, and Davis dug his fingernails into Everett's shoulder, the sound coming from him low, guttural, like an engine revving up to speed. Again, Davis bit his lip, nodded, then smiled, then laughed, then—twice!—he said, "Yes." He lingered on the *s*. "I will marry you."

Everett can still hear that *yes*, conjures it anytime he wants—both the memory of it and, with a few flicks of his hips or his tongue or his fingers, the real thing, from Davis in real time.

His phone buzzes when a text lights up the screen. Everett's twin brother, Connor. *Be there in 10. Dad and Caleb close behind.*

Everett remembers that Davis never grabbed a cup of coffee. Quickly, he makes one, pouring the coffee into an oversize mug over some half-and-half. He spoons a dash of sugar into the mug as well, still hot, still steaming, and brings it to the master suite, where Davis will be getting ready for the wedding.

He knocks. "Babe, I'm going on a run with the guys. Can you grab a T-shirt for me? I brought you a coffee!"

He waits by the door; seconds later, it opens just a tad, Davis shoving first his arm through the opening, and then his face. Everett swipes the tee, then kisses him one more time, a peck. "For good luck!"

"For the wedding?"

"For my run! You know how the Caldwells get."

Everett smiles to himself as he pulls the T-shirt over his head, bounces down the stairs, and slides his feet into his running shoes. He's still thinking about Davis coming into the room like a Tasmanian devil. It will be a wild ride, their life together; he's ready for this, ready to get it under way.

FIVE

Davis listens as Everett retreats down the hall, his footsteps receding into the distance. He moves to the window, watching as Everett bounds from the front door into the commotion of his brothers and father. He touches his fingers to his lips, watching as they envelop Everett. The Caldwell men are enthusiastic; any greeting with them includes a bear hug and a heavy-handed thump on the back. Though he can't make out anything they say, Davis hears the clamor of their voices, then their bodies as they take off running. He backs away from the window after a few seconds, grateful that he wasn't spotted.

Davis loves watching them greet Everett. Their joy, their love is infectious; he wants to breathe it in, wrap it around himself. And yet it's also punctuated with a sense of loss felt somewhere in his own chest, a sharp, momentary tightening. Davis isn't greeted by them in the same way, hasn't been since his first visit when he was entirely overwhelmed at the bigness of their affection, and Everett, in a moment of deep perception, found the words to kindly ask them to tone it down a few notches for Davis, who was new to all of them, and who didn't come from a family like theirs.

Davis holds his coffee mug close to his nose in both hands. He wants to feel the steam rising to his skin. There's a particular waterfront restaurant—the Marina—where the Caldwell men will have breakfast before any other customers arrive. There's a booth they love that will almost certainly be free. They'll sit, they'll talk, they'll eat, they'll laugh, and though Davis wonders what goes on at these breakfasts every time he accompanies Everett to Montauk, and though he is always invited to join, he never does. Neither does Charlotte, Everett's mother, nor Courtney, Everett's sister-in-law. It's understood that it's for the boys, and Davis's feeling—which he's never revealed to Everett, and which he doesn't mind because he has no interest in running—is that it's not for him.

Soon enough, his best friend Phoebe, whom they've hired as their photographer, will arrive; shortly after, so will their other best friend, Zora, to help with makeup and styling. They've known one another since the first day of freshman year at Juilliard. As far as Davis is concerned, other than Everett, they're his family. Phoebe insists on taking pictures of him getting ready, but he wants to be showered and shaved by the time she arrives.

Standing in front of the mirror, he looks at his face. There is—around his lips, lining his jawbone, and covering his neck—the faintest stubble. He hates to look at it, to even acknowledge its existence; to do so feels like humoring some kind of optical illusion. He hates the darkness of the hair against the hue of his skin, hates how it sometimes curls underneath before puncturing the surface when it grows. Davis hates that regardless of how recently he's shaved, the beard shadow is incredibly easy to spot because his hair is so dark and so coarse. He hates how the new hair sometimes gets infected, never puncturing the skin at all, merely causing painful, ugly, pus-filled bumps all over the bottom half of his face. And of all things, he hates the amount of time and intention it takes for him to manage all of this if he wants to be clean-shaven and clear-skinned. Which, of course, he does.

Zora has taken the liberty of matching his skin tone with a foundation. As Davis looks in the mirror he can barely contain his excitement. What will it look like, he wonders, his face freed from any trace of unwanted hair? Zora has also promised to wax any strays, and to make his cheekbones pop.

In high school, it took a long time for him to grow facial hair. Davis made it well into his senior year without ever being asked to shave. Until one day it started coming in, and the only reprieve from the hatred he felt was that no one seemed to notice it. Not the Reverend, not Olivia, and not the teachers at school. He'll never forgive the boy, a blond baseball player named Cub—whose parents had purchased a brand-new Lexus SUV when he turned fifteen, and hired someone to drive him to and from school until he passed his driver's test—who pointed out to the dean of students that Davis wasn't shaving like the rest of them, and that he was therefore in violation of the dress code. He was given a demerit, returning the next day clean-shaven, his formerly flawless skin now covered in painful bumps barely concealing ingrown hairs all over the bottom half of his face.

But this is his wedding day, and by letting it grow out just a tad, he has timed it perfectly. He begins by washing his face, the running water and the fear of a bath offending Bam-Bam. Davis glances behind him as Bam-Bam runs for cover, crawling under the bed. "Sorry, friend. Your daddy likes me clean-shaven."

As soon as Davis says it, he hears the lie. Everett doesn't care if he sports facial hair or not; he couldn't care less. Everett thinks he's beautiful no matter what. It's him; it's Davis whose compulsion to look as young as possible, and as pretty, too, dictates so much of his life, causes him so much inner turmoil.

He turns on the shower, knowing it'll take a few minutes for the water to heat up. He begins by covering the bottom half of his face with shaving cream, scented with lavender and vanilla. It's thick, a true cream, meant to moisturize and soften the stubble before he shaves it. Davis massages it into his skin, enjoying the sharpness of the stubble against his fingertips and the feeling of blood flowing to the area. He loves the scent of the vanilla and the calming effect of the lavender. He closes his eyes, takes a deep breath, thinking back to a different mirror, and a different face.

SEVEN YEARS AGO.

He was soaked as he ran from his parked car with his backpack and viola into Olivia's building. It was a stone's throw away from the Cleveland Clinic back in the years when she was doing her residency. Charlie—the older doorman, friendly, with the bowl of butterscotch candies on his desk—didn't say anything when Davis arrived, just phoned up to Olivia's apartment to let her know her baby brother was on his way up. When he stepped off the elevator, she was poking her head through her front door, bonnet-adorned, nightgown-clad. With each step he admonished himself: *Don't cry, don't cry, don't be a fucking crybaby.* And then she hugged him, pulled him inside, and his tears fell. Her questions were constant.

What happened? Why are you here?

He hadn't wanted to make a scene.

Davis takes the blade, wets it, and begins to shave. From the bottom of his neck, he shaves upward until he reaches his chin. He fans out from the center, shaving up to the jawbone. For the hatred he feels toward his facial hair, the actual act of shaving feels nice, almost like a precise, incisive massage. He moves quickly, by now an expert at this. When he finishes with the neck, he takes a lighter touch to his cheeks, where his skin is more sensitive. As he shaves, his face transforms back to the face from that night so many years ago. His eyes are wider, brighter; his skin seems to catch the light. He can see his cheekbones. With every stroke of the blade, every flick of the wrist, the person he really is begins to peek through.

At first Davis was evasive when it came to his sister's questions. She fed him, made him some hot cocoa. She placed his bags on the bed in her second bedroom, handed him a plush towel, and sent him to the bathroom for a hot shower, all while asking again, "What happened? Why are you here?"

"Can't I just be here? You said I could come here anytime I needed to get away."

"I realize that as a teenager, you think attitude is your God-given right, but please check yours at my door. And yes, of course you can be here. Anytime."

"I don't want to talk about it!" He started the shower, turning the knob to the hottest it would go.

As the mirror began to fog, as he closed the door to the bathroom, her voice receding in the distance: We're not done with this!

He spent a great deal of time in the shower that night, running soap, several times, over every part of his body. He held his hair directly under the water, its heat managing to loosen his muscles. When he stepped out, the tile floor shooting cold through his feet, he felt better. He stood in front of her mirror studying his face, searching for answers that he already knew to questions that had already been asked.

When he opened the bathroom door, she was sitting at the foot of the bed.

"I have a headache," he said.

Olivia brought him some Tylenol and a glass of water, ice cold, just as he liked it. She sat in a chair in the corner and pointed to the floor in front of her. He sat with his back to her. She squirted some oil into her hands and began to massage his scalp.

"Are you being safe?" Immediately the conversation became clear to Davis. He sensed resolve in her voice.

"You called the Reverend."

"I needed to let him know where you were, and that you're safe."

He tried to turn his head to look at her. "Olivia? Does the Reverend have a drinking problem?" She kept her hands on the sides of his head, kept his face looking straight ahead. He felt it when she nodded.

"He's been sober for a long time, but yes. The Reverend is a recovering alcoholic."

"Why didn't anyone ever tell me?"

Olivia paused. "The only person who would've told you is me. And it hasn't been an issue in so many years that I honestly never thought to tell you. Other than one slipup, he stopped drinking before I was born."

"Well he got drunk tonight."

"I know. I could tell on the phone." For a few minutes she said nothing.

Davis tried to focus on the feeling of her fingers moving around his head, now kneading his scalp, applying pressure to his temples. "I've never seen him like that."

"I have," she said. "Once, sort of."

Davis nodded, not wanting to ask for any further details. "I'm being safe, Olivia. I promise." He felt her nod again.

"So you're gay?"

He smacked his lips, then nodded. "Yeah."

She leaned forward, bringing her body against his shoulder blades, her head close to his as she wrapped her arms around him. "Okay," she whispered. "As long as you're being safe." She sat back and continued massaging him, working her way up and over the crown of his head until her thumbs reached his hairline.

"Olivia?"

"Yes?"

"He told you about Jake."

"Yes, Davis. He did."

Davis felt his voice catch in his throat. "Did he tell you that he hit me?"

Olivia's hands, then massaging his face, stopped. "No."

"Well he did."

"Like what? He spanked you?"

Davis sighed. For a few seconds, everything was still. He listened to the light on the bedside table flickering, and the raindrops landing with authority against the roof of the apartment. "Yeah," he said. "He spanked me."

She pressed her first fingers along his hairline, and dragged them across his temples. "You can stay here as long as you like. You two probably need some time apart."

Sometimes Davis feels bad for not telling her the whole story. Sometimes he feels like a hero. His sister still has a relationship with their father because of him. In recent years it seems she and the Reverend have grown closer. Davis wonders if his new life in New York City, which doesn't much include her, has driven Olivia to rekindle her sense of family with the Reverend. He supposes he can't blame her for that—but he and the Reverend always seem to float past each other. If she moves closer to one of them, the other will inevitably step aside, getting out of the way. As Davis sees it, his life has led him elsewhere, in a different direction.

He hasn't set foot in that house since that night. He fled, took safe haven with Olivia until school ended, before running off to Vermont for a summer-long chamber music camp, then Juilliard directly from there for a bachelor's, a master's, and, as of this past June, his artist diploma.

All of it impresses upon him the weight of his journey to this moment. *This* is where he is. He gets to marry *this* man, be part of *this* family. He smiles; it's all about perspective, really. By now the water is warm. He taps the razor against the sink, rinses it off, and steps into the shower.

Six

When they run together, they move like a unit. The Caldwell men: feet pounding pavement, shoulders broad, spines tall, arms shifting back and forth opposite legs. Christopher leads always, father forging ahead, foremast holding steady. Connor and Everett run side by side in the middle, mainmast, tallest, broadest, the energy and axis of the Caldwell family. Twins in every sense, though fraternal: Everett is an inch taller, thirty-two minutes older, his skin a hair darker, eyes a soulful green and hair a deep brown. Still, Connor and Everett are more alike than different. College athletes, professional family men, strong and steady, calm of head and heart. Natural-born leaders, ambitious and charming. Caleb brings up the rear, the mizzenmast, the quintessential youngest son, unmarried, untethered—all the potential, none of the drive. Christopher has resigned himself to the fact that it will take longer with him.

Christopher has resigned himself to a lot of things. For one, his oldest boys are taller than him! And none of them will carry on his sandy blond hair. He is a retired U.S. Navy man; every year he sends his sons new sweatshirts boasting the seal. From day one he immersed his boys in sailing, from onesies patterned in sailboats and the United States Navy seal to owning and operating a sailboat of their very own. He took them sailing first one by one, and then, as they grew up, all together. It was important; he felt the structure of a ship was a metaphor for that of a family. Christopher was an exceedingly proud man, had moved into business following his years in the navy, then toward the end of his career, local politics. They are, of course, Democrats—of the Kennedy tradition.

He turns back, his boys only feet behind him. What a job he and Charlotte had done. Three boys, now three men. Two of whom understand their place in the world, a reflection of the family, the ever-present Caldwell name. A third who was working on it, but had, at least, managed to complete his BA. They are men through and through, capable and strong, holding up the spars and the rigging, supporting the sails flapping in the wind, just as he'd taught them. Keeping everything and everyone safe, on point. Afloat. Christopher Caldwell's dedication to the Navy is second only to his dedication to his family, though he'd fought and raged when Everett surprised them all twenty years ago by choosing Dartmouth over the Naval Academy.

Christopher hadn't spoken with his son for the entire first term; this despite Everett's immediate excellence, academic, athletic, and otherwise. It hadn't occurred to him in those days that a man could follow in his father's footsteps a little too closely. He turns back and glances at Everett—his oldest, tallest, sturdiest. Once Everett graduated, he enrolled in business school, met a nice, pretty girl named Danielle studying to be a teacher. He hadn't wanted any of his sons to marry so young as twenty-five, but Everett was forging his own path, and he seemed to love the girl. She was suitable and sweet. Her similarities to Davis ended at that particular brand of feminine sweetness, but Christopher couldn't help but chuckle: It seemed, for all the differences between Danielle and Davis, that his son did, in fact, have a type.

That marriage hadn't lasted long. Just under two years, the breakdown quiet, the conclusion nearly silent—damn near unnoticed by the Caldwells. A busy time in their collective lives—they were on the brink of a broken economy. And death: Christopher's mother, then Charlotte's father, seven weeks apart. Everett was quiet and moody through his divorce, odd behavior for him, but he was a man unused to failure of any kind. No one thought any more of it than that. The following summer, when Everett was the first to arrive at the Montauk house for their annual Fourth of July sojourn, he walked into the house like a man on a mission, like his old self, Bam-Bam trotting behind him and rushing right up to Charlotte. While the dog tried endlessly to jump up to her face, Everett poured himself and his father a bourbon on the rocks, and his mother a pinot gris, and sat them down on the rear patio.

"You look good, son," Christopher said, and they raised their glasses. Bam-Bam stood by the sliding glass door, his tail wagging steadily like a windshield wiper, *shwoop, shwoop, shwoop.*

"How're you holding up?" Charlotte took a sip of her wine and rested her chin in her palm, her elbow on the table.

Christopher remembers the way the smile spread across his son's face all the way up to his eyes. The way he laughed like he hadn't in years. He watched his son take a sip of his drink. "The divorce final yet?"

Everett nodded. "Yes."

"Good. You were fair to her?"

Everett laughed. "Yes, Dad." He paused. He glanced beyond his parents, out at the beach. A small family was walking close to the water, a mother and father holding hands behind their young daughter, who was squatting, scooping wet sand into an orange bucket. Christopher watched his son watching that child, and the easy way Everett raised his hand to that couple when they looked toward the house, before turning his attention back to them.

Everett leaned forward, looked them in the eye. He set his tumbler down; Christopher will never forget the sound of the glass landing solidly against the metal table. "You know, I've been seeing a therapist," Everett said. Christopher watched how his son's eyes moved between his parents, as though sizing them up before taking them out back for target practice. He felt the hair on his arms start to rise. He breathed in but did not breathe out.

"Okay," said Charlotte. She leaned back, her chair squeaking. "I suppose that's common in New York."

"It is. It's been really helpful. And . . ." He hesitated for a moment. "I've been thinking." He turned to his mother. "You know how you named me after Uncle Everett?"

"Your middle name," Christopher said, the surprise evident in his voice. What was his son getting at, bringing Charlotte's brother up out of the blue like that? He remembers how Charlotte sat back even farther in her chair, how she stuck a finger in her wine, swirled it a bit, her thin lips in a tight half-smile. She and Christopher glanced at each other.

"Yes, Dad. My middle name."

Christopher watched his son turn to his mother.

"I've started going by Everett. I'm not Carter anymore."

He stared intently into his mother's eyes for a moment, before looking again at Christopher. No one said anything—he and Charlotte just let their son's words sit there, breathing, taking up space like another person seated around the table, a presence invisible but important, nonetheless. Charlotte sat with one leg crossed over the other. She was a woman with a habit of bouncing her leg endlessly, and by this point her ballet flat had become loose, its fall to the ground punctuating the conversation. Christopher watched as his wife startled, looked at her shoe on the ground, shoved her foot back into it, and stood up.

"Well, honey, that's fine. That's just fine." She smiled, one of those half-hearted little things, and walked over to her son. She bent down and kissed his hair, and when he looked up at her, she kissed his forehead the same way she had back when he had been the little boy who played hard outside, who came into the house every day with scratches and bruises and always gritted his teeth and clenched his fists when she treated his cuts and scratches with peroxide.

"Turning over a new leaf. I think that's a sweet way to do it. Your uncle would be honored." She spoke with her cheek next to his, quietly, but not so quietly that Christopher didn't hear it. Then she returned to her seat and took a long gulp of her wine.

"Wait a minute, wait a minute!" Christopher remembers the way his hand hit the table hard, the way the liquid in their glasses danced, the way his son's car keys rolled over. He felt confused, unmoored, lost at sea. "Your name is Carter! That's a family name!"

"Yes, and my middle name is Everett. And that's a family name, too."

Christopher watched his son spread his legs, take a deep breath, clasp his hands. He felt the condescension as surely as the summer heat bearing down upon them. His son had known this moment was coming. His son had rehearsed this, probably with that blasted therapist.

Charlotte turned to her husband, voice low, eyes on the table. "Christopher, Everett is his name, too." She shook her head.

Christopher did his best to project calm. "Yes, Charlotte, I'm aware of that."

"Then you're also aware that our son is an adult."

He exhaled loudly. He pushed his chair back and stood up. He put his hands on his hips and started pacing the patio. He huffed. "What's this really about, Carter? What happened in your marriage?" He walked back over to the table, balled his fists, and leaned down, just inches from his son's face. "I don't want you going around telling everyone your name is Everett, telling everyone you're named after your uncle. I don't like it." He and Everett locked eyes. "Am I understood?" He was roaring now, anger coursing through his body as though it were a bomb only seconds from detonation.

It seemed that around them the world had gone silent, and they were invisible, their conflict like a bubble keeping at bay the view of the outside world. A name meant something to Christopher; the name Carter meant something to him! His grandfather's name was the first gift he had given his son. There was a lot of history in his names—both first and middle—that his son didn't know, and to trade a grandfather's name for an uncle's was dismissive, lacking all gratitude and respect. Though perhaps, it dawned on Christopher, there were things in his son's life that he didn't know about. He watched a battle rage in his son's eyes: First they hardened in anger, then they softened as though defeated. He knew his son, knew that Carter didn't rest for long, knew that he wouldn't accept his father's word as law.

He was not the kind of man to take it lying down.

And he looked as though he might cry. Christopher wouldn't have that. He wouldn't have it, and he damn sure wasn't going to watch it.

"Do what you want," he said. He backed away from his son, a man who seemed suddenly unrecognizable considering how small it was—in the grand scheme of things—to change one's name.

And in all of this, really, the only person whose feelings truly mattered to Christopher were Charlotte's. Charlotte who, in one swift motion, had risen to her feet, picked up her wine glass and thrown it against the wall of the house. Charlotte who shrieked at her own eruption and looked at Christopher now as though he were the devil himself. She grabbed him by the hand, leading him through the shattered glass into the house, leaving their son to stare at the wine dripping down the wall, sipping his bourbon, one eyebrow raised, one corner of his mouth lifted in a half-smile much like his mother's, as though utterly bemused by the whole thing.

Christopher turns around. They have slowed, are jogging for the moment. The Caldwell boys have aligned themselves in a row, Everett in the center, flanked by his brothers, his groomsmen in his first wedding. Even now, as grown men, they immediately quiet and look at their father, deferential, respectful, waiting for his command.

"Race you to the Marina," he says.

He continues to jog as his sons take off, quickly passing him, sweatshirts rippling in the wind, feet furious, once more, in their pace. He just wants to watch them run and laugh, an old man watching his sons race one another in the joyous way of boys.

SEVEN

At the Marina the Caldwell men have their pick of tables, but it doesn't matter. It never matters—there's only ever one table they want, a large round corner booth, situated next to floor-to-ceiling windows. As boys, Connor and Everett would run around outside playing, waiting for Charlotte to step out and call them in when it was time to eat. Everett thinks of this now as he slides into his seat, as his twin slides to his left, and Caleb to his right. It occurs to him for the first time that Caleb might not have the same memories, being so much younger than they are. Everett extends his arm along the back of the booth, behind Caleb, and for a moment grips his younger brother's shoulder.

Christopher sits on the other end of the booth, next to Connor. Everett watches as his father reaches into his pocket and pulls out a pair of glasses—his "readers" and his balding head his only signs of aging. Christopher keeps his eyes on the menu, something entirely unnecessary given that they've been coming to the Marina for more than forty years. Everett watches as his father starts to shake his head.

"Well, I just don't know what to get, boys. It all looks so good."

Each of his sons laughs, shakes his head. Christopher watches them, looking at one another, laughing with one another.

Everett goes first, picking up his menu, lowering his pretend readers to his nose. "Um, Evelyn, what would you recommend today?"

Caleb puts a hand on his hips, pretends to puff a cigarette, adopting a husky smoker's voice. "Stop playing with me, Christopher Caldwell. You know as well as I do not a goddamned thing on this menu has changed in over forty years, not even the Wonder bread."

Playing the role of Charlotte, Connor sits prim and proper. "Evelyn, while my old fart of a husband struggles to make up his mind, may I have a cup of Lipton, with lemon on the side? To eat I'll have the Senior Special Number Three. Hash brown patties, please, and hold the prunes, don't need 'em." He playfully pushes his imaginary readers up his nose and crosses his arms. "You know what, Evelyn? You might as well get that started. If I waited for my husband to make up his mind before eating, I'd have been dead and gone twenty years ago."

"Now, boys," Christopher starts. They all shape up as Evelyn walks over, ready to take their orders. When she leaves, Everett looks conspiratorially at his brothers. "That was close."

Connor pours all of them a glass of water and gives an exaggerated "Phew!"

They laugh, looking past one another through the windows, thinking of their past selves. Town begins to stir, a few people run along the shore, occasional dogs in tow. A few early diners walk in, tipping their hats or waving.

Christopher wipes his readers. "When was the last time we were all here together?"

Everett snorts. "Dad, it was the Fourth of July."

Caleb shakes his head. "Not all of us. I stayed in the city."

"Oh." Everett nods. "Right."

Caleb looks at him, momentary hurt written all over his face, before he turns and sits back. Everett grips his shoulder again. "Sorry, buddy." He laughs. "I guess you're the forgettable one."

Caleb smirks at Everett, then looks away.

"All of us?" Connor says. "Had to be . . . Thanksgiving?"

"Yes," Christopher says. "That's right. Trusty Turkey Day." He pauses, looks every one of his sons in the eye. "What a moment. To be here now, watching my oldest get married."

Caleb grunts, then mumbles, "For the second time." He smirks, again, at Everett.

Evelyn returns with a tray of glasses and a carafe of orange juice for the table. She sets it down hard, smacking her gum, and walks away.

"The first time I brought Davis here, she frightened him. That's the exact word he used: 'frightened.' He called her Miss Evelyn and said, 'She don't play!' I think he's still scared of her."

Christopher laughed. "He should be. Evelyn doesn't like newcomers—and to her, you three are still newcomers."

"Dad, Connor and I are almost forty years old."

Christopher shakes his head, swipes his arm at his sons. "Newcomers, the lot of you!" He clears his throat. "But back to business. Everett, I just wanted you to hear from us, son. We're proud of you." He looks at all his sons in turn. Caleb is the first to raise his orange juice, but the others follow suit, clinking glasses.

"Everett," Connor says, a mysterious glint to his eye. "You never told us the story of how you popped the question."

"That's right," Christopher says. "Now that you mention it, I seem to remember a lot of suspicious evasion of that question when we were all here for Thanksgiving." He strokes his chin, feigning being pensive. "How did we get here?"

Everett laughs, looking down as he blushes. When he looks back up at them, he shakes his head. "Not getting that story; sorry. That's just for Davis and me."

Caleb looks at Connor mischievously. "You know what I think."

"We all know what you think, douchebag." Connor kicks his younger brother under the table, but not before Caleb forms a circle with his thumb and first finger and points his other first finger through it a few times.

Everett smacks his brother's head from behind. "I was actually thinking of proposing to Davis last summer, a few months before it ended up happening. It was June, the night of the Supreme Court marriage equality ruling."

Christopher looks knowingly at his other two sons. "Your mother and I almost called you that night. I can't remember why we didn't."

Everett shakes his head. "All of New York City was out. People were dancing, partying in the streets; just getting home was a nightmare. And then I walked into an apartment where Davis was curled up on the couch, a pile of Kleenex surrounding him. He was watching a YouTube video."

At this, Christopher balks. "What video?"

"Earlier that day was the funeral for the victims of the church shooting in Charleston. Davis's father is a minister. I hadn't thought much about it because they don't even talk; Davis seemed fine, the shooting had happened the week before. But I came home, and he was practically catatonic."

Connor's voice is low. "That funeral."

Everett glances through the window, then looks directly at Connor. "Bingo. He was watching the video of President Obama singing 'Amazing Grace.' And he just kept hitting the 'play again' button when it ended."

"Damn," Connor says.

"Bleak." Caleb looks away, his eyes traveling through the restaurant.

Christopher picks up his orange juice. "What did you do?"

"He didn't even notice me when I came in. I just dropped everything on the floor and ran over to him. And when I touched him, and he saw me, he had this look of horror like I was an intruder he didn't recognize. And once he did, he just collapsed into me. If a person can dissolve, that's what he did."

Christopher shakes his head. He stares at the carafe in front of him.

"It was like he thought his father had been killed in that shooting. They're from South Carolina originally. I mean, Davis was born in Ohio, but his family. The whole thing felt way too eerie, too close to home. I just held him. We kneeled on the floor in front of the couch. I'd never seen him so sad, so scared." Everett looks at them all, pausing. "So small. He's been through a lot with his family, you know?" He takes a sip of his orange juice. "I don't even know all of those details, but I know that by marrying into this family, he'll never feel so alone again." Everett looks at each of them one by one. Caleb, Christopher, and, finally, Connor, who nods back at him. Everett chuckles. "And then he asked me if I would detangle his hair."

Caleb wrinkles his brow, squinting. "I'm sorry, Davis asked you, Everett Caldwell, to detangle his hair?"

Everett laughs. His eyes twinkle at the memory. "He had to talk me through it, but I got the hang of it quickly. You start by dividing the hair into sections and gathering each section with a clip so it's out of the way. I had to spray the section I was working on with water until it was dripping wet, and then work in the detangling conditioner—which is different from the leave-in conditioner. It has more slip." He pops his lips on the p and points his first finger at his little brother. "You start at the root of the follicle and comb it through using your fingers. If there are any tangles, that's when you work them out with the special brush, or a wide-tooth comb. And then finally, you finish with the leave-in conditioner and some oil for shine." Everett looks around, nonchalant, each of the Caldwell boys staring back at him, dumbfounded. "What?" He shrugs. "I could've done it for hours."

"The word 'follicle' just came out of your mouth," Caleb says, shaking his head. He turns to look at Everett. "Who even are you?"

Evelyn arrives with their food. "So, I hear you're getting married today," she says to Everett as she sets down everyone's plates.

"Yes—yes, ma'am."

"Town talks," she says. When she finishes with the food, she looks straight at Everett, smacking her gum the whole time. "I like that young man. Calls me 'Miss Evelyn.' Wouldn't it be nice if the rest of you did that, eh? You, too," she says directly to Christopher. She turns and walks away. "Bring him next time."

"Guess you're still a newcomer after all, Dad." Connor laughs.

"Yeah," Everett says. "Guess Montauk is still Mom's town."

"Everett doing hair—Black hair, at that." Caleb's astonishment is broken when Everett smacks the back of his head again.

"The point, dumbass, is this: Davis normally stands in front of the mirror in the bathroom with the door locked when he detangles his hair. I didn't even know this was a thing he does. And then he just asked me to do it—out of nowhere. He said one day we might have a child, and if we did, that child would be Black, and I would need to know how to do their hair."

"Son, are you saying—"

"Stay focused, Dad. You're not getting grandkids from us anytime soon."

"Sorry," Christopher says.

"Let me tell the story."

Christopher mimes zipping his lips and throwing out the key.

Everett continues. "We didn't say much. He just kept playing that video, and every once in a while, I'd kiss the top of his head or wrap my arms around his shoulders. In that moment, for that night, it was the thing I could do to make sure he felt loved and protected. I got to care for him in this simple, quiet, unexpectedly intimate way. And as I did it, I realized that a time was going to come when I would ask him to marry me, and that when it did—and *I* did—he would say yes." Everett drops both his hands on the table, looking at his brothers first, and then his father. He shrugs. "You asked how we got here; that's how we got here."

With that, they eat. When they stand to leave, Everett checks his phone for the first time since leaving the house. There's a text from Davis:

My sister is coming.

"Guys, I'm going to run ahead, but I'll meet you back at the house." Everett waves at his brothers, hugs his father, and takes off.

EIGHT

Davis lays his phone on the dresser, face down. Around him are the voices of the foremost women in his life: Phoebe and Zora, deep in conversation with Charlotte and Courtney. Part of him wants to ask them all to step out, to give him a moment alone. The other part of him wants them to gather round him, to dispense some wisdom that will fortify him in the wake of the text message he's just received from Olivia. She has landed in New York City and is on her way to the wedding. Initially, she'd sent her regrets.

Then Charlotte steps away from his friends, begging his attention. "The caterers are arriving soon, along with the florist. Courtney and I will have a look around and make sure everything is ready." She looks him in the eye. "It's going to be a perfect day." She steps toward Davis like she's going to hug him, thinks better of it, and steps out into the hallway with Courtney.

Davis stands there, his brain momentarily delayed. Phoebe chooses that moment to snap a candid shot. "Be right back," Davis says to his friends as he steps out into the hallway.

"Charlotte! Charlotte!"

Davis scampers down the stairs where he meets Charlotte in

the foyer. He grabs her hand and pulls her aside, into the family room.

"What's wrong, sweetheart?"

Davis wants to cry or scream or throw something, and he doesn't even know why. So many feelings rush through him, but he collects himself. "My sister just let me know that she's going to attend after all. I don't know why she couldn't let me know before she landed in New York City, but here we are." He pauses, rolling his eyes. "Can you make sure the caterers know to add a table setting?"

"Oh, this is wonderful news! Yes, of course." Charlotte begins to walk away. "Davis, I assume you'll want her to sit with us, right? With family?"

Davis nods, but when he speaks, his voice is barely a whisper. "Yes, with family."

Charlotte, never breaking eye contact, walks back over to him. The two are close in height, so when she hugs him, her mouth is near his ear. "Don't you worry about a thing." She pulls back, still gripping his arms, gifting him the kind of smile that reaches her eyes. "It's going to be marvelous." Then she turns away, just as the door opens, just as someone who needs to be directed looks around and enters the house.

When Davis returns to the master suite, he jumps immediately into action. He sits in front of the vanity. Around him, he hears the shutter click of Phoebe's camera as Zora pats a brush in powder.

"Just a subtle beat. A little pink in my cheeks, and cheekbones as sharp as you can make them." He folds his hands in his lap, like an obedient schoolboy.

"You did a great job shaving, Davis." Zora slowly examines his face, her brow furrowed in concentration. "I don't even need to wax your upper lip." She leans close, brush in hand. "You ready?"

Davis nods. He's never worn makeup for anything other than a party in college; this is something both Zora and Phoebe are well aware of; in fact, it was their suggestion that he wear some for the wedding if he didn't want there to be any beard shadow.

"You excited for today?" Zora's voice is like a purr in his ear. Davis turns, looks at her, really looks at her. "Keep your head straight," she says, her gaze trained on his face.

"For the makeup? Or the wedding?"

"Both," she says. She touches the brush to his skin. The bristles are soft; Davis is taken by the feeling of luxury that comes over him.

"I'm very excited. I feel like a rich white lady."

"I'm glad you were open to wearing makeup, Davis."

"I've always wanted to try it."

"It's just going to enhance your beauty."

"You've been telling me I was beautiful since day one."

"Because you are."

Davis turns and looks at her again, and smiles. "Thank you." Then he turns and looks once more, in the mirror.

"I wish this day could last forever."

Zora shrugs. "It will, in a way. Isn't that what marriage is? The forever?"

Davis is struck, in that moment, with how young they really are: himself and his girlfriends. Their wisdom buoys him, and yet there's a way in which it feels false—as though they are children playing an elaborate game of pretend. It makes him fearful, nervous; he doesn't know what he is doing, and neither do they. None of their friends are anywhere close to getting married.

Through it all, Phoebe continues taking pictures, occasionally opening the camera and replacing the film. Davis had wanted an older, classic look to their wedding photos, so he does his best to ignore her, to give her the candid shots she's looking for, but he knows that not every shot will show him looking joyful. And in a way, this calms him, makes him feel seen.

WHEN IT'S TIME to get dressed, Davis pulls Phoebe and Zora into the walk-in closet with him.

"Don't touch anything," he says. "It's all mostly Charlotte's, but if you look in the corner, in the plastic bins, there's all kinds of things from Everett and his brothers when they were kids. I know, because I snooped earlier this week while Everett was working out." Davis points, as he slowly makes his way to the back of the closet. "There are art projects in here, and costumes from the local summer parade in there, and knickknacks from the Strawberry Festival."

"The what?" Zora asks.

"Girl, I don't know. These locals really love strawberries."

When he reaches the end of the closet, he pulls a garment bag down and throws it over his arm. He turns around to exit.

"Davis, I think you forgot something." Phoebe bends down and grabs a matching box that sits on the floor, next to where the garment bag hung.

"Oh, you can just leave that there." He looks away, but Phoebe lingers.

"It's wedding stuff, right? I want to see!" She grabs the box.

"Girl,"— Davis sighs, waving her off. Phoebe makes a victory fist and brings the box out with her, where she sets it on the bed.

"Zora, I'll need you to help zip me into this." He unzips the garment bag, pulling from it an ivory, open-back jumpsuit.

"You're going to look amazing in that! You have the best back," Zora says.

"And shoulders," Phoebe adds almost absentmindedly as she begins to pry open the lid of the box.

Zora runs a finger up and down the front of the jumpsuit. "It's so soft."

"I was never going to wear a suit—obviously—but when I found this, I really liked it. It's sort of inspired by the elements of a tuxedo, while still being really soft and beautiful." Davis looks at it proudly. "The pants were flared so I had them redo them for a straighter fit."

It's Zora who looks away first, watching as Phoebe pulls aside white tissue paper, a ruched strapless white gown in her hands.

Zora gasps. "Davis!"

Phoebe holds the gown, staring at it, her hands gingerly fingering the ruching. "Okay, Davis, why is this in a box in the back of your closet when you should be wearing it?" She holds it up, points to it, dumbfounded. "This is stunning!"

Davis blinks, then looks between the two of them. "I know," he says. He bites his lip.

Zora and Phoebe look at each other. Zora steps forward, toward Davis. "So why aren't you wearing this? The jumpsuit is great, but, Davis, this gown is everything."

"Be serious." Davis looks at Zora, then Phoebe, who has placed the camera on the bed. "I can't get married wearing a gown." He says it derisively, as though it's an absurd notion.

"Davis," Phoebe says. "Why not?"

Davis closes his eyes, takes a deep breath. "Why not?" He looks between them both. "You know why." He waits another few moments before walking closer to them and rolling his eyes. "Can you just help me?"

Zora looks at Phoebe. "No, I really don't know why you can't wear this. It's beautiful."

Phoebe stares at Davis as Zora takes the jumpsuit from him and lays it flat on the bed. "Do you want to wear it?"

Davis nods, shrugs. He glances out the window, then stares at the floor. He can barely say the words. "Of course I want to wear it. I bought it!"

Zora steps close, puts an arm around him. They sit on the edge of the bed.

"But I can't. I can't do it."

"Because your sister's coming?"

Davis had almost forgotten about Olivia. He nods, the movement slight and slow.

Zora narrows her eyes. "That's not really the reason, is it?" She crosses her arms. "Since when have you given a fuck what anyone thinks?"

Phoebe starts rubbing his back in wide, comforting circles. "God, your skin is smooth."

Davis laughs. "I bought it because I wanted to feel like a bride. That's how I've always imagined it. So I went to a boutique, had a fitting, and almost an entire bottle of champagne—"

"Uh, where were we?" Zora fakes indignancy.

Davis looks at her as Phoebe passes him a tissue.

"Blot. Gently."

"I loved it, so I bought it. And the minute I walked out of that store, I wondered what I had done because I was never going to wear it." Davis picks it up, folds it over his arm, pulls it close, almost hugging it. "I just wanted the feeling, I guess."

Phoebe leans close. "Why didn't you return it?"

Zora stands. "I know why! Because if he wasn't going to wear it, he didn't want anybody else to wear it, either." She looks Davis directly in the eye. "Did I get that right, Katie Petty? Petty Wap, Petty Mayonnaise, petty is as petty does?"

Davis chuckles. "Pretty much."

Zora nods, kisses him on the cheek, then looks away from him at the floor.

"I have an idea," says Phoebe. "Why don't you try it on? Just for us. We'll take some photos, just here—in this room—so you can have that feeling today and capture it forever. And then you can change into the jumpsuit."

"I love that," Zora says. "You're doing it."

Davis rises slowly. "I don't want them getting out. When you send me and Everett the wedding photos, send these only to me."

"I have an even better idea," Zora says. She pulls a disposable camera from her purse. "I brought it for fun!"

Davis looks Zora up and down, then shakes his head, awed. "Slay, my vintage queen."

NINE

Everett slips into a comfortable pace as he runs, leaving behind the men in his family who will walk back to the house. If he's honest, he would've run ahead of them anyway, even if Davis hadn't sent that text. The entire rest of the day will be consumed by friends and, in particular, family—his family. Breakfast at the Marina, and this breakfast specifically, is as tame as they get. He appreciates a few minutes to himself.

And there's Davis to think about. They love him, as much as Everett loves him. But there's a way in which they treat him sometimes—not as a visitor, per se, but as a much-loved oddity. A person on display. He'll be on display today; they've chosen a wedding when they could've chosen the courthouse. They've chosen the consternation that comes with planning a major life event when they could've chosen simplicity. Everett is thrilled that Davis is getting the beachside wedding he's always wanted—really quite modest in the grand scheme of things, far cheaper than Everett's first wedding—and he really is tailor-made to be the belle of any ball. He's beautiful and charming and funny and oh so very bright.

And different.

But as Everett runs, he admits to himself that if Davis didn't want Olivia to come, if her presence was going to stress him out, then he shouldn't have invited her.

When Everett runs, he keeps his eyes trained ahead of him. They live in the city, in the West Village. The streets, on certain blocks, are brick-laid or cobblestone, but the more treacherous terrain is the sidewalk. At all hours, filled with people—arms linked, walking hand in hand, giggling or drunk or pushing strollers. Or ambling around, stepping into shops. Everett loves it, but it makes for a difficult run. But here in Montauk, at this hour, he can alternate between looking down and looking ahead. When Everett runs, he likes to avoid the cracks in the sidewalk. On a day like today, everything feels like an emotional minefield. For Davis, yes, but also for him and his family.

There's history in this house, and that's part of why Everett wanted to get married here; they are making new history—*their* family history.

He wants to avoid the cracks—he is avoiding the cracks—and yet Everett knows he's running directly into an emotional land mine. He thinks of one night a few months earlier, when they'd been out with some of Davis's friends on a humid summer night, a rooftop bar. Davis was celebrating booking a concert as soloist with a well-known chamber orchestra, when his cellphone rang, a Mozart ringtone. The call was from Olivia. When Davis looked at him, Everett shook his head. *No, don't take the call. Not here, not now.*

Davis took the call, stepping aside.

Everett doesn't know much about the conversation, but he knows it got heated. Davis moved from the side of their table to indoors, to a locked single-stall bathroom. Everett had to knock when he came to check on him.

"Davis?"

He repeated himself a few times before Davis unlocked the door and pulled it open.

Everett looked him up and down quickly. "Baby, you have to

come out, you're holding up the line." He laughed at the way Davis just pulled him in, ignoring the sign telling him not to. "They're going to kick us out; they're going to think we're fucking."

His eyes were red; there were several tissues balled up on the counter. Davis returned to where he'd obviously been standing in front of the mirror, trying to get himself together. Everett came behind him, wrapped his arms around Davis's waist, looked at the sight of the two of them—one teary-eyed and flustered, the other standing tall, composed, but quietly concerned.

"I'm awful. I said something awful," Davis said.

Everett kept his voice deep. Low. Calm. "I told you not to take her call. We're out with your friends. You've been working so hard."

"Not helpful."

Everett was quiet for a moment. He held Davis tighter. "Why *did* you take it?"

Davis pressed himself back against Everett's chest and sighed wearily. He crossed his arms. "Clearly, because I'm awful. I was happy and excited, and I wanted to say something petty." He closed his eyes. "And I did."

Everett kissed his cheek. "What did you say?"

Davis ignored that question.

"She was so good to me. She's my sister, Everett."

"I know."

"Why am I like this?"

"You're not 'like this.' If things are difficult between you two, that's not entirely your fault." It was something he'd said before, something he believed. He cupped his hand against the mound of Davis's ass, his thumb slipping into his underwear. Everett caressed the soft, bare skin, and pressed himself harder against Davis, saying, "You're not awful."

There was a disturbance on the other side of the door—the sound of clinking glasses, tumbling silverware, a plate smashing to the ground. A body falling against the bathroom door. Someone had tripped.

Everett watched in the mirror as Davis closed his eyes and let his head fall forward against his own chest. He put his hands on Davis's shoulders, started gently rubbing his neck. "Listen, do you want to get out of here? Some of these people are kind of"—he made a face—"basic. They're kind of basic."

Davis laughed. "What? You love my friends!" He turned around and smacked Everett's chest, still laughing.

"I love you," Everett said. He kissed the nape of Davis's neck. "And I want you." He kissed his cheek. "On your back." He kissed his other cheek. "Or your stomach." Davis jumped up and sat on the sink. He opened his legs and pulled Everett close. He placed his palms against Everett's chest, his statement seemingly rising from nowhere: "I want to take your name." He looked at the ground. "Would that be okay?" He kissed Everett again. "I need a clean break, or a new beginning, or some shit."

He hopped down, grabbed Everett's hand, and pulled him out into the hallway, back to their table, back to their friends.

And Everett must admit: Davis taking his name wasn't something he'd given much thought to until that moment. But he'd loved the idea of it then, and he loves it now. He knows it's primal, rooted in the patriarchy, and perhaps unexpected on the part of Davis. But it's real, and it's a thing Everett can hold on to.

As HE NEARS the house, Everett picks up his pace with ease. He flexes his hands, stretches his fingers, before curling both into fists. When he walks in, he finds his mother directing the caterers in the kitchen. Everett thinks of Davis, of what he'd said earlier about his own mother, and he runs quickly over to Charlotte, sweeping her into a hug, a little bit tighter, a little bit longer than usual.

"Mom, I don't say it enough: Thank you." He clasps her hands, kisses her cheek, then runs upstairs to the master suite where he finds the door closed, Davis and his girlfriends in fits of laughter. He pauses. Everett runs back downstairs, back to the kitchen, where he grabs a bottle of champagne and three flutes. He takes the stairs two at a time, knocks on the door to the master suite. Zora opens it just enough to stick her head out.

"Everything okay in there?"

Zora looks behind her, into the room, then back at him. "Yeah."

Everett lowers his voice. "Is he okay about his sister? Sounds like you're having a good time."

Zora turns behind her again, then gives him a bright smile. "He's okay. Better than okay—he's marrying you! Nothing can ruin that for him." She winks, and Everett passes her the champagne and the flutes. Zora thanks him, closes the door. Behind it, he hears a waterfall of laughter, imagining perfectly the way she holds the bottle of champagne like they've just won some kind of prize.

TEN

Returning to the house, Christopher and the Caldwell brothers walk past Charlotte—the woman who bore them, who bandaged their scrapes and sang them to sleep, who fed them and kept them comfortable. Who drove them to thousands of practices, and washed uniforms and maintained hockey helmets and lacrosse sticks. Who taught them how to slow dance. His boys love their mother, Christopher knows they do. They show her all the time; and yet in one particular way they still seem to be boys: They saunter right past her, up the front stairs two at a time, deep in conversation, possibly not even seeing her.

While she stands there, clipboard in hand, directing vendors to their proper places.

Christopher hangs back, watching her—his little mouse, with her bangs that bounce when she walks and the hands she never seems to know how to occupy. Even after all these years, to him she is still the most beautiful woman in the world, his Helen of Troy. She's all joy, her smile bright as the lighthouse farther down the beach. It stretches across her entire face, seeming to reach every corner.

Except her eyes.

Gray. Soft. Swirling like paper-thin storm clouds. He knows what she is thinking, and whom she is thinking about. As his boys scamper upstairs to start getting ready, he takes a moment.

"Hi," he says shyly, like they are young lovers, exploring, questioning, just feeling each other out.

Charlotte furrows her brow, clearly startled by his sudden presence. "Hi, there!"

She is all energy, full-on mom. *Go, go, go*, he imagines her saying, the way she did as she cheered her sons from the stands during Little League games.

"Are you . . . ?"

She nods. She closes her eyes. She is still for a moment, one hand cupping her forehead, the other on her hip. "There's just so much to get done, I can't even think right now."

"I know." He pauses, glances at his watch. "Can I help? Your old man can still get those boys down here pronto."

She shakes her head, eyes shut tight, a dam she's unwilling to burst. "I have to get through this," she says, her voice breaking for a moment.

Like a mitt catching a ball, Christopher's hand catches hers, giving it a squeeze. "I'm here, honey. I know I wasn't back then, but I am now."

She looks up at him, a thunderbolt of anger flashing across her face. "Back then you were the problem." Christopher's heart breaks a little, but she squeezes him back.

And then she's off, running around the side of the house, shouting at the florist and the men carrying the standing heaters for the tent. And the caterers, who are well on their way to taking over his kitchen. Christopher bounds into the house and up the stairs as well, to the room Everett has chosen, the guest suite at the other end of the hall where they will get ready in the way they do—as one unit, one vessel, his boys now men and yet, in his eyes, still boys.

"SHE'S ALREADY IN the other master with Davis." Everett stands on one leg negotiating his pants up the other. "The photographer, I mean."

Christopher wants to laugh; how familiar this moment is, so much like it was when Everett first got married. "Son, you need to take a quick shower. Go on. Your suit will be waiting and so will the photographer."

"I don't have time!"

He walks over to Everett, puts a hand on his shoulder, looks him straight in the eye. "You have plenty of time. What you won't have is Davis if he walks down that aisle to you and you smell like a six-mile run."

"Take your shower." Caleb frowns, struggling to unfold the ironing board.

Christopher sighs. "The photographer will take more time with Davis anyway, so she'll be late coming over here, and there is plenty of time."

Everett looks at him. "You sure?"

"You're the groom—one of the grooms—she has to wait for you."

Everett nods, enters the bathroom, and closes the door. Seconds later, he opens it and pokes his head out. He points to Connor. "Beer?"

Connor grins. "You got it." He points to Caleb and Christopher.

"Just bring a six-pack," Christopher says. "Two six-packs!" He nods as his son runs off, as Caleb joins his brother, leaving him in the room alone. He glances out the window, then decides he might as well do the ironing for Caleb, who likely hasn't seen or touched an iron since he burned a hole into a dress shirt in college. He grabs the pants, which are crumpled in a pile on a floor next to his son's suitcase.

I really ought to buy him a garment bag, he thinks as he plugs the iron in and turns it on. He holds his son's suit pants up, inspecting them. Clean enough, and wrinkled, but he can work the crease back into them. He dips his hands into the pockets to clear them out, knowing that Caleb would have probably forgotten this minor detail. He realizes as he does it that he is also playing into Caleb's manipulations: The boy is used to having everything done for him!

But Christopher can't find it in himself to be mad at him, partly because today is not about him. Everett is getting married, and with his marriage, they are breathing new life back into this house.

Christopher's fingers close around some change and he pulls it from the pocket. In the other he finds a cigarette—no, a blunt, he sees as he pulls it out. He's not surprised, he was just hoping they wouldn't have to smell it on Caleb today in front of their guests. And there is something else, a folded-up piece of paper, which he places on the edge of the bed, along with the blunt, the change, and the keys to Caleb's Brooklyn apartment. He's not sure he's ever known Caleb to fold something so neatly—certainly not his clothes.

The boys are loud bounding up the stairs, then into the room, their feet quick and heavy as they move, a trait it seems all the Caldwell men share. They shut the door behind them, each carrying a six-pack and an open bag of ice. Christopher folds his son's suit pants and lays them across the ironing board. He watches as they march into the bathroom, listens as they mutter amongst themselves in the casual way of brothers. They laugh. He hears them pour the ice into one of the sinks in the bathroom vanity. Smart move.

Connor and Caleb walk back out, and Connor tosses Christopher a beer. He catches it, then keeps ironing.

Caleb tips an imaginary hat as he sits down in a chair and opens his beer. He puts his feet up on an ottoman and crosses his ankles, his other hand propped behind his head.

"This favor I'm doing you is not permission for you to just sit around." Christopher pauses, makes his voice less playful, more gruff. "I found everything in your pockets." He nods toward the bed, then watches as Caleb sits up straight and plants his feet firmly on the ground as though he's in trouble, sitting in the principal's office waiting for Christopher—or more likely Charlotte—to arrive.

"Everything?"

Christopher nods but doesn't say a word. The truth is, he lights up himself from time to time, though it's been years. He was once a young man, too, and did all the things young men do. But at twenty-eight he was married to Charlotte with twin boys on the way. Meanwhile, Caleb seems unable to hold a steady job, unable to find any sense of direction at all. He doesn't deserve weed, hasn't earned it, is what Christopher thinks. And what stings the most—though Christopher has never said this to anyone but Charlotte—is how their oldest son is marrying a boy three years younger than Caleb, a boy with a promising career, something of distinction, something that requires intense focus, rigorous study, and has already taken him all over the world. Something that keeps him disciplined and competitive. Something through which he consistently achieves excellence; something that has already made him some money and will one day soon make him a lot of money.

"Dad?" Caleb's face becomes serious. He leans forward in his chair. "I want you to know that I haven't made a decision yet. I was just exploring my options."

"What options, son?"

His mind is back on Charlotte, on what this day must be like for her. Tomorrow, after the wedding, he will take her to the gravesite. He glances at Connor, who puts down his phone, and they both look at Caleb.

"Um, nothing. Nothing!"

He looks like a pogo stick, the way he bounces up and moves toward the bed. But Connor, sitting on the bed, is faster. He lunges for the blunt and his hands grasp the flyer. Christopher watches as Caleb stops and groans, and Connor unfolds the paper. He feels the way all three of their hearts stop, like synchronized swimmers, just dancing along and then frozen, stopped.

Arrested.

Legs straight, eyes bulging.

Then Connor, his loud anger like an asteroid, the room suddenly no more than a crater left in its wake.

"What the fuck, Caleb?"

"What?" Christopher asks. "What is it?"

Connor reads, his voice coated in disgust: "*Make America Great Again!*"

He slaps the flyer down on the bedside table. "This is the option he's talking about. It even has a little red hat at the top." Connor turns back to Caleb. "What the fuck? I mean what the actual fuck, Caleb? You're voting for that imbecile?"

For a moment Christopher thinks he knows what it is to feel your soul leaving your body. He moves with the speed of his youth, but once again, Connor is faster. He is in Caleb's face, shouting, pointing, his body shaking with the combustibility of his rage. "Quiet!" Christopher doesn't want Everett to hear this, nor Davis, nor Charlotte. And the house, while large, while well-built, carries an echo the way children carry sickness.

Which, he thinks, is what this is.

"Quiet," he says again, his voice softer but every bit as harsh. He steps between his sons and grabs Caleb by the collar. He is quiet, his voice low, but his disappointment searing. "Are you considering this, son?"

"I don't know. Maybe."

Christopher lets his son go. He watches as Caleb rubs his neck, smooths down his shirt, looks at the floor, then the door. He watches anger swoop down upon his son like a cloak. "They fucked over Bernie, Dad! Drain the swamp!" Caleb jumps up and down like a boxer prepping for a fight. Out of the corner of his eye, he sees Connor rummage through Caleb's duffel bag.

Christopher steps closer to his youngest son. Memories come and go in an instant, a kaleidoscope of moments. He thinks back to that summer when Caleb was six and Charlotte was away visiting her mother for a week. He'd called the boys for dinner, and Caleb, who'd been unusually quiet, came clomping down the stairs in a pair of his mother's high heels, his entire face covered in five different lipsticks. He thinks of how he allowed Everett and Connor to make fun of him all through dinner, and how Caleb sat there and took it, his face resolute, as stern as though he were a little soldier.

He thinks of how he yelled later, and he sees the way his son flinched, the way his son cried and then sobbed. He thinks of how Caleb is eleven years younger than his brothers, how he spent many years living as the only child in their home, his brothers grown and gone, Christopher off on frequent business trips, only Charlotte there to raise him. He knows Caleb often felt like an only child, but he'd always said it was a good thing, like he got the best of both worlds: parents who spoiled him and brothers who looked out for him but weren't there to eat all the food or take the best bedrooms. Christopher thinks of these things, and his heart, which for the past few moments has felt so hardened against his son, begins to break, cracks moving throughout. And yet his anger and disappointment seem to fortify it.

"How can you stand here, at your gay brother's wedding, thinking of supporting that man?" Christopher shakes his head.

"It's just one vote, Dad." Sweat mists Caleb's brow. Christopher watches his son turn in a circle.

"I think he's high," Connor says. He holds up an orange pill container, shakes it, the pills banging against the plastic.

Caleb doesn't notice. "You know, not everything he says is bad."

"Oh yeah?" Connor goes off. "'Grab 'em by the pussy'? Mexicans are rapists?"

"Mocking that disabled reporter," Christopher adds, sadness flowing through him.

Caleb shrugs. "Yeah, well he doesn't hate the gays." He adds a bitter laugh, steps closer to his father, gives him a light punch on the arm. Smiles. His voice is louder now. "Speaking of, I know we're all PC and PFLAG and shit, but, man"—he pauses and takes a breath and looks his father in the eye—"you must be glad your son's not the bitch, right?"

For Caleb, the fight is over before it begins: In two seconds Everett stands over his brother who writhes and moans on the ground; a single strong right hook was all it took to land Caleb on his back. Christopher hadn't heard the shower stop, hadn't heard the bathroom door creep open, or seen his oldest son peering at them, listening to every word. But Everett was there in an instant, towel wrapped around his waist, hair stringy and dripping wet, in only two quick strides having moved from there to here, stepping past his father, past Connor, to take care of his little brother himself.

"Get out," he says, his voice low. "Get the fuck out of here, Caleb."

And there is Caleb, sprawled like the head of a wet mop on a closet floor, slowly pushing himself up with his hands, shouting back, "It was a fucking joke!" Once he rises to his feet, he runs a hand through his hair, then turns to Everett. For a moment it looks like Caleb is going to charge his brother. "Jesus fucking Christ!" He cradles his jaw in the palm of his hand.

It feels to Christopher like a tennis match between a player of the highest caliber and an amateur, a child—one whom the star player might humor with their attention. But any fight between his boys, and these two in particular, is not a fair contest. He tries to step in, but Everett, once again, stands only inches from his brother, chest out, shoulders back, stance erect, both hands folded into fists. Ready for strike number two.

But Christopher knows his oldest son, and he knows it won't happen. He waits a few seconds, and watches as reason comes back to Everett. He watches him relax his stance, unclench his fists, and step even closer to Caleb. His voice is quiet, and yet Christopher can hear the hurt pumping through his words, sure as the blood that pumps through his veins. "You have to go," he says. Then he turns to his father, gesturing with his thumb over his shoulder. "He's gotta go. I can't even look at him. Fucking pathetic."

He steps back, turns around, hands on hips. He sighs. Connor moves next to Everett, puts an arm around him. They whisper, and after a few words are exchanged, Connor pats Everett on the back and Everett walks away, back into the bathroom.

There is a knock on the door, and before anyone can say anything, it's opened, the photographer poking her head through.

"We're not ready, sweetheart, not yet," Christopher says. The girl narrows her eyes at him, then pushes her glasses up her nose.

"It's Phoebe."

"I'm sorry?" he asks.

"It's Phoebe, not sweetheart." She smiles at him like he is a doddering old man. He remembers now: She is one of Davis's friends. "But that's fine. I can continue with Davis and check back in a few minutes, if that works?"

Christopher nods, then glances at Connor and Caleb, both of whom are pacing near a window. "Yes, perfect. Thank you." When the door shuts behind her, he ventures to the bathroom and knocks twice on the door.

"Yeah?" Everett's voice pulses with controlled anger.

"Connor and I think your brother is high." Behind him, Caleb groans.

"Okay," Everett says.

"So I don't want him leaving the house." Behind the door he hears Everett place a glass or a jar of something heavily on the counter.

"Well, I don't want him around Davis. Or me. Not today."

Christopher hears Everett's feet walking to the door. He opens it slightly, and when Christopher sees Everett's eyes, he knows immediately how furious his son still is. "I know," he says. "But you are the oldest brother."

"Fuck that."

"Everett . . ."

"This is our day, mine and Davis's. And if I have to see him again, I don't know what I'll do."

"Today is your day but this is my house, and he is my son, too. And I know he didn't mean that."

"Like hell I didn't," Caleb grumbles. "I'm tired of all this shit." Christopher hears his son plop down on the bed.

"Connor, get your brother some water." He waves behind his back, hears Connor shuffle from the room. "Listen, Everett. I understand. If he weren't high, I'd kick him to the door myself. But he is, so he's staying here. You won't have to see him. He'll stay in one of the other bedrooms all night. But I'm not sending him away. Not like this." He turns and speaks directly to Caleb now. "No matter how vile he's being."

He turns back to Everett. "Now, keep getting ready. Try to forget this even happened."

Everett looks at his feet. "I need to be the bigger man, I know, I know."

Christopher shakes his head. It surprises him, the way his pride in Everett suddenly settles inside himself, the way he knows it will carry him forward through this day and beyond it, too. "No, son. You are the bigger man. You make me proud every day." He wants to reach through the door and touch his son's arm, to somehow transfer any extra strength he carries to him.

Everett, never one to cry or show any weakness whatsoever, blinks several times and steps back, closing the door. Christopher grabs Caleb by the arm and pulls him to his feet. At the moment, it seems words escape him when it comes to his youngest son. He marches Caleb down the hall—the chaos of the final pre-wedding hours in full swing below them—to one of the bedrooms in the middle of the house, overlooking the front lawn. He is filled with disappointment at the mess the boy has become.

Christopher doesn't know what to do with himself. Or with Caleb.

But he does know this: Caleb will stay in this room, this pirate-themed bedroom decorated in wallpaper covered in trunks and treasure. He will read one of the magazines or play games on his phone or stare out the window that faces the front lawn, the only window in the room. Caleb won't so much as cast his eyes upon the wedding or the reception, and he won't be around his father all day, either. In this Christopher finds some small nugget of relief.

He can breathe easy, because Caleb, for all his problems, has always been able to see through his father in a way the other boys never could. And Christopher fears—no, Christopher knows—that Caleb has seen something in him. Something small, but not insignificant.

Christopher loves Davis, and he loves Davis for Everett. But even with everything he's learned over the years, all the ways in which the world has changed, and all the things he's learned to accept, there is still a certain sensation that comes over him—a thing he hates, a thing that long ago burrowed deep inside and covered itself in the flaps and folds of his person.

As he closes Caleb's door behind him and walks down the hall and past the master bedroom where Davis and his friends are getting made up and posing for photos, he thinks that he has to name it if he's ever going to cast it completely aside.

Shame.

Entirely theoretical, given the way things are, but real and present all the same. Because it would be his shame—Christopher's, no one else's—that would volcanically erupt their family if Davis's and Everett's roles were reversed. If it were his son walking down that aisle with a bouquet of flowers while Davis stood up there like he was the man. If it were his son that covered his face in all kinds of creams and oils and plucked his eyebrows. If it were his Everett, his Carter—his mainmast!—who'd been proposed to, like some blushing bride right out of a movie. Christopher hates that he feels this way, but it's easier to accept all that when it's Davis. He's young and small and pretty. You don't look at him and expect anything different. And most important, he's someone else's son. Christopher won't say anything, and really, there's nothing to be said. But if the situation were reversed?

He can't begin to consider how he would handle that.

ELEVEN

Slow down. Breathe. In and out.

The Reverend begins at his feet, with his toes. First he tries to flex, then point them. The right foot, then the left. It dawns on him that he doesn't know if he was successful because he can't feel his feet, nor his legs. He tries to turn his head to the right, then the left. He can feel his neck; he knows there was no movement. He tries to move his eyes. Out of his right eye, he can make out the shape of his right hand, even in the darkened car. The Reverend tries to point his first finger. He feels heat, energy moving through his arm to that finger. Ever so slightly, it moves.

All is not lost, not yet, but he will have to be patient.

Father God, he says, mouthing the words. A plea, a prayer, a repentance.

There are so many things he needs to say to Davis, so many truths: like how badly Davis had been wanted by both his parents, how long they had waited. How many years they had prayed for him. Some things the Reverend never thought to say, other things he avoided because by not saying them, he thought he was doing the right thing.

Like the fact that, in a way, Davis had come from nowhere.

He just appeared one day—in a vision, to Adina—and then again every day for the rest of that week. It was many years ago, when Olivia was in middle school. Adina had always been a woman of robust faith, but only once was she gifted with prophetic vision.

Adina had started drinking tea in the afternoons. One Monday, as she waited for the water to boil, she flipped through the mail that had arrived that day. She listened to the hummingbirds and cardinals bounding from branch to branch, and she thought of the wonder of the Lord, the wonder of the world he had created for his people. As she flipped through a magazine, she caught a glimpse of a baby in the pantry. The baby wore nothing but a smile and a diaper covering his bottom.

Adina knew, somehow, that he was a he, and that he was hers.

Her son waved, charmer that he was, then turned his attention forward. He wrinkled his face in concentration, his heavy little feet wobbly as he took uncertain steps across the pantry. Adina watched him—her breath temporarily taken—her body frozen in place. She crossed her arms, rested her chin atop her knuckles, her magazine by then fallen to the ground in a messy heap of pages.

She watched the boy stumble, then fall in a similar heap to the floor.

Then she watched as the boy pushed himself back up—calm, collected—already wise enough to understand that falling was the great occupational hazard of living. And as this boy resumed his pace, slow and steady, moving almost like an elderly man, Adina began, quietly, to weep.

In the pantry were preposterously well-populated cabinets, shelves lined with canned and boxed goods, noodles and cookies and coffees and teas. It was like a little grocery store, with a ceiling so tall a stepladder was needed, much like the one in John's study. And there was a drawer, a specific, hard-sticking drawer that neither Adina nor the Reverend had ever successfully opened. It was small, the sort of thing you might use for odds and ends in a hallway credenza: Post-its and tape dispensers, tea bags and yeast packets and take-out menus. Perhaps a book of matches and a few tea lights.

That Monday, when the baby arrived in front of the drawer, he stumbled again, falling backward this time, landing on his plump rear end. Seated, legs crossed, his eyes found the knob, painted in gold sparkles. His goal, the object of the sojourn. His eyes never left that knob as he sat, hand raised high in the air, stretching toward it. Something about this motion made her understand, immediately, that this baby would grow into someone who knew, at all times, exactly what he worked for, exactly what he wanted out of life. There would be no confusion there. A gift, Adina thought.

On Tuesday, crossing the pantry, getting his hands upon the knob seemed the baby's singular focus. He ended up on his knees, taking a moment and bowing his head as though saying grace before dinner. When he looked up, his tongue pushing out between his wet pink lips, his eyes narrowed in focus as, once more, he stretched his arm skyward.

Like that he waited until he vanished before Adina's eyes, gone as quickly as he'd arrived—nothing more than smoke and mirrors.

In part, she began to look forward to the daily visitation. Each was different from the last; each showed this baby in a new, more fully human, light.

On Wednesday, he fell again, wailing as though stabbed squarely in the chest, tears streaming down puffy golden cheeks that shimmered like sand in the sun. Adina had never seen such a beautiful baby. She wanted to kneel, pick this baby boy up, and sniff his perfect baby smell. It radiated from the top of his head where loose, wispy curls sat, a garnish carefully placed.

A cherub's crown, a veritable wreath of curls.

He was bleeding, his knee badly skinned, and Adina felt that pain as though it was her injury. The baby didn't make it to the drawer that day, and Adina felt as though a little piece of her heart broke for her boy. Forever bonded, mother and son.

On Thursday, the baby walked with intention and purpose, holding his body tight with the discipline of a soldier marching to duty. How cute, she thought. He would be a soldier for the Lord. He'd learned how to shoot his legs straight out in front of him. How to hold his arms taut, down by his sides. His focus, as usual, never left the knob. There were no falls that day, no tears, and when he arrived in front of the drawer, he casually grabbed onto it with both hands, one on top of the other, pulling easily—surprised when the drawer didn't budge.

His body went slack. His brow rumpled; his eyes narrowed. He put his whole body into trying to open that drawer. Bending his legs, spreading his feet, as though he felt the burden of carrying something heavy, something from which he couldn't entirely free himself.

Nothing worked.

He disappeared, the same as he had every afternoon that week.

On Friday, when Adina walked into the pantry, the baby had already made his way to the drawer. He was a toddler suddenly, a very serious little boy. His curls had tightened, some hanging forward, long enough to be bangs. His diaper had been replaced by a set of underwear inspired by *Goodnight Moon*, dark blue briefs with bright green trim, and a white star smack dab in the center of his rear. He saw her notice them, and she understood that he now recognized her as his mother. He looked down, pointing and laughing. She gasped. The baby was communicating.

He giggled and waved at Adina with both hands, his face an expression of the purest, most enthusiastic joy. She knelt in prayer. *Father God, forgive me for my sins. I know I haven't always been the most faithful servant, Heavenly Father, but I need to know: Is this my baby?*

She lowered herself farther, bending at the waist, her hands flat against the floor. *Please, Father God.* She trembled. *We need him, all of us.*

She opened her eyes. Once more, the baby held the knob clasped in his hand. He tried to open the drawer, pulling with all his little boy weight and strength. After a few moments the boy paused, turning to her, eyes pleading.

"Mama," he said. This was the first she'd heard of his tiny soprano voice. A buoyant, lilting, musical thing. Something else she understood immediately: Her son would be talented, just as she was talented. Still on her knees, Adina brought her face skyward. She gazed at the heavens, then turned and faced this boy. She was moved, so she sang to him. *"You are my sunshine, my only sunshine. When you're not happy, my skies are gray."* They stared at each other, mother and son. Adina watched as disappointment, then frustration, moved through him, briefly passing over his face when he realized Adina couldn't come to help him. He turned his attention back to the drawer, stood once more on his tiptoes, and tried again, to no avail.

Adina tried again to move closer; she wanted, desperately, to help. She wanted to hug him, clutch him, smell him. She wanted to help her son open that goddamned drawer.

Her stasis was not of her own accord. She could only watch, lifting her eyes as a large male hand descended from the heavens. Adina studied it: muscular outstretched capable fingers, prominent knuckles, visible veins, smooth skin. They were kind, the hands of a nurturer.

She looked at this boy as he held on to the knob, his body twisting to the left so he could watch the hand of the Lord. He giggled in recognition, giggled as though they were long-held comrades, this boy and the Lord. As the hand came closer, the boy turned his attention back to the golden knob on the drawer. His concentration was of the utmost intensity; he pulled as hard as he could, emitting the most helpless, high-pitched grunt Adina had ever heard. He kept pulling until the hand of the Lord came down upon him. For a moment Adina felt secure. She understood that this boy would be watched over. He would live a long life. He bowed his head. Adina watched the hand tense, the knuckles turning red with effort. God's strength, in concert with the baby's tiny hand, made one attempt, then a second, to open the drawer.

To no avail.

For several minutes she watched as the two of them worked together, her boy and his heavenly Father. She watched them jiggle the knob, shifting energy this way and that for a drawer that was determined to stay shut. Eventually she had to step away. It was too much, the struggling hands, the baby's growing frustration with himself for something he couldn't help; it was all just too much.

Adina walked away. She paced around the first floor of the house. She needed to think. She stepped into her rain boots and opened the door. Outside, she knelt in prayer, her knees getting soaked in mud, the rain bounding down upon her. She bowed her head. A ray of sunlight peeked out from behind a cloud. Adina felt its heat; she felt the hand of God resting on the crown of her head. The rain continued to fall as she prayed for safety, a safe transition from that realm to this; safety for her son's long and healthy life. When she was finished, she saw through the falling raindrops that the sun had come out. Moments later, the rain stopped. She stood, clasping her hands, thanking the Lord. They would have this child; she was sure of it. Adina ran back to the house, back to the pantry. When she got there, dripping wet and panting, tracking mud through the house, all was silent, gray, empty, the sky overcast once more.

Gone without a trace, her boy. The knob, still gold; the drawer, still closed.

As though he had never been there, and never would.

THEN THERE WAS the Reverend; there was his wanting.

It was different, not purely the desire to have another child in and of itself. In a way it was for him, about him, this desire to father a son. He liked parity, that was part of it, had always wanted one of each. But it went beyond that. There was something about being a man—and being a Black man—about guiding another Black man to follow in his footsteps. He was careful; this wasn't a vanity project for him. While Adina's need for a baby was more acute, and the Reverend saw that, he couldn't allow it to move him until he felt his motivations to be aligned with God.

When they moved from Philadelphia, they chose Chagrin Falls for the quiet, and for the trees. It was oh so silent in the wee hours, eerie-like. The Reverend checked that all the doors were locked, that the stove was turned off, that the lights in the hallways hadn't lost their yellow glow from a battery gone dead, or a cord fallen from a loose outlet. Inevitably, he found himself back in his study, praying, his mind racing with thoughts of the Lord.

A call came after midnight, the phone ringing loudly, waking them. Adina never kept a phone close to the bed. She felt they were too available; she insisted that her husband allow them some bound-aries, now that he was no longer serving as pastor to a single church. That night the phone kept ringing, so John rose and answered it, but not before it woke Adina, and possibly Olivia, too. He went to answer it, while Adina went to Olivia's room. Who could it be?

A burning brick had crashed through the window of a new church, a young man and his young wife, the pastor and First Lady. This was at a time in the night when the saints should've been sleeping in their beds, prayers said, foreheads glistening from anointing oil, dreaming only of pearly gates and golden-paved roads.

As the young pastor spoke, the Reverend pictured him and his young wife standing on the sidewalk, a blanket around their shoul-ders, huddled among the broken glass, gigantic flames roaring in front of them, and the red and blue lights of two cruisers and a fire truck somehow offering more comfort than some of the white men who drove them. In the background of the young pastor's call, he heard the fire hose. He heard good men shouting, rubber boots clomping to the pavement. How fearlessly they must've galloped into that blaze, determined that this little church, a life raft for some in East Cleveland, remain in place, sturdy and tall. Safe and untouched.

These men were too late, of course. The flame spread, its target the aged wood, the building's weak foundation. It had never really been sturdy or tall. The young pastor called the Reverend because it was his job to call, his words calm but his voice distraught. *Sorry to wake you, so sorry but this has happened and I'll need your support, we all will. What can the association do? Of course there's no need to drive down tonight, you're nearly an hour outside the city, we'll be fine, we'll be fine, we'llbeabsolutelyfine,* the young pastor said, his cadence ringing in the Reverend's ear.

And then, a whisper: *But what are my wife and I to do?*

He heard it in the young man's voice clear as day: self-doubt spreading through him like fine cracks. This could be a man's undoing. A young pastor and his wife, reduced to bystanders in the wake of a threat so powerful their lives and livelihood were at stake. And their faith? Maybe not shattered, but neither was it unscathed. Though they were right to be thankful—they, themselves and their congregants, were not prematurely sent home to the heavens in a roaring blaze.

Counsel was needed. This was his job.

When the Reverend arrived, he held the young pastor and his young wife tightly to his chest. He studied the way the light from the flames illuminated their skin, shadowy embers dancing, mysterious and gleeful. They stood behind the yellow tape, held back by cruisers, the blaze unbridled. They stood among the crowd of those who'd come to watch, the neighbors who'd called 911—many of whom had never set foot in this church or any other, but were sympathetic nonetheless.

The Reverend took the young pastor aside. He spoke of things like insurance and lawsuits, hate crimes and rebuilding. *Of course we'll help,* he said, *that's why the Cleveland Baptist Association exists—for support during troubling times. Don't worry about a thing, you'll be fine, you'll be fine, you'llbeabsolutelyfine.*

The young pastor spoke of hope, his words and timbre becoming more like a sermon. Easier said than done, but as his voice grew in assuredness, bystanders moved closer, forming a circle around the young pastor. The Reverend watched the young pastor as he spoke, watched how his gaze moved north, his eyes following the skyline, moving past Lake Erie. He could see the pastor was thinking about escape, departure, considering whether or not he was ready to cut his losses. To start fresh, to land elsewhere, somewhere new. When he stopped speaking, and the crowd moved back to where they had been standing, just behind the yellow tape, the young pastor cleared his throat and nodded his head in the direction of his young wife. She had, by now, fallen asleep in the backseat of a cruiser, her husband's jacket draped upon her like a blanket.

"My wife," he later said when the Reverend pulled him aside. "She's pregnant."

The crowd was dissipating by then.

She can't be. Three words that lodged themselves in the Reverend's mind, sitting there like a tiny pebble that had found its way into a well-loved, well-worn shoe. He knew not where they came from or what they were doing, but there they were. *She can't be.* He felt the young pastor's panic—another mouth to feed, another body to house and clothe—and yet he showed no sign of such feeling. That was his job, and he was doing his best. The Reverend took both his hands and covered them. He called him *son,* told him again that all would be well, that he and his young wife would be well. He held his hands to his own chest, tried his best to breathe his steadiness and faith into the young pastor. It occurred to him then that this intense desire to transfer any strength he held to this young pastor might be exactly what it felt like to father a son. He thought of the boy from Adina's vision, and of all the moments he would worry for that boy. The Reverend hoped for rare moments when he wouldn't worry, when he would know that his son and daughter were safe, cared for, supplied with everything they needed. In his head he said a quick prayer for the two of them, himself and the young pastor.

In the years since that night, the Reverend had transposed Davis's face over that of the faceless, nameless, theoretical son he'd pictured that night. He led the young pastor in prayer. He did so quietly, in private, around the corner and away from the fire, of which the men had finally gained control.

By the time he arrived back home, the sun had risen over the trees and hills of the valley. It was a beautiful day. As he turned in to the driveway he saw a light in the kitchen, which told him that his wife had risen for the day, and perhaps by this point his daughter had as well. He intended to head straight into the study and issue that young pastor a generous check. The association was equipped to offer some help, but it would be nowhere near what was needed. But Adina wore a thin cotton bathrobe. She stood by the window warming her hands with a cup of tea. He longed for her. Adina was a place where he could lose himself entirely. Where he could forget. And there was so much he needed to forget.

The Reverend didn't want to disturb his wife from her reverie, so he closed the door quietly behind him. He dropped his jacket on the counter and kicked his shoes off. He walked in his socks until he was behind her. She knew he was there.

He leaned in close behind her and slid his hands around her waist. He rested his chin on top of her shoulder, nuzzled his nose in her hair, kissed her neck. She leaned into him, turned her head as though pressing her cheek into his. She sighed, then turned back to the window. "You hear that?"

He listened. "Hear what?" he said.

"Silence." She squeezed his hand. "That is silence." She took a deep breath in.

He nodded, his nose and lips still buried in her neck. He squeezed her waist tighter and she leaned her head back farther, her gaze now skyward. Her lips parted slightly, and as she rolled her head to the side, she said in a whisper, "Olivia is still asleep." She brought her husband's fingers to her lips. She placed the mug on the counter and led him up the stairs to their bedroom, where she closed the door. From there he sank into his wife. His lips went first, but it was his tongue that pulled him headfirst over the edge, so that he tumbled and twisted in the air as though he were a child who'd tripped into a well. He lost himself in the well of Adina, thought only of her womanhood, inhaling only her skin. He sank deeper and deeper, knowing that if he was to survive, if he was to emerge, he could only forage further.

THEY AGREED THEY wouldn't tell anyone—not Olivia and certainly not the association—that they were trying for another baby. Adina was steadfast in her faith that conception would happen, and that she would give her husband the son he finally wanted. She had a feeling the baby would arrive during summer; come June, she walked around with a sly little smile on her face, the knowledge hidden in the fiber of her being that she might already be pregnant, or would surely soon become. In the solace of their home, her hand gravitated toward her belly, rubbing it in circles as though her womb was already occupied.

The following spring, Adina woke bright and happy one morning, whistling and singing and eager. "I'm late, John. Eight days!" She hummed while making breakfast, a joy and lightness of being that John hadn't seen in years coming over her. But a few days later he came home from the office and found her sprawled across the bed, a mountain of crinkled Kleenex on one side of her and a deep red, almost purple stain on the other, spread like a continent over a map near the edge of their silver comforter. She couldn't look at him when she spoke.

"I'm not late anymore." She tossed a Kleenex into the air. "This is my white flag. I wave it proudly." Her laugh, an ugly bitter thing, like no sound he'd ever heard from her, hung in the air between them. "Imagine me, a mother to a newborn, at forty-one! What was I thinking?"

He still remembers how she looked at him, how she looked to him: eyes bloodshot, hair like Medusa's, her knees bunched to her chest, her arms wrapped around them as though they, too, were children who needed tethering. He had only wanted one more child—a son—but he knew then that he would raise as many babies as Adina wanted if it prevented her from feeling this way ever again. He was overcome with a wave of desire to raise and provide for another smiling, strong, healthy, dignified Black child. The desire to take his turn at raising a man, to one day look upon his son and see the men that came before, and the men that would spring forth. There was something scintillating about this. To know that his son would be one in a lineage, in a nationhood that would survive.

And of course he wanted to see his wife fulfilled. Happy. Of the simple variety.

The sort of happy that ignites joyous smiles and sentimental laughter and contented sighs. Rose-colored reflections and light-heartedness. Adina deserved this. How he misses, to this day, the sound of her contented sighs. Her slow breaths in and out, the pushed-out air landing against his cheek or chest when she was happiest of all. The way her hands and arms draped across him, sending warmth, touching him because life is better when there's physical connection. When you are touched. When your pieces fit together.

When you know your place in the great procession.

All this he thought in seconds as he dropped his briefcase to the floor, kicked off his shoes, and ran to the bed. He pulled his wife close, cradled her head in his arm and against his chest. He rocked her back and forth. He tenderly kissed the crown of her head and stared out the window. The night was clear, stars would soon be visible.

"It's okay, baby. I want him, too. I want our boy, too."

HIS WIFE'S PREGNANCY with Davis had been difficult, high-risk. *Geriatric* it was called, which she'd hated. The Reverend still feels in his legs the way he jumped up from his desk and bounded up the stairs when his wife screamed for him at the sight of blood between her legs, streaking between her thighs all the way down to her knees. He was grateful that Olivia was out of town overnight, visiting a college with her youth group.

He rushed Adina to the hospital where they waited, briefly, until they were sent to a private room. The Reverend was well-known at all the area hospitals—the work of a prominent clergyman—and in turn, he knew the hospital well.

They were willing to do him a favor because it turned out his son would be arriving that night, or in the wee hours of the next day— early, by more than a month. The Reverend is forever grateful to his calling, if for no other reason than his wife's survival that night. He'll never forget the visits, day or night, at all hours, usually two and three times a week, to any and all people who were under his spiritual guidance. Because the Reverend didn't pastor just one church, but instead ran a multi-racial coalition of more than forty churches in the greater Cleveland area, it was the pastors—who looked up to him, who deferred to him—who so often called on him in dire times. It was as though they believed his presence, his prayers, held more weight in the eyes of the Lord. *The Reverend's job is never done;* he'd said this to Davis many times as he walked out in the evenings, as he closed the door behind himself.

But then it was his wife, his son, whose lives hung in the balance. He felt naïve, in a way, realizing that even though he knew better, he, too, carried some sort of implicit belief that his proximity to God would protect his loved ones from the same trials and tribulations that everyone else faced.

Adina suffered a placental abruption, the event having gone unnoticed despite heavy monitoring because of the nature of her pregnancy and despite her having complained, repeatedly, of discomfort. The Reverend was allowed in the delivery room until the time came—at which point he was rushed out—so the baby could be cleaned and transported to the NICU, where he would live in an incubator while they monitored his lung development.

He felt, still feels, that he should've gone straight to the chapel, prayerfully covered his wife and newborn son in the blood of the Lamb. He couldn't bring himself to do it, perhaps couldn't humble himself in that way, so he sat in the waiting room, telling himself that he needed to be easily found for any and all updates.

He moved freely between the sitting area and the NICU. He watched his son's calm, quiet breath, lying flat on his back, legs spread and knees bent, skin pink and thin and translucent. The Reverend isn't sure he has ever been so proud, neither before nor since, of the way his little son, this tiny creature, was fighting for life before he even knew what life was.

You couldn't tell the Reverend that fighting wasn't God.

He might not have prayed, but he held his son with his eyes, and his wife with his heart. He listened when the doctors found him, when they deigned to update him. He signed forms and made quick decisions. He did his part and he trusted the Lord to do His.

WHEN OLIVIA RETURNED home, eyes sparkling and voice cracking at the mere possibility of Spelman, the Reverend brought her to see her mother, then her brother. When they reached the NICU, he stood back a bit, allowing her to stand as close to the glass as she wanted, to find her brother on her own. She identified him immediately, tapped the glass with her pointer finger, a knowing smile creeping across her lips.

It was a moment of rare quiet, no babies bellowing, only the sound of monitors beeping, and farther down the hall, a nurse's sneakers hurriedly padding to a hospital bedside. The Reverend stepped closer to Olivia as she turned back to her brother. He listened closely as she said the words, "Hi, baby; hi, baby; hi, baby." She didn't take her eyes off the baby. She waved her hand, as if he were an old friend, as though they had seen each other before, had said goodbye before. Then, from nowhere, she said, "You should name him Davis."

He laughed—the first time in days. "His name is John."

"You haven't named him yet." She pointed at the incubator. "It says Baby Freeman."

"Olivia, a baby boy comes to this earth with his name already chosen. Just as mine was and my father's before me."

She turned, her eyes boring into him as though made of steel. Mouthy. "He deserves his own name. And after what Mom went through, you should honor her."

"I can't name my son Adina."

"I'm talking about Davis. Davis Josiah Freeman. Her maiden name. It has a nice ring to it, don't you think?" She looked at him again before walking away, back to her mother's room.

Later, he and Olivia took the baby to his mother and placed him in her hands. Olivia leaned in close, her hands on her mother's shoulders, as they both stared into Davis's eyes, watching him squeal and giggle and wiggle his toes. His eyes roamed until they settled on his mother.

"Davis Josiah Freeman," he said, his voice a near whisper. "Davis Josiah Freeman."

He watched his son close his eyes, drifting off to sleep in his mother's arms. She trembled, and then smiled through tears, looking between her daughter and her husband.

THE REVEREND DOESN'T know if Davis plans to keep his name. In fact, he knows nothing of his son's plans because they don't talk. Everything he thinks he knows he's gleaned from logging into Olivia's Facebook account and poking around.

He's seen pictures of them, his Davis and this Everett. He knows how they sleep, what it looks like—their bodies lying next to each other, Davis on his side, just as he's always slept. When he was a boy, he folded himself against a stuffed animal or a body pillow. Now it's Everett—this is something the Reverend is sure of. Legs entwined with legs, arms around torsos, brown cheek resting against pink chest. He pictures them under cover of night, their bodies tumbling and dancing, always linked, connected, limbs coming together like silent chords in unsung hymns.

He's studied Everett: his perfect teeth and open-mouthed laugh, the aggression in his eyes when he's running with a football, chased by his brothers. Shots of him in a suit on the streets of New York, a portfolio in his hands. There's a picture of the two of them on a sailboat, Davis holding a glass of champagne, Everett holding a beer and standing behind him, one arm wrapped around him. He looks fierce, protective, and it occurs to him that Davis, having never learned to swim, probably shouldn't even be on a sailboat, orange life vest notwithstanding. He wants to be angry at the mere possibility of this white man playing fast and loose with his son's life, but even he can tell that when Everett is around, his son is safe.

Tomorrow Davis will marry a man with a firm grip and brazen handshake, a man who barrels his way through the world, certain of himself and his desires. If Everett has ever been afraid to go after what he wants, he's the kind of man who's more afraid not to. He's seen the way Everett looks at his son, and understands the nature of how Everett touches his son. He sees how small, how delicate Davis looks next to Everett. Here's another truth he needs to admit to himself: *In this marriage, my son is going to be the wife.*

TWELVE

Olivia Freeman sits in her car, gripping the wheel at ten and two. In ninety minutes, her brother's wedding will begin.

She would prefer the next few hours to pass like a Hallmark movie. She would prefer to be lighthearted enough to bask in their romance, to easily socialize with Davis's friends and new family. They might not be close anymore, she and Davis, but her brother deserves a wedding day filled with laughter, joy, and hopeful omens about the coming years. She wants this for him.

She can't believe the way they've grown apart, the place they're in right now. She's ashamed of it, even though she doesn't really think it's her fault. Olivia knows she is lucky to have even been invited—it's far more than the Reverend got—but there was a time in their lives when she felt like the center of her brother's world, and he the center of hers. She'd felt as though he was her baby. Not in parentage, not at first. But then there he was, walking and talking and being; having opinions, wanting and needing things, and always—always!—growing. And then suddenly, in what felt like the space of a breath, he was this tiny precious thing thrown into a motherless existence: Adina was gone, her body disintegrated from sickness in a matter of weeks.

He was the most sister-like brother a girl could have, and he was an angel. But from the very beginning, from the difficulty of his birth to the loss of his mother—throwing the Reverend into a tailspin—his young life seemed mired in difficulty. It had felt like a process of elimination at the time, but Olivia became the one: She was the one who made sure he had what he needed, that he was properly well cared for. She was the one who made sure he knew he was loved. She was the one who impressed upon him the knowledge that one day he would go out into that great big world and do something important with his life.

She knows that Davis remembers quite clearly how the Reverend retreated into his work after his wife's death and never really came back. She also understands that Davis couldn't know all the ways in which she stepped into that cavernous absence throughout his childhood. She doesn't begrudge him this lack of knowledge; she doesn't feel as though he should know. Every child is entitled to be loved and cared for. She would not want him to feel as though that love and care was some kind of charity, or anything other than what he should expect from his life. But here she is, sitting in her rental car after having purchased a last-minute flight, after having RSVPed no to his wedding—an answer that had surprised no one—because she'd thought it would be easier to simply not go.

They often had words when they spoke, and their last conversation had ended with his. So levelheaded, so cutting in his calm: *And what, Olivia, do you know about love?*

The things he doesn't know.

She'd thrown her phone across the on-call room. She resented his smugness, the way he dismissed her. How childish he'd seemed, given the fact that they were discussing something as grown-up, as profound as his wedding. And yet here she is, having made a last-minute sojourn to the Hamptons to be at his wedding, where she isn't even sure she's wanted.

It comes down to this: No matter the past, the three of them are a team, whether intact or fractured. The Reverend, Davis, herself. This is a fact, a true thing, but it feels like no one ever sees it but her.

OLIVIA IS GREETED by Charlotte the minute she walks into the house.

She notices, as Charlotte welcomes her, as Charlotte wraps her into a hug as though they were lifelong friends, that they are roughly the same size. For a moment, Olivia is sure that Charlotte feels her heart thumping through her chest.

"Your brother," Charlotte says, looking into her eyes as she pulls back. Hers is a smile that extends forever. "He's something special," she says. "Whatever part you had in raising him, thank you."

Olivia is speechless while her mind races.

"I imagine you're looking for Davis?"

"Yes," she manages. Charlotte guides her through the first floor, her hand on the small of Olivia's back, talking the entire time about the house: when it was built, how long it's been in their family, how Davis and Everett decamped to it a week ago to get some much-needed time together before tying the knot. Olivia nods, occasionally makes a sound, wanting Charlotte to know that she's listening. When there's a momentary break in Charlotte's soliloquy, Olivia jumps in.

"Just to be sure—you're Charlotte, Everett's mother?"

"Oh yes, I'm so sorry." Charlotte, for a moment, looks sheepish, before turning her attention back to climbing the stairs. When they reach the top, she points down the hall to a set of French doors. "The house has two master suites, and Davis is in that one. He'll be coming out for photos shortly, so I'm sure he's decent. You can go on in."

BEHIND THE DOOR to the master suite, Olivia hears her brother with his friends. Laughter, clinking glasses. Fabric moving and feet shuffling. He is happy and busy, and it's been a long time since she's seen him this way. She knocks, then pushes the door open without waiting for permission.

She has never been one for excess, and in this way, among many others, they are opposites. She sees first not the room, not the friends gathered round, nor the beautiful white jumpsuit. Not the makeup, nor the braids tied into an elaborate updo. She sees Davis, who first lays eyes on her through the vanity mirror. She sees the way his face evolves over the course of a few seconds, and she appreciates it— the way his brow furrows, then relaxes; the way his smile shrinks, then expands to a full-teeth, full-lipped, open-mouthed beam. Davis has sparklers for eyes, and in that moment Olivia, too, relaxes, and knows in the depths of her bones that she is right where she's supposed to be, and that all will be well.

He turns around, stands, opens his arms, and beckons her into the room. "I'm happy to see you." His smile is wide, bright, confident, his voice delicate, yet strong. She's never seen him dressed like this, not in person. Only his website. He hasn't performed yet as a professional in Cleveland, and she hasn't traveled to New York since his undergraduate commencement. It hits her in a way it never before has: Her baby brother is no longer a baby.

But when she hugs him, she's reminded of how diminutive he is. She steps back, hugs Phoebe and Zora, both of whom she's met once, at graduation. For a moment they exchange pleasantries, as warm and friendly as she remembers.

"We thought you weren't coming," Phoebe says.

Davis looks at the floor.

Olivia smiles at her, then at Zora. "So did I." Then she turns her attention to Davis. When he continues to look away, she steps closer to him, curling her finger under his chin, turning his face to look her in the eye. "I'm so glad I changed my mind." She nods, for emphasis, then steps back again. "Let me look at you."

What a beauty he is. Striking. She almost feels as though she's been slapped across the face with the force of it, the force of him.

Standing in this room, flanked by his friends, his expression serene and joyful. In an instant his life flashes before her eyes and she marvels that in the midst of so much early loss, he's found for himself exactly the life he's always wanted.

Olivia is astonished at how naturally he commands the room.

He reminds her of their mother.

His clothing is nothing more than adornments, embellishments, playing the role of accented lighting to him, the beautiful painting. They could fall from his body to the floor, leaving him standing there entirely naked, and he would look just as stunning. He was born to walk down that aisle to Everett. Implicitly, she understands this now.

After a few minutes, Phoebe and Zora make themselves scarce.

As she continues to study him, he turns his head so he can view himself in profile. He sends a furtive glance her way. "What?" he says. He chuckles, uncomfortable with her attention. She feels a twinge, the way their mother used to pinch her arm when she was little and had fallen asleep in church. Davis used to live for her attention.

"Nothing! Nothing at all. You look really beautiful, Davis. You—"

She pauses, stumbling over her words. Davis, who's now bent over the vanity inspecting his lips, looks at her expectantly.

"You really look like Mom."

He stops in the middle of reapplying his lipstick. "Wow."

"What? Something wrong with looking like Mom?"

Davis shakes his head, then sits. He turns, meeting her eyes, the emotions on his face so genuine it's as though he is literally transparent. It's a relief to know that she can still see inside him, all the way down to his core. To her, this has always been the beautiful thing about Davis. He is so capable of hiding what he thinks and how he feels, and then there are these moments when he's caught off guard and all that training, all the deftness that's always on display simply vanishes. In those moments his soul is laid bare, out in the open for anyone to see.

"It's ironic, that's all." He fiddles with one of his braids. "Because you're telling me I look like her. Meanwhile, I'm starting to forget what she looked like." His voice cracks at the admission.

In her chest Olivia feels a hand close into a fist.

Davis nods, bracing himself against the vanity. She can see how determined he is not to cry so he doesn't ruin his makeup.

"Well, that's understandable. You were so young." She takes a few steps toward him.

"Olivia, I don't have any pictures of her. They're all in Chagrin Falls."

She takes a few more steps. "That can't be. You didn't bring any with you when you went to Juilliard?"

Davis shakes his head. "I ran out of the house, straight to your place. Then to camp, then to school."

"And you haven't been back."

He shakes his head. "I haven't been back."

Olivia feels like a fool. There she was, not fifteen minutes ago extolling her virtue as a big sister, surrogate parent, when she never even thought to make sure he had pictures of the mother who died when he was five years old. "Oh, sweetheart. I'm so sorry." She's right behind him now. She puts a hand on his shoulder.

He winces at her touch. Immediately, she knows why: She's touched him in a way that the Reverend would have touched him.

Instead she moves her hand lower, to his exposed back. She rubs her palm in gentle, wide circles against it. "I'm sorry," she says again. Behind him, she marvels at how soft his skin is.

"This is the biggest moment of my life," he says. "I'm getting married. I need my mom." He continues looking down at the vanity when he says it. She understands he doesn't mean it as a rebuke at her presence.

Olivia walks over to the bed where she'd dropped her purse. She sits, opens it, scouring it for her wallet. After a moment, Davis stands at his full height and turns around. Olivia finds what she's looking for, a picture of their mother. She stands on a small stage, microphone in hand. Her smile is big and bright, her lips painted a bold, matte red. Her vest, denim. And her hair: black, waist-length braids.

"Come here," Olivia says, waving her brother over.

When he sits next to her, Olivia hands him the photo, a Polaroid. "You know she was a singer, right?"

"I know." He leans into, and against, his sister.

"Good. Every Friday night, for a full year, she would sing jazz at this coffee shop in downtown Cleveland. She never wanted me to go, but sometimes I would, just so I could take pictures."

"She looks so beautiful. Like Janet in *Poetic Justice.*"

Olivia leans close, gazing at her brother while he continues looking at the photo of their late mother. "Your entire life, all people have talked about is how much you look like her." Olivia looks at him conspiratorially. "And rumor has it that coffee shop was a haunt for Janet when she was filming another project and that she dropped in to sing a few times."

Davis blinks.

"Okay fine, that rumor has a circulation of one: me!" For the first time in years, she laughs with her brother. "Now, you said you need your mom. What is it that you need?"

Davis throws his hands up. "I need her to tell me it's going to be okay." He runs a hand over his braids. "That I'm not going to ruin this man's life by marrying him. I need my mom to tell me I'm making the right choices."

Olivia shakes her head before Davis finishes speaking. "I don't think you do, actually."

"What do you mean?"

"I don't think you need anyone telling you you're making the right choices here."

"Olivia . . ."

"When have you ever depended on that?"

Davis stares at her, unsure of how to respond.

"For as long as I've known you, you have always done exactly as you see fit. You collect the requisite information, you make a decision, and then you act. And you don't ask for permission."

"Olivia, what are you talking about?"

"When you were ten, and you wanted ice-skating lessons: You didn't ask me or the Reverend to get them for you."

Davis smiles. "I walked to the rink and asked for a list of private teachers and called them up myself. Then I told you and the Reverend I had a lesson on Saturday and that someone needed to pay for it."

Olivia laughs. "You had no patience for asking what I, or anyone else, thought. And when you ran away? You came straight to me. You didn't ask me what to do, or if everything was going to be okay. You asked for a place to stay, like a little old man. And I must admit: It's impressive." She clears her throat, then keeps going. "You got yourself to camp, and then to college, and you never looked back. And you never, ever asked if you were doing the right thing. When I asked you if you needed any help, what did you say?"

"I said, 'It's handled.'"

"You sure did." Olivia looks out the window for a moment. "You have never waited for someone to tell you that you were making the right choice—so why would you start now?" Olivia stands. "Look at your life. Look at the man who loves you. Look at his family that adores you."

Davis nods. "You're right." She watches as he closes his eyes, as he takes a deep breath. Something inside tells her to wait.

He starts shaking his head. They've never had a conversation like this before. "Everywhere we go, there are people, multiple people, who make it very clear they want to sleep with my fiancé. Men, women, gays, and theys, and I'll be right there, next to him, holding his hand—very clearly his partner." Davis shoves his engagement ring in her face to prove it. "And it's like it doesn't matter. Either they don't see me—like they literally don't see my body right there—or it never occurs to them that he would be with someone like me."

"Does he ignore it? I'll bet he ignores it."

"Actually, sometimes it pisses him off. Everett can be sort of . . . primal. He doesn't take well to anyone disrespecting me. But sometimes I wonder if he'll decide he wants to be with someone different than me. Someone masculine." He turns and looks at her again. "Someone white."

"Davis, if he wanted butch or white, I don't think you'd be here right now."

"He's never loved someone like me."

Olivia shrugs. "Now he does. What, like, it's hard?"

Davis remembers when Olivia took him to see *Legally Blonde* in theaters every week for the entire summer, just because he loved that movie.

Olivia shakes her head. She takes his hand in hers. "Don't play these games with yourself. Don't be more worried about what-ifs when you can be excited about what is."

Davis nods. "You're right." He shrugs. "When you're right, you're right."

He stands. "I guess that on some level I never thought this was actually going to happen. Meeting Everett was completely surreal. An unbelievable dream that was always going to end. He can have anyone he wants, guy or girl—"

"So can you!"

Davis turns so quick his hair, for a moment, is airborne. "No, I can't. I can't, Olivia! That's not how my world works!"

"Of course you can."

Davis shakes his head. "Do you know Everett was my first boyfriend since Jake?"

"Davis, you were in high school seven years ago. I know that must feel like a lifetime to be single, but trust me, it's not."

Davis puts his hands up in surrender. "The point is that this—all of this," he says as he gestures to the room around them, the house they occupy, "was never supposed to happen for me. In the gay world, I'm not the prize."

Olivia doesn't know what to say, so she waits.

"Do you know that Everett is the only person I've had sex with since . . ." For a moment he quiets. "He's the only person who has introduced me to his friends and family, the only person who's brought me to work functions." He walks over to the wall-mounted mirror, which Olivia has been admiring since she entered the room.

Davis stands as tall as he can, his left foot in front of his right. He leans forward, inspecting his face. He is not a smoker, has never been a smoker, is, in fact, an asthmatic. And yet he suddenly finds himself wishing for a cigarette. "My cheekbones look really good." He turns around.

"Good contouring," Olivia says.

"Boys"— Davis lowers his voice—"people like me? We don't get the guy. We don't end up married with two-point-five children and a white picket fence and matching SUVs. And when we do, we don't end up married to *this* guy. No matter how many times this guy tells us he loves us, this guy leaves us. And most of the time I'm not worried. Most of the time I'm very secure. Everett shows me he loves me every single day, and I believe him." Davis steps closer, pointing his finger at her. "But today, I'm getting married. Today, it feels like every single feeling I've ever carried has to make an appearance."

"Okay," she says. "I hear you, I do. But riddle me this: You already got the guy." She smiles, she shrugs. "Maybe the others don't get this guy. But that's because you have him." She gets in his face now. "He's yours, baby. I met his mother. She thanked me for you! I know for a fact that he's down the hall and can't wait to marry you. Doesn't that count for something?"

Davis nods. "Sure it does. But the magic will wear off at some point." He sounds as if he might cry, though his face only shows a hardness she hadn't realized he knows. Olivia moves to stand next to her brother, holding his hand. Sometimes she marvels at their shared genetics considering how different they look. Both short, both Black, but that's where the similarities end. She is dark-skinned and shapely, with close-cropped hair. He knows, and has voiced in very pointed ways, her own struggles, the eerie ways in which they have walked the same barren streets looking for love. She wants him to know that he is not alone, but then she remembers that this would, in a way, be beside the point.

Davis is not alone. They are here celebrating that very fact. All she has to do is snap him back into it, talk him back from the ledge.

"No, baby. Your magic isn't going to run out because it's not magic. It's just your life. You get to be happy, and you get to be loved. And you get to trust it. Lord knows you've earned that much, at least." She adjusts her feet; self-conscious about the way she wants to fawn over him, the same way she did when he was a boy. "And, Davis, perhaps the rules of this world you speak of don't apply to you because you've found the one man who is not of that world. I'm guessing Everett doesn't give a fuck about that world. So why should you?"

Davis turns to his sister and smiles, their hands still entwined.

"Well," she says. "I should get down there and find my seat." When she tries to pull her hand away, he clings to it.

"Walk me down?"

They are the only two people in the room. A single voice like a strain of music migrates in through the slightly open window. Guests are welcomed; jokes are made. Davis squeezes her hand again. "Please?"

And then there are no sounds, no voices, no words. Only his eyes, welling and trembling and filled with something pitiful.

"Davis, why aren't you happy?"

"I am happy, Olivia. I am insanely, deliriously, unbelievably happy." He waits, bites his lip, glances at the window, and then meets her eyes again. "And that's what I'm afraid of."

She nods, takes a deep breath. "Not today, you're not." She turns around, pulling him with her. They link arms and walk out of the room. Once they've reached the first floor, gently going down the stairs, Olivia releases him. "You know where you're going?"

Davis turns to her, watching as she steps back. He nods.

She shoos him forward. "Okay, go on now."

She watches as he brushes a braid out of his face and steps gingerly over the threshold of the front door. She knows she's supposed to go stand by the back door—where she and Davis will walk down the aisle. But they're going to be taking pictures for a few minutes, and she wants to watch. She quietly sneaks all the way up to the front door.

There they are, Davis and Everett.

Wow, she thinks. They stand like lovers. Davis gazes lovingly at Everett, his arms linked at the wrist and stretched upward, wrapped around Everett's neck. She watches as they kiss—tender, sweet, soft—as Everett leans back and picks Davis up. She watches her brother bend his knees, his foot suddenly pointing upward. She listens as he giggles, as their laughter grows. She watches as they strike a pose, Davis looking away, turned toward the ocean; Everett holding his hand, but stepping back, letting him take the lead.

Life is filled with beginnings, and this is one of theirs. Olivia wonders how many more beginnings are in store for her.

After a moment she retreats into the house, where she sticks her hand in her pocket and pulls out her phone. There it is in Facebook Messenger, the note from Ben—bolded as though she hadn't read it at least a hundred times since she first saw it among the hidden messages that come from spam accounts. When she happened upon it while clearing out her social media accounts, her heart dropped through her knees, all the way down to the ground.

Thirteen

The diagnosis came fast, the symptoms arriving all at once, their strength gathered like a hurricane. Stage IV lymphoma. An almost immediate prognosis of rapid decline. Night sweats, weight loss, fatigue so severe that Adina was often left unable to pick Davis up or keep up with his endless five-year-old energy. Coughing turned to vomiting blood. They did their best to hide her sickness from him, but in a matter of weeks, she was hospitalized for good.

John regrets now all the times he didn't bring Davis to the hospital. All the things he did because neither of them wanted the baby of the family to see his mother in that condition. If they could've stopped the formation of memories, they would've. Nothing more than skin and bones, cheeks sallow and sunken in, tubes running in and out of her. A five-year-old was too young to understand. Olivia took time away from school; a sister suddenly left to care for her baby brother. But one day, nearing the end, Adina asked for him, asked to see her miracle baby, to hold her Sunny Boy. She asked Olivia to bring him to her, and the Reverend no longer had it in him to deny her their child.

That first afternoon, Davis looked terrified as he slowly entered the room. He held part of his blanket up to his mouth. It was so long it would've dragged behind him, train-like, on the hospital floor had Olivia not been holding it up, walking ever so gingerly behind him.

"Go on," the Reverend said, his voice cracking.

Davis didn't move and all the Reverend could think was that he'd have to toughen the boy up because his mother wasn't going to be around to baby him for much longer. He picked his son up and placed him in the bed, alongside Adina. Lying next to her son like that somehow overemphasized how much weight she had lost, and how quickly.

"Sunny Boy," she said simply, her voice weak and soft and thin, like air bubbles wheezing from a balloon. She put an arm around her baby, pulling him close to her. The Reverend felt her joy in his bones, and in the exact same moment, he was hit with a profound sadness when he thought about all his boy was losing so young. He watched as Davis, just a little tyke—on his knees, his feet curled beneath him, still in his yellow Keds—leaned closer to his mother, to the soft warm body where he found his comfort, and his love. The Reverend watched as his boy reached out a hand to touch her, as though she was new, unfamiliar. He watched his wife watching her son, his eyes glued to her as she leaned closer and turned, bringing her cheek to meet her baby's open and outstretched palm. He watched several tears descend his son's cheeks.

"Mommy, what's wrong?"

At that point he was still having trouble with his *r*'s. He hadn't been told anything yet, other than that he would finally be seeing Mommy, whom he'd been missing for weeks, whom he'd taken to crying for in the darkest hours of night.

Adina pulled him as close as he was willing to be pulled, kissing him all over his face, his plump, round cheeks, his forehead, still shiny from the olive oil the Reverend had used to anoint him in the blood of the Lamb that morning—protecting him in the name of the Holy Ghost.

Mother and son needed privacy. The Reverend saw that, and he turned to his daughter, brushing his hand across her shoulders. "Come on, let's take a walk."

For a while they walked in silence, father and daughter, first around the hospital among the beeping machines, the hushed voices of doctors and nurses, many of whom they'd come to know personally. It was strange to be on this side of it, to be there needing help as opposed to the ones providing spiritual counsel. The doctors and nurses now used those same hushed tones when talking about Adina, her sickness, her treatments, and her drastically shortened future.

The Reverend led his daughter outside, where the warmth of spring was fading into the coolness brought by night. The wind picked up, and he offered her his jacket. He wanted to grab her hand, to feel the warmth from her skin and the life coursing through her body. He wanted to feel her mother in her.

As they stepped out of the main entrance of the hospital and walked around the campus, Olivia asked him a simple question, one for which he had no adequate answer. "Are you ready, Reverend?"

"No." He shook his head. "Are you?" They were both looking down at the asphalt as they walked.

"No."

"It's left to God," he said. He put his hands up. "It's above me now."

Olivia grabbed her father's hand for a moment, stopped, and looked him in the eye. Her life flashed before his eyes: her high school graduation, her four years in college, when she got her white coat. "Most of the time God makes it plain. We know how this is going to end."

He nodded, wiping away a tear. "Yes, we do."

They started walking again.

"Sometimes you treat him as though you never wanted him."

"Olivia."

She continued looking right at him, her gaze unfaltering, unending. "It's true. Mom has said so, too."

He took a deep breath and kept walking. He dropped her hand, which suddenly had begun to feel like a hard, hot stone. They continued walking until it became too chilly to remain outdoors.

WHEN THE REVEREND and Olivia returned to the hospital room, Davis lay stretched in the bed by his mother's side, sleeping once more, thumb in mouth, cheeks streaked with tears. He was held by Adina as she mustered the energy to stroke his forehead. She continued to kiss him every so often, even as Olivia and her husband entered the room. She scrunched her face and brought a finger to her lips, so they knew to keep quiet. Olivia settled into a chair and pulled a book from her bag, but could not tear her eyes from her mother and the child. The Reverend stood next to his boy, trying to pry him from his mother so she could rest, but Adina shook her head and instead gestured for him to bend close. He put his ear by her mouth, his hand atop hers.

"Be different, John. Be softer. He needs you to be soft in a way you weren't for Olivia."

He nodded.

"I'm serious," she insisted. "Olivia had me. He won't."

She stretched her neck and kissed him, then Davis. Olivia rose and stood by her mother, opposite the Reverend. She placed one hand on Adina's shoulder and with the other she held her brother's hand, stroking the inside of his palm, which was turned upward to the heavens while he slept, as though he held within it an offering. Like that they remained: quiet, clinging to one another, praying that it might be enough.

It wasn't.

The first time Davis screamed, hours after the funeral, not long after the guests had departed and his father had packed away food in the dark, Olivia woke, bounding from her bed, and ran to her brother's rescue. It was she who stood beside him, unsure at first of what to do as she witnessed him twisting, turning, shrieking like a thing possessed. Sense gone. Limbs flying every which way. She turned on the bedside lamp, took a seat next to him, and wrapped her arms around him. She pulled him close, rocked him like a newborn.

The next morning the Reverend sat at the kitchen table, head aching in his hands, doing his best to listen.

"I stayed with him until his arms stopped moving, until he stopped kicking," she said. She was pouring coffee into a travel mug, her suitcase by the door, her back turned to her father. After she set the coffeepot down, she went to the refrigerator looking for milk. "You're going to need to watch him. He could hurt himself. He was asleep the whole time." Her voice was low and serious.

"Olivia?"

"What?"

She stirred a packet of sugar into the mug and glanced at him when she tapped the spoon twice against the mug's brim. Her face didn't change—not a smile, nor a glimmer of softness. But she answered his unasked question.

"I can't stay. I have exams."

He remembers the sound of her boots clicking across the hardwood floor as she walked from the kitchen through the living room, pulling her suitcase behind her. How much she looked like her mother—short, darker skinned, with a head nearly shaved like hers. She stopped in the foyer and turned around, for a moment looking at him, eyes wide, round, blinking. Incredulous.

"How could you not have heard him screaming like that?"

John closed the door behind her and slumped against it, his cheek sticking to the glass. Olivia had worn her mother's perfume.

THE REVEREND DID his best to forget the bourbon he kept in his desk in the study. His drinking was under control. He could have one when writing, or thinking, or studying, or conferring with other clergy. Sometimes he needed to sit back, take a load off, and have a moment to himself.

Three nights in a row he helped Davis move stuffed animals from the rocking chair to the double bed where he slept all by himself. The boy needed company. There were giraffes, pigs, monkeys, and a cherished koala bear named Wally, into which his mother had recorded herself singing his favorite Christmas carol, "The Little Drummer Boy." All he had to do was squeeze Wally, hold him close, and her voice rose like a phoenix from the ashes. For three nights after the funeral, the Reverend sat all night long watching his boy sleep soundly, the same as he had always slept: flat on his back, his right cheek against the pillow, and his right arm flung above his head, bent at the elbow. Olivia had slept the same way until she turned thirteen. He wondered if she'd ever told Davis that.

He enjoyed the nightly ritual of getting his son ready for bed— helping him brush his teeth, setting out his pajamas, watching him climb into bed and under the covers after plugging in his favorite night-light. It quieted the Reverend, shushing the constant traffic that now ran through his head—visions of Adina, her full thighs, her sharp cheekbones, the three bangles she wore around her wrist. The way she always called him "my love," whispering it in his ear when he woke in the morning; and the way she kissed him good night.

Each night as the Reverend tucked Davis in, he'd watch him fight to stay awake. Listen as he tried to talk his way out of sleep, and instead talked himself further into it, his words slurring and his eyelids drooping. Three nights the Reverend observed with care, waiting for those screams that pierced the night like claws, leaving his slumber tattered and worn. He paid attention to the ways his boy shifted in his sleep—to the right, to the left. If he curled into a ball or turned his body around, the tops of his feet searching for the coolest patch of pillow. Davis slept with his mouth slightly open, his pink lips wet as a puppy's nose, with each breath parting just enough to release a breezy whisper. Nothing more than air passing through those lips, those lungs, that heart.

Everything was normal; his screams from the night after the funeral seemed a fluke, a one-time thing. So for the next two nights, the Reverend waited until Davis had fallen asleep, and then he returned to his own bed where sleep was elusive.

On the sixth night he broke down, tired and weak and mournful. He poured a drink. It started as nothing much, a nightcap. Enough to conjure his wife flitting around the room as she always had, a single lit bulb on her vanity framing her face in a soft yellow bloom as she readied herself for bed. So many nights he'd watched her—lying on his back, feet crossed at the ankles, arms crossed behind his head, a Bible resting on his chest and his reading glasses slipping down his nose as he danced in and out of sleep. That night it was a plastic cup that managed to maintain its balance as he slept, even as his chest bobbed up and down with each slow, measured breath.

The next morning, he woke, not remembering when, or how, he had fallen asleep. And he'd rolled over, the plastic cup crushed underneath him, the remaining drops of bourbon staining the sheets.

On the seventh night he woke with a start, the wind careening the valley, skimming the creek, screaming with reckless abandon. He stared at the emptied plastic cup, this time placed near the edge of the nightstand. It took seconds that felt much longer before he realized the awful sound was coming from the room across the hall—the room where Davis slept.

His vision blurred when he stood up, but still, he ran. Momentarily blind, he sped through the room, across the hall, and opened the door so hard it smacked into the wall, its knob crashing through the drywall, chunks and dust splattering to the carpet.

He saw nothing. No ghost in the closet. No monster under the bed. No intruder. Only his son, his perfectly innocent baby boy sitting upright, his little mouth stretched as wide as it would go, his body whipping around. Teardrops fell from blotchy eyes. He had never seen a body move like that—disjointed, uncoordinated, as though held together by nothing more than a piece of thread that might fray at any moment.

He grabbed each of his son's skinny toothpick legs with one hand and held them down. Then he mounted the bed and used his shin to hold his son down by his ankles. He needed both hands to trap Davis's arms. Palms open. Palms closed. Twice Davis slapped him before he caught both arms and brought them down against the bed where he held his son, captive to him as he was to his own demons.

From a window, moonlight poured across his son's darling little face. And he was a cherubic little boy. His skin was honey-golden in that light, his loose curls hung in ringlets framing his face. As his body calmed, Davis opened his eyes. They were the color of amber, filled with panic and confusion—as though the Reverend, his father, this dark-skinned man not far from elderly, was somehow unfamiliar, someone threatening.

He was startled by that look, so he released his son and leaned against the headboard, motioning to Davis, guiding him until he sat between his father's legs. He leaned back against his father's bare chest. The Reverend wrapped his arms around his son and began to sing into his ear, "Hush Little Baby." He felt the boy relax into his body, heard his breath settle back into its normal rhythm. He was Davis again, as though his own spirit had exited, and then re-entered, his body. With one hand the Reverend wiped away his son's tears when he finished the song. Davis turned around and saw his father crying. He placed one hand against his father's chest, and with the other he traced the trail of a tear down his father's cheek. He pulled himself up until he brushed his lips against the Reverend's.

In his memory, the Reverend has always felt as though his spirit left his body at the same moment his son's re-entered his. He felt this way because he was a father comforting his young son, and yet he jerked away from his boy, pushing his little body away. "No," he said. "That was only for your mother to do."

Disgusted, he peeled Davis from him as though he was someone other than the scared and grieving child he actually was. The Reverend stood from the bed and went close to the door. "Go back to sleep, boy." He drew the curtain closed so Davis would be enshrouded in darkness. "Under the covers. Now."

His son slid under the comforter and scrunched up his face, readying himself for more tears. He remembers thinking he was onto Davis—but onto what?

"None of that," he said.

He watched as Davis pulled the comforter all the way up to his chin. Then he backed out of the room. "Good night," he said, as he shut the door.

The Reverend walked quietly to the bathroom. He stood at the sink, turned on the faucet, and splashed his face with cold water. He studied himself in the mirror, trying to see himself through his son's eyes: the thick-skinned wrinkles of his forehead. His wide-set nose and fat nostrils. The mole on his left cheek with the hairs growing out of it. Adina had loved this face.

He turned the water off. He went back to Davis's room, pushed the door slightly open, and squinted in the dark until he could make out his son's shape under the covers, clutching a stuffed animal against his scrawny chest, quivering.

Asking, quietly, for his mother.

THE REVEREND CAUGHT glimpses of the quarry when the car tumbled down the hill. He couldn't see the water once he landed, only scattered shards from the shattered windshield.

At its surface, the quarry is frozen, but not far underneath the water rushes fast and powerful, so fast he might be swept away had the car not stopped in the nick of time. Somehow, he's not scared, not yet. He's awed by its power, reminded of the force God imbues into the natural world. He's alone, but not alone: The rush of the water underneath its icy surface is rhythmic, carrying a distinct cadence. The rustle of leaves fallen to the ground, the snap of branches broken by woodland creatures. He, too, feels imbued with something divine: peace. He feels suddenly overcome with the hope that his son, his boy, his Davis, will one day know the things his father so desperately wants to tell him.

Frigid air drapes the Reverend's body, sinking into his skin. He's never in his life been so cold. Movement, other than his eyes darting left and right, gradually nears impossibility. His body feels like a lie, a hollowed-out tree trunk. So he waits. And he listens, praying for help to come. He will either wait and die or wait and be saved.

FOURTEEN

Everett takes a moment, and a deep breath. He tugs on his suit jacket, squares his shoulders. He turns around, smiles once more at his twin brother and his father, who smile back. They confirm; he looks good.

"Better than your first." Connor steps close, claps Everett hard on the back. "I'm proud of you. You followed your heart." For a moment he looks choked up and brings a fist to his mouth.

Christopher rises, joins them by the door. "Do you want us to walk you down to the front door?"

Everett, finding it hard to speak, nods. A flash of something—regret, perhaps—moves through him. Caleb should be here; he should be walking with them.

Everett shakes his head. He should not—not after what he said about Davis. There has always been, Everett thinks, some kind of weirdness about Caleb, and how he talks about Davis, looks at Davis. The youngest of them, the most liberal education, and yet quietly homophobic.

When they reach the front door, Everett turns. Quickly, he is engulfed by both men, and despite being tallest, he somehow feels small, cared for, in their embrace.

"This is where we leave you, son." Christopher nods—short, curt, serious—and then he and Connor walk back to the back door, and to the patio.

He and Davis elected not to have a wedding party, not to have anyone standing up there with them, but Everett finds himself wishing he could be flanked by his father and his brothers. He'd expected to be filled with emotions today, to be happy and to feel at peace. He had not expected to feel the sense of pride that courses through him. But he feels it as he steps out onto the front porch, as he greets the photographer, as she directs him to stand a little way away.

"Here," she says, and points toward a wooden fence. So many memories climbing that fence as a boy; they flash through his mind in an instant: playing tag with Connor, and with his uncle. And years later, as a young man chasing Caleb, gently tackling him to the ground, he and Connor, a two-pronged Tickle Monster. "Lean against it. Look casual, unbothered."

Everett, who does a pretty good impression of a douchebag, strikes a pose. He laughs, changes it immediately to something more serious, pensive. He listens as the shutter opens, the camera taking shot after shot. He's gazing away, looking toward the road when everything seems to go silent: the shutter, the birds chirping. Everything stops. The photographer gasps quietly. Everett turns toward the house just as she raises the camera and starts photographing Davis, who steps gingerly onto the stoop. He looks down, grabs a part of his jumpsuit in his hand as he slowly walks down the steps.

Everett's heart beats a little faster. Davis has never looked more beautiful in his life. A vision, forever his.

When he reaches the stone path, Everett jogs over to him and holds out his arm.

"MY HERO," DAVIS says. Everett laughs. They walk over to their designated spot, Everett aware of Davis's sister back by the house. Standing, watching.

"How'd it go?"

When they reach the fence, Davis lifts his arms and links them around his neck. "It was like old times." They kiss, Davis's eyes like sand, glittering in the sun. "She's going to walk me down the aisle. And your mother already saved a seat for her with your family."

"That's perfect," Everett says.

"What about you?"

Everett shrugs. "I took care of some mess. Now I'm here—with you." He turns Davis around so they both face the same direction, and he pulls Davis against him.

"All in a day's work," Davis says. He leans back against Everett. He's never felt more calm, more peaceful, in his life. *This,* he thinks, *is what my life gets to be.* His joy soars through him. It's atmospheric, infectious.

The photographer directs them down a path toward the beach, away from their wedding tent. They hold hands, Everett leading the way. Davis studies him, studies this man whom he's chosen, and who has chosen him. He looks closely at his hands; at the way his fingertips go pink where they touch. He studies the hair on his knuckles, the perfect shape of his fingernails. He's putty when it comes to Everett; he'll follow him anywhere, anytime. It doesn't even feel like a choice. And this is how Davis likes it.

When they reach the beach, Everett bends down on one knee.

"Again?" Davis asks.

Everett looks up, squinting in the sunlight. "I'm going to take off your shoes so the sand doesn't ruin them." Everett holds him steady with one hand and pulls off each shoe with the other. His hand migrates, briefly, up Davis's calf, all the way up to his thigh. Davis listens—among the waves rushing the shore and the seagulls, he hears, distinctly, Everett's sharp intake of breath. He basks in Everett's desire. When the shoes are cast aside, they step onto the beach, into the sand. They only take a few pictures, the photographer insisting that she's got the shot. After Everett puts on Davis's shoes once more, he rises to his full height.

"So, I've got to go over there"—he jerks his head in the direction of the tent—"and get married. You're invited, you know."

He smirks. Davis swoons and leans close. They kiss. "Next time we do that, you'll be my husband."

Everett, remaining close, brings his palm to Davis's cheek, brushes his thumb across Davis's lips. "And you'll be my husband."

Davis laughs, smiles. "Will I? I feel like I'm the wife in this scenario."

Everett laughs, but doesn't break eye contact. "I'm not complaining." He looks down, then up at Davis, his smile permanent, his voice calm and smooth, an engine rumbling before takeoff. "See you over there."

Davis nods. He watches as Phoebe's assistant follows Everett, dancing around him, taking shots from every angle as he walks behind the house, along the beach toward the white tent whipping gently in the ocean breeze.

Davis and Phoebe walk slowly, gingerly along the stone path. She leans close, grabbing Davis's hand. "I've got gorgeous shots of him removing your shoes. The way he was looking up at you? You took his breath away." She shakes her head, then stops. "I'm just saying, I think you could've worn a paper bag."

Davis can't think of a time, a moment, when he's been any happier than he is right now, on this day. Phoebe puts an arm around him as they approach the house.

LOOKING OUT AT the ocean, a memory arrives in an instant, miraculous, an extra balm for Davis on his wedding day. His mother's face:

clear, high-definition, as though she is walking right next to him, in Phoebe's stead. He sees first her full lips, remembers how soft they were when they kissed his cheeks. Then her nose, rounded at the tip, and she'd had the longest, fullest eyelashes he's ever seen, and great big brown eyes, filled with every feeling a person could hold inside of them.

He feels her, too: Her arm wrapped around him as she kneels close, pulling a seashell from the sand. She holds it up to her ear, smiles, then throws her head back, laughing, before she holds it up to his ear. *If you listen closely, you can hear the ocean.* Her voice drips over his ears like honey; soft, lilting, filled with joy, brimming with wonder. She moves the seashell quickly away from him—there it is, there it isn't! In its place she plants a sloppy wet kiss on his cheek. She grabs and tickles him as they tumble backward into the sand, laughing.

Until she stops. She coughs hard, scary, into her fist, then rubs it around in the sand. "Isn't it a beautiful day?" she says to him, her voice choked but her smile bright once more. She slowly stands up, offers him her other hand, and pulls him to his feet. "Come on, the Reverend is down there."

"I'm tired," he says. He remembers sticking his thumb in his mouth.

He wraps his arms around his mother's neck as she tries to lift him. After a moment she puts him down and kneels, crouching next to him once more. "You know what, Bug? Why don't you run over to the Reverend? Down there." She points at her husband, at his father, standing close to the water, his eyes on the horizon. "Go on. I'll catch up." Davis can still feel the two tiny pats to his rear as he started running in the sand. Other memories have faded over the years, but this one returns, so close to him it becomes part of the atmosphere, impossible to grab and yet, somehow, coating his skin with its wetness.

He was a little thing; he hadn't understood what was going on. He's almost embarrassed; how sick she must have been that day, how weak, and there he was asking to be carried like a big baby when he could've just as easily walked.

In a way it feels like a premonition: a reminder that life will not always be filled with this kind of bliss. It's part of why he loves Everett, part of why he loves their life. He wants to believe in the safety of his smallness; that if he just shrinks into Everett, into Bam-Bam, into this life he's found, and this love that's found him, he can wait out the loss; he can go unnoticed, painful memories and the possibility of a painful future might pass him by. All five-foot-four of him, standing tall, on the precipice of the biggest day of his life.

But it also brings him joy, makes him feel as though his mother is secretly a part of his day, holding his hand in hers as he walks down the aisle. When they reach the house, he takes his sister's hand.

"Are you ready?" she asks.

Together they walk through the house—the front hall and the living room, navigating around the kitchen, occupied by caterers, until they reach the sliding glass door to the patio. In these few seconds, the clouds clear. Sunlight beams down on the tent.

"As I'll ever be," he says.

FIFTEEN

The Reverend sees embers of sunlight refracting in the scattered shards of shattered glass; he's certain of it. Hours have passed, morning isn't far off; he's certain of that, too. As he waits, memories flood his senses. He sees his children—his daughter, his son; his sun, his moon—moving through their lives. Olivia wearing pinafores to church as a little girl; Davis at the mall as a toddler, sucking his thumb sitting on Santa's lap.

He feels them, too: their newborn skin against his fingertips, their beating hearts against his chest. And perhaps, most powerfully, he can hear them. The evolving timbre of their voices; their laughter, their terrified screams, the somber way they began to speak as they got older, as they weathered unthinkable loss. He hears Davis most of all, hears his music. The Reverend closes his eyes as strains of classical music delight him. He'd always loved Davis's playing, even though he hadn't wanted Davis to go to music school. For many years the Reverend stood by his stance that playing the viola was a great hobby; it need not be any more than that.

The Reverend knows that not all memories he takes to his grave will be good ones. His mind turns to when Davis was a senior in high school; when he was supposed to be practicing for the final round of his college auditions; when he was still just a boy.

The Reverend was headed to an evening meeting at a church where the pastor had run off with a deaconess. He was running late, had returned to the house for whatever he'd forgotten, and as he rummaged through his office and then the kitchen table, where he also sometimes worked, he caught a movement from the corner of his eye. It was outside, in the backyard, under a zealously overcast sky. What was Davis doing out there? It occurred to him then: Why wasn't the house thrumming with music from the Bach suite Davis had mastered, and now performed by heart?

The Reverend followed the flutter he thought he'd seen. He moved through the kitchen, opened the sliding glass door, and stepped carefully into the grass. A dense fog sprawled across the valley. He cursed the early morning rain and the mud that would cake the soles of his shoes. He was walking toward the gazebo when he noticed the back, the shoulder blades of another boy—a white boy, shirtless, standing upright in the gazebo. The Reverend slowed, but crept closer until he could see the boy's exposed skin, pale, almost red in places. He studied his lengthy athletic frame, the baseball cap he wore backward, the Reeboks on his feet, and the jeans that were bunched around his ankles. He watched the boy move rhythmically, aggressive amid the thickening, unhurried mist.

It was Davis who lay flat on his back on the bench inside the gazebo, legs apart, heels pointed skyward. The Reverend watched the way that white boy moved slowly over his son's body. He watched those pale hips collide violently against his son. He listened as this white boy grunted, growled, and in the same moment, he listened as his son said *yes*. His Davis, his Sunny Boy: so light, so effervescent. A rose petal flitting around the valley.

The Reverend tried to look away, but he couldn't. He watched as that white boy bent down and kissed his son's bare chest. He watched his son arch his back, inviting this boy to slide an arm underneath him. In one swift movement that boy straddled the bench and lifted Davis upright, so that he was now perched on that boy's lap. He watched that boy's hands move with abandon and authority over his son. They roamed freely, invasive and possessive: The Reverend watched that boy slowly insert two fingers into Davis's mouth. That boy touched Davis as though he owned him, kissing him with practiced hunger. And then it dawned on the Reverend: This was not the first time this had happened.

The Reverend felt his blood pressure rising: He had not raised his son to submit to any man except his father and his Father. He didn't raise Davis to be touched by a man, let alone a white boy, as though that boy possessed him, dominated him, had any claim to his body. He didn't raise his son to shudder and whisper some man's name in the way that a wife whispers a husband's name.

The Reverend tasted bile rising in his throat. He thought he might throw up in his mouth, so he backed away from what he saw. He stalked through the kitchen and the downstairs hall and went upstairs to the master bedroom. In a corner of his closet, tucked underneath his ministerial robes, was his shoeshine kit, filled with black polish, cream, and several brushes. He grabbed it and went downstairs to his office, where he pulled a bottle of whiskey from his desk and poured several shots into a tumbler. He returned to the kitchen table, took an upholstered chair, turned it to face the sliding glass doors, and plunked it down with a violent thud.

The Reverend sat, spread his legs, and placed the kit on the floor between his feet. He removed his shoes, then the lid from the box. From there he pulled out several small rags he'd commandeered from Davis's old T-shirts, a horsehair brush, and a tin of black polish. The whiskey warmed him like an old friend, easy and smooth. Giving in to temptation was dangerous, but if Davis had, then he could, too.

THE HEAVENS OPENED.

The Reverend heard the boys before he saw them: Davis's joyous shriek at the sudden downpour, the chaos in their voices as they gathered their clothes and shoes and ran together toward the house. This has been true of Davis all his life: A happy laugh was like a jolt of sunlight on an overcast day.

Sunny Boy.

The Reverend rose, standing inches from the window, feet planted firmly on the ground. He flipped the light switch and lifted the tumbler to his lips. When the two of them emerged from the fog, he saw them together—Davis's body curled into that boy's, his cheek against that boy's chest, that boy smiling and talking, his hand linked in Davis's. And then they both stopped. Davis was looking at that boy, and that boy was looking past him, at the house, where the Reverend stood watching. They were only feet from the house now, thunder growing louder, the claps more severe. Davis turned, looked at the house, and saw his father. The Reverend had seen fear cross his son's face many times—at the start of a recital, or on the first day of school. But this was different. It became clear to him then, in the way that white boy touched his son, in the way he pulled Davis closer to him, and the resolute look he wore—his hardened jaw, his tightened grip—that that boy saw the Reverend as someone Davis needed protecting from. As though he was the threat, he was the man who'd broken and entered, and that boy had taken it upon himself to see to it that Davis was safe.

It was then that the Reverend got a good look at the boy, how much taller and stronger and bigger he was. He barely looked like a boy at all; he nearly looked like a fully grown man. He tried to push Davis toward the door, but Davis stood his ground. The Reverend nodded; Sunny Boy was well trained. The Reverend would not have stood for that boy leading Davis to the door as if this were his house, thinking he could challenge the Reverend. He was young, entitled, and foolish. He was a boy after all.

It wasn't until Davis looked like he would burst into tears that the Reverend beckoned both boys forward and into the house. This was a thunderstorm; he wasn't going to be the reason some rich white boy caught pneumonia and died.

Davis nodded and allowed that boy, his hand on the small of Davis's back, to guide him those last few steps. The Reverend opened the sliding door and stepped aside so the boys could enter. He studied the boy, who stepped back and waited for Davis to enter first. The Reverend recognized him from the local paper—he was excessively tall, went to school with Davis, had won that school a state championship in swimming. He extended his hand to the Reverend, who refused to look up at the boy, and instead closed the door behind them.

"This is Jake" was all Davis could say, his voice shaky.

"Put a kettle on. I'll go get you boys some blankets so you can warm up. When the storm subsides, Jake can leave." He turned around and climbed the stairs. It was all he could do to speak to his son, to be reasonable in front of that boy, that arrogant boy whom the Reverend found himself wanting to fight.

He wasn't happy to hear their voices moving through the house like disembodied spirits. Davis, always so understated, sounded almost giddy—perhaps the weight of his secret lifted, a bubble burst. And that boy's voice, deep and sonorous like a man's, a low rumble traveling through the house. The Reverend couldn't make out their words, not exactly, but he felt unmanned in his own home.

When he came back down the stairs, he crept quietly, avoiding the steps that he knew creaked. He stopped at the bottom of the stairs in the foyer. He wondered how long he would have to allow this white boy who was fucking his son to stay in his house. He waited, feeling the need to announce his return, which was perhaps the most disconcerting feeling of all.

He saw that he'd interrupted them when he returned with the blankets. Davis had been speaking, Jake's hand on top of his as though trying to reassure, though he retracted it when the Reverend returned. He handed Jake his blanket first, then draped the other over his son. He felt Davis's bony shoulders in the palms of his hands. He opened his mouth to speak, but once again found himself speechless.

"Mr. Freeman," that boy said, extending his hand once more.

"Reverend Doctor Freeman," he said, the words escaping his mouth like bullets. "You have some nerve." He didn't offer his hand, though he poured himself more whiskey.

"Reverend Doctor Freeman," that boy said, standing and extending his hand once more. The Reverend stared at him, but once again, did not offer his hand. After a moment, Jake nodded, took a step back, but refused to look away. Part of the Reverend was impressed with how foolhardy Jake seemed: He showed no weakness, no fear, but perhaps he could manage some respect.

Just as the Reverend sat down, the kettle began to sing.

"I'll get it!" Like a spring, Davis popped up to retrieve mugs and pour boiling water over chamomile tea bags, leaving his father and the boy he'd allowed inside him to their thoughts, and to each other.

THE TROOPER CAREFULLY removes his hand from the Reverend's shoulder, pulling it back through the damaged car. The Reverend listens to the trooper's boots crunching against the snow as he moves away from the vehicle.

"Please," he cries out, his voice merely a whisper. "Don't leave me." He catches a few of the trooper's words as he speaks with the other men who arrive in quick succession:

Assistance. Dangerous. Life. Hurry.

The trooper returns, kneeling beside him once more. So does an image of Davis: kneeling on a white rug in an apartment, his mouth open, his reflection dancing against a floor-to-ceiling window.

"I have a son, too." The trooper braces himself against the snow. "How old is yours?"

The Reverend sees that Davis's eyes are closed, that his head tilts backward, that his right arm reaches around the front of his neck.

"He's twenty-five." Is Davis praying? Does he somehow know?

"Sir, you don't look old enough to have a twenty-five-year-old son." The trooper smiles kindly. "Mine is seven months."

"A baby," the Reverend says. "Those were the days."

The white rug is not a rug, but a quilt on a bed. The arm reaching around Davis's neck is not his own. The Reverend pictures how their bodies move together, how Everett presses himself into his son.

The Reverend has never been so cold.

He wants to tell this man, this young, compassionate, kind-faced man, that children rarely turn out the way you expect them to. He wants to tell him that fatherhood will turn him into a monster, into a monstrous thing—and that it happens in the blink of an eye. He wants to tell him how confusing it can all be: the rage that will over-take him, blinding him, sometimes at the simplest, smallest thing. The confusion lies in the love that will flood him, too—when he least expects it—and how it will make him do crazy, awful, wonder-ful things.

The Reverend wants to say all of this, but he's too cold to move his lips, too cold to feel his tongue.

He closes his eyes, hearing panic in the trooper's voice. "Stay with me, sir! Stay with me!"

The other men begin to work.

In time, voices. Movement. Rubber boots clomping through the snow. The Reverend knows it's bad. He can no longer open his eyes. From an emergency vehicle parked at the top of the quarry, a steady beam of light shines down upon him.

Then Adina—her presence, her voice—beside him, her hand in his.

He knows the men will do their job. He will hear them doing it. He will feel them as they tear apart the car, hope rising within him as they pull his body free.

SIXTEEN

Before Davis knows it, he's standing across from Everett, their hands linked. Olivia sits with Everett's family, all of them watching intently.

Dearly beloved, we are gathered here today. The words are like an incantation; Davis and Everett are spellbound.

Everett finds himself acutely aware of every detail. Every time Christopher coughs, or a large gust of wind ripples the tent. Every word, in fact, every syllable uttered by Connor, whom Everett had asked to officiate. Phoebe and her assistant quietly snapping photographs, silently moving with the agility of ninjas to capture each moment from all the right angles. Zora reading a poem, bringing nearly everyone in the audience to tears. The moment when Davis surprises him, cuing Bam-Bam who trots obediently over to them, carrying a Tiffany blue ring box in his mouth.

Davis shakes his head, laughing. "I didn't think about how gross this would be."

"I love you," Everett says, also laughing, overjoyed at how Davis found a way to involve their dog; impressed at the thought of all the training this must've taken. Everett breaks, ever so slightly, when

Davis bends down to grab the box, opens it, and slides the ring onto his finger. He sheds a few tears, and proudly looks over at his family, loving the way Davis holds his hand even tighter. Then a few moments later, Connor stands and pulls an identical ring box from his suit jacket and hands it to Everett, whose hand quivers as he slides that ring onto Davis's extremely steady outstretched finger, next to the diamond engagement ring he'd surprised Davis with after proposing.

For Davis, it's different.

He and Everett are in their own little soundproof bubble. He feels as though the entire world is cut off—their family and friends have disappeared, the sounds of the seagulls and the ocean are muted. Only Bam-Bam—and only for a moment—pulls his attention away from Everett. For these few minutes, the world is rid of ghosts and pasts, and forward is the only direction in which they can look.

When they speak their vows, when they say *I do*, when they kiss, and everyone who's gathered to celebrate them stands and claps, the spell doesn't break; it opens, its warmth spilling forth, inviting everyone in.

After the kiss—their first married kiss—they join hands. Davis flashes a brilliant smile, poses. Everett kisses him again, tender yet insistent. Davis tingles everywhere Everett's hands touch. After pulling apart they walk back up the aisle, Everett pumping his fist into the air, and Davis feeling closer to Everett than he ever has, carried away into his future, into the life he wants, and by the man he chose.

"Not sick of me?" he asks Everett.

"Not a chance, Sunny Boy."

BY THE TIME the first dance comes along, night has fallen. Waves rock gently against the shore, the moon full, the stars bright, any lingering clouds having dissipated. Tea lights hang from the tent and bunches of flameless candles light the dance floor. As Everett leads Davis to the center of the dance floor, to the whistles and hollers of the audience, and the first pensive chords of the guitar are struck, all eyes are on them.

They move simply at first, a basic slow dance—left, back, right, forward. Their bodies appear almost glued together. Davis looks up at Everett, one arm around his husband's shoulders, the other hand resting on his chest. Tears well and stream down his face. Crying seems the only way to express his joy at the evening they're having, and the gratitude that fills him.

This is his life. This is his family. He breaks from Everett's gaze and glances at his feet.

Yup, still standing.

He glances around the tent at the happy, drunk, smiling faces, swaying to the music, all staring back at them. Olivia waves, then smiles, wistful. Part of him wants to run to her, to drag her onto the floor to dance with them. *Look what's happened,* he wants to say to her. He can feel Everett's hands tighten on his waist. He turns his attention back to Everett, who leans his head down, who caresses his cheek, who asks, "You okay?"

Davis nods, leaning his cheek into Everett's palm. He opens his mouth to affirm, but Everett sweeps him into a soft kiss. As he does, through his peripheral vision, he sees several bodies step from the shadows and join them on the dance floor in simple black leotards and tights. He looks closer and sees several of his dancer friends from Juilliard. There's Macy and Amber, Jordan and Clark, Nellie and Sierra, Jabari and Neil. Davis watches his friends, clapping along with the guests, as they begin an interpretive dance. He glances at Everett, not believing what he's seeing—that Everett, who constantly asked Davis to remember that he'd been married before, and to not go too overboard, planned something this elaborate, with Davis none the wiser.

"Did you . . . ?" He trails off as the dancers immediately start moving, their choreography in unison at first, then diverging into different patterns and poses, their bodies at different angles and levels.

Everett nods, then places a finger to his lips. Davis turns around and leans into Everett. Like that they slow-dance, turning in a circle so they can watch the pairs twirling and leaping and pirouetting around them.

FOR THE REST of his life, when Davis thinks of the moment during the reception when his sister came up to him holding her phone, he will think first of the way his chest tightened at the mere mention of the Reverend. Then he will think of the way his throat dried up and his tongue felt like sandpaper as she repeated herself. He will hear the crash of the champagne flute he dropped. He will remember the way he stumbled past her, past all the other guests on the dance floor because he needed Everett. He needed to find his husband. He will think of how in that moment, when it seemed the entire world might crumble underneath him, he knew exactly who and what he needed.

There will be nights when he wakes suddenly, sheets drenched in his sweat, from the appearance of Zora's face, and the expression she wore as she took a sip of champagne and looked up at him as he moved wordlessly past her. He will forever feel a thousand hands, those of his guests, reaching out to touch him, to stop him, to dance with him, to tell him how beautiful he looked. His body will relive the weight he felt in his limbs, the blurred vision that suddenly afflicted him. He will remember the way he got up and left Olivia, and the way she followed quickly behind him. For years to come his hands will instinctively gather and lift the fabric of whatever he's wearing at the memory of hurriedly running up the stairs of the veranda.

THE BALLS OF his feet feel the pounding. Dusk sets in behind him, the lights inside the house blind him. He pauses, momentarily feeling like an intruder in an unfamiliar home. He doesn't know where to go, where to look. He only knows that he needs to find Everett.

He sees the kitchen through the library, light beaming through the hallway. He runs to it and arrives at the island where a waiter approaches him offering a leftover appetizer. "Have you seen my husband?" he asks. He feels invisible for the lack of care they take to answer him, anger rising inside him like a genie awakened. Then Olivia appears beside him, her hand sliding into his as she clears her throat and calmly repeats the question. "Have you seen the other groom?"

Their faces tell him they don't know where Everett is, but the head caterer approaches Davis and Olivia, placing his hand on Davis's shoulder. He bends down to Olivia and points her toward the staircase, saying something in a French accent about the family. They rush through the rest of the house, brother and sister, yet when they reach the stairs, Olivia stops him. They hear Everett's mother knocking furiously, a fist banging in perpetual motion against a closed door. "Caleb? Caleb!"

She is not a loud woman, but her voice is as loud as it can be, traveling as far as it can travel.

"He locked the door, Christopher."

"He's mad at me. He's fine, Charlotte."

"You put him in the treasure chest room."

"So?"

She knocks again. "Caleb?" Still, nothing but silence on the other side of that door. "Caleb, honey?"

Davis takes one step before Olivia blocks him with her arm. She places a finger to her lips, then to his lips.

He hears Everett. "Mom, what's the big deal?"

Charlotte's voice has depth and fortitude that Davis has never heard before.

"You don't understand, honey. Neither of you does." She knocks again. "Caleb? Honey?"

Her voice becomes increasingly loud, her energy increasingly frantic. Davis and Olivia look at each other as they hear her moving upstairs, the floor creaking underneath her.

"I should go up there," Davis says.

Olivia shakes her head.

"What? I'm family now."

She shakes her head again.

Upstairs, Charlotte begins to knock again, harder and faster.

"Mom, stop it, you're going to hurt yourself!" Everett says. Davis pictures her tears; he sees the way her body begins to shake with fury at the situation before her.

"Kick the door in."

"What? Mom!"

As Davis takes another step and begins to climb the stairs, slowly and quietly, he sees how Charlotte is standing, feet shoulder-length apart, arm up as she points at the door and looks between her husband and her oldest son. "Kick the door in! My son is in there." Her anger rips through them, an invisible force. "He's sick! I need to know he's okay!"

"Charlotte!" Christopher says.

Then she roars. "Get that door open now!"

As Davis rounds the corner, he sees the way Christopher lifts his wife from in front of the door. He sees Everett plant himself in front of it, his suit jacket flung to the floor beside him. He watches as Everett, in one swift movement, kicks the door open. Charlotte rushes past Everett, gasping as she enters the room. Davis rushes to Everett's side and feels Everett's arm slide around his waist and pull him close. He loves the ease of this movement, how automatic it is for Everett to hold him so close. "Everett, what's going on?"

His voice is quiet. He watches, alongside his husband, as Charlotte bends over the edge of the bed, trying to wake her youngest son. He watches as Christopher runs to the attached bathroom and fills a glass of water.

"Come on, Caleb. Come on, honey!"

Charlotte lightly slaps Caleb's face, many times over, uttering another gentler command. "Caleb, Caleb, Caleb, come on, sweetheart. Come on, honey, wake up!" She pauses for a moment, staring at him, and then falls to her knees, bending until her face meets the carpet. "Wake up!"

Davis steps in. "Charlotte!"

He points. She follows his finger, Caleb beginning to stir, her husband splashing water in his face. Caleb pushes himself up, and looks at his mother and father, his brother and Davis. "Mom, what gives?" A confused expression shapes his face.

She looks at him, then rises and runs to the bathroom. They hear the sound of her vomit splattering into the toilet. Davis and Everett back out of the room and turn around. Behind them, Christopher places one hand on Everett's shoulder, the other over his mouth as he begins to breathe harder. "I can't believe I forgot," he says, astonished. "Her brother fell from the window in that room."

Christopher walks away from them then, down the hallway, still covering his mouth, still looking shell-shocked at his own lapse in memory. They don't use that room. Charlotte hasn't been inside that room in twenty-five years.

Davis hears Caleb get up from the bed and walk to the bathroom, where he addresses his mother. "Mom, I'm okay. I was just asleep." Everett enters the room, standing in the doorway as his little brother bends down close to his mother and pulls her into his arms. "It's okay, Mom."

Davis grabs Everett's hand. "Everett."

Everett turns to him, startled. He sees that Davis is filled with feeling for the moment. He sees how his eyes shine bright, filling with tears. He sees how small he looks standing among this family of giants. All else vanishes as he leads Davis back to the master suite. Once inside, he presses Davis against the door, eagerly kissing his neck and running his hands up and down his body, his anger at his brother only enlarging his love for Davis. "My family is a fucking mess. Do you know how much I love you?" he whispers into Davis's ear. "Do you?"

Davis's body is still, trapped between the door and Everett. He turns his face to the side, and then places a hand against Everett's chest. "Everett, stop."

Everett removes his hand from behind Davis and steps back, watching as Davis moves furtively to the closet where his suitcase is stowed away. He listens as Davis tells him what he's just learned from Olivia: that the Reverend's body was found hanging upside down in the car he'd bought Davis when he was sixteen. Davis is scant with details, not knowing many himself. But Everett sees it— the Reverend's body, hanging in that car having rolled over the edge of the highway somewhere in western Pennsylvania.

"We're lucky," Davis says, repeating what Olivia's told him, "that the car stopped where it did because if it had rolled any closer to the quarry, the car would've drowned and he might never have been found."

Everett unzips Davis from the ivory jumpsuit, watching as he steps out of it and finds a pair of jeans and a sweater from the pile of clothes he tossed into his suitcase. "So she and I are flying to Cleveland. They've sent him to the morgue, and we have to identify the body."

Everett nods, then wordlessly starts to pack his things. He is deep in thought as Davis stops, watching him for a moment. "Everett, what're you doing?"

"I'm coming with you."

"You are?"

He looks at Davis, standing across the room staring at him like he's an alien. "I'm your husband. I come with you."

He watches as the smile he knows so well and loves so much returns to Davis's face, a brief apparition, but there all the same. "Right. You're my husband." Davis drops the clothes in his hands and walks quickly over to Everett.

He places his hands on Everett's cheeks and kisses him, throwing all of himself into it. He wants to forget everything and everyone for just a little bit longer. "You come with me."

Davis buries his face in Everett's chest. Everett wraps his arms around him, squeezes tightly, picks him up, then puts him down; Everett's fingers trace circles against his back as he stands, shirtless, in the center of the room trying to figure out what to wear. Standing only feet away from where they were that morning, as though the day has been wiped clean. Poof! Invisible—a blank slate. As they pack in silence, Davis thinks only of the lie he'd told in bed that morning: *If I'd wanted him to come to the wedding, I would've invited him.*

BOOK TWO

ONE

Davis throws his head back, laughing at some joke Everett's made. They stroll hand in hand along Forty-second Street. They're headed to the bowling alley where Connor and his wife, Courtney, made reservations for the four of them, and they're running late. But Davis doesn't care; he is truly and unapologetically happy. Surrounded by tourists, waiting for the light to change, Everett slips his arm around Davis and pulls him close for a kiss. As their lips meet, a fat snowflake lands on Davis's cheek, and when they break apart, he looks skyward. Davis finds himself looking at plump, puffy clouds, and thinking about the word *heaven.* It makes him enormously grateful to be exactly where he is.

As they wait, he turns in a circle, watching the flakes fall to the ground. He listens vaguely to the people around them and their conversations, and the horns honking in the backed-up traffic. He turns in place, Everett's arms around his waist, Everett's eyes on the light, waiting for it to turn green. For a moment the city falls silent; Davis feels like the dancer at the center of a snow globe: the special girl, the one the world revolves around.

"You're adorable," Everett says—almost, Davis feels, as though his mind has been read. "C'mon, the light's green." He takes Davis's hand and leads him across the street.

"Thanks for getting me out of the house. I needed this. But bowling?"

When he turns to look at Everett, Everett winks. "Connor suggested it. We loved bowling when we were kids." He shrugs, slides his hand just below Davis's waist, and lowers his voice. "Maybe we don't stay out too late."

Davis shivers, then smiles at the heat emanating from Everett's hand. He's not so sure about ducking out early. He's still getting to know Connor and Courtney, and this is a rare chance to hang out with them without the specter of the entire family hanging over it.

WHEN THEY ARRIVE at the bowling alley, Connor and Courtney have already rented their bowling shoes and chosen the lane. Each of them holds a fruity-looking cocktail with an umbrella in it.

"These are disgusting," Courtney says when she hugs Davis. "Way too sweet."

He laughs. "Can't they just pour in another shot? We're in Times Square!"

It takes Davis a minute to unzip his coat, take off his hat and gloves and scarf, and pull off his boots—black leather, knee-high, three-inch heel—in favor of the bowling shoes. Courtney sits down next to him, puts an arm around his shoulders. "Those boots!"

"Impulse buy," Davis says. "I've never worn heels before, but I love them." Before Courtney can comment, he continues. "I also haven't been bowling since I went with my church youth group in seventh grade." He stands, shrugs, looks around. Not a minor in sight. "Bowling alleys sure have changed." A waitress comes over, and Davis orders a gin martini. "Ice cold, please."

When the waitress leaves, Courtney leans close to Davis. "I don't want to ask how you are, but . . ." She clicks her tongue.

Davis is quiet as Everett and Connor, both choosing bowling

balls, stop their conversation and look over at Davis and Courtney. Davis walks to the racks of bowling balls and grabs the smallest one—a pretty blue ball with glitter swirling all over it—and carefully sticks his fingers inside it. "I would much rather be here."

"The funeral was today, right?" Courtney looks at him, and Davis wonders what she's thinking.

He nods. "He hasn't been a part of my life in years. I don't see any sense in changing the course now." Davis looks at Courtney, hoping that he's gotten his point across. He takes his position at the top of the lane, as though the game has started. He closes his eyes, holding the ball in both hands. He knows his talent for bowling is next to nothing; knows that in this contest, in this family, he will almost certainly finish in last place. But he thinks back to those youth group outings; at some point he'd caught the hang of it, and he knows that muscle memory is real, and that if he concentrates really hard, he might manage to hit a strike or two.

He can just make out Connor's voice, quiet next to his wife. "Hey, babe, we didn't plan this so that Davis would have to talk about his dad if he doesn't want to, okay?"

"I know," Courtney says, annoyed. "But he might want to. When you're going through these things, you never know what you're going to feel, or when."

Davis is trying to drown them out when he feels Everett's cheek by his ear, then Everett's hands around his waist. "Don't you worry 'bout a thing." He kisses Davis on the cheek. "Do you want any pointers?" Davis nods, thinking mostly of Everett's lips against his skin, Everett's hands caressing his body.

THEY'RE HALFWAY THROUGH the first game, well into their second round of drinks, when Everett gets up to use the bathroom. Courtney and Davis sit together, commiserating over their respective standings thus far, third and fourth place.

"At least you're pretty decent. You could actually beat those two.

And I hope you do, so they have to admit to their father that they were beaten by a girl. Plus, everybody loves a comeback story."

"You know," Courtney says, almost conspiratorially, "Caleb is even better. He'd be wiping the floor with them. None of us would stand a chance. Where is he, anyway? He loves to bo—"

Courtney stops talking when Connor raises his eyes and clears his throat.

"What?" Davis looks between them as he gets up to take his turn.

Connor shakes his head. "Nothing. We just thought it would be more fun tonight without him. It's your turn. Take your shot; try to hit some pins this time."

Davis stands still, his eyes moving between the two of them. "Is something up with Caleb?"

Connor is quiet, looks at his feet. It's Courtney who speaks first. "You know, Davis, something did go down between Everett and Caleb, but I don't actually know what happened, either." She gets up, walks over to Connor, and sits next to him.

"But Everett and Caleb haven't seen each other since the wedding," Davis says. "It's only been a month."

Courtney shrugs, feigning obliviousness. "Yeah, Connor! It's only been a month! So, what happened?"

Connor looks at her, his frustration with her obvious. He whispers audibly, "Seriously?" He sighs loudly, looks around for Everett, who remains in the bathroom. Then he walks over to Davis. "Look, Caleb got high the day of your wedding."

"Right, Everett told me that, at least. I'm sorry, I thought he was doing better with that."

"So did I. We all did. Anyway, it got a little heated and—"

Davis nods. "What did he say?"

"Connor!"

Connor stops talking. Everyone turns to Everett who's returned, who walks up to the lane staring at Davis. "I leave you with Davis for five minutes!" He barks these words at Connor. His walk is quick, aggressive. He's pissed.

Davis turns to Connor. "So whatever he said, it was about me."

"Connor?" Everett says again, his tone a warning.

Davis ignores Everett. "Was it racist?"

He watches as Courtney's eyes widen. "Oh my God, was it?"

Connor shakes his head. "Everett had your back. That's all that matters."

"So it *was* racist."

"No, baby," Everett says. "It wasn't racist."

"But it was bad enough that you're icing him out?"

Everett sits and begins to re-tie his shoes. "Can we please focus? I've got a bowling game to win."

"Yeah." Davis nods. "Okay. Sure."

This time, when he releases the ball, it travels down the lane in a straight line, perfectly center, knocking down every pin. When he bowls again, he knocks down every pin but one. At the end of the night, all of them are laughing again, the momentary tension almost forgotten.

When Everett goes to return his shoes and pay the tab, Connor sits down next to Davis. "You know how much he loves you, right?"

"I do." Davis nods.

"He punched Caleb in the face, banned him from the wedding."

Davis gasps. "Holy shit. He did that?"

Connor puts a hand on Davis's shoulder and squeezes.

Davis is reminded of Olivia, and of that night so many years before, when he'd run to her for safety, when she'd kept him, fed him, but never addressed with their father what he'd done to make Davis run away in the first place. He thinks about the fact that he's been here in New York City since the news of the Reverend's death, that he did not, in fact, return to Cleveland with Olivia. He wonders, briefly, about the funeral, held earlier today, a full month after the Reverend died so churches across the country could send their pastors and bus their congregants to Cleveland. He thinks about the hole his absence will have left in the pew reserved for the Reverend's family.

Davis rises to his feet, grabs the bowling shoes, and walks over to the shoe rental counter next to Everett. As he waits for an attendant to come and collect them, he turns around, his back to the cubbies filled with shoes, the bowling balls housed in a glass display case. Everett kisses him, pushes him back against the counter. All is fine, he thinks, as Everett's tongue works its way between his lips. Olivia had said she understood why he wasn't coming home for the funeral. He sits in a new family pew now.

WHEN EVERETT HAILS a cab and opens its door, he stands back so Davis can slide in first, just to the center seat. Everett tells the cabby where to go as he relaxes, extending his arm over the back of the bench. Davis leans against him, and every few minutes Everett turns and kisses the top of his head. They don't speak until they reach the West Village, when Davis turns, looking up at Everett, who pulls out his phone to pay the driver. "Caleb must've really said something awful to get you so angry at him."

"I'm not telling you what he said."

"Okay," Davis says. "Can I say one thing, though?"

"Of course."

"You're gonna need to forgive him someday. He's your little brother."

Everett looks away from Davis, through the window. "I know."

The car pulls to a stop in front of their building. Everett opens his door. "Someday. But not today."

Everett walks around the back of the car, joining Davis on the sidewalk.

"I can promise you that whatever he said, I've heard and survived worse."

"I know you have," Everett says. They walk into the building, and when the elevator comes, Everett pulls Davis inside it, against him. "It's one thing when you're out there, running around in the real world. Look at who just got elected. Shit is only getting more and more dangerous. But when it comes to us? You're going to be safe with me, Davis—mind, body, and spirit. I won't allow my family to threaten that, not even Caleb. I don't care if it's an accident; I don't care if he's high." He pauses, tightening his grip around Davis's waist. "You're what matters most to me."

As soon as they enter the apartment, Everett pushes Davis against the wall. His lips are hungry, his kissing urgent. In that moment he wishes he could be Davis's entire world, his protective bubble.

They haven't been intimate since the night before their wedding. Davis has been, understandably, preoccupied.

"I miss you," Everett says, almost breathless. He runs a hand along Davis's thigh, lifting it, wrapping it around his waist. His other hand strokes Davis's neck. "You know, technically, we haven't made love as husbands."

"I'm sorry," Davis says. "I want to." He looks up at Everett, eyes big and bright, hands running the length of Everett's torso. "Now."

Everett pauses, looking into his eyes. Davis puts his leg down, takes one of his hands, and leads him down the hall, through their bedroom, and into the master bathroom. He turns on the shower, and then he backs himself up against the counter where he hops up, sits, and spreads his legs.

Everett growls as Davis lifts his arms. He pulls off Davis's sweater, then his own. He smashes Davis's lips with his in between removing their clothing, and by the time they're both naked, the water is hot, the mirror covered in steam. Davis jumps down and leads him into their shower, where he positions himself under the shower-head. Everett wraps his arms around his husband. They kiss long-ingly. Everett spanks his ass gently; Davis moans. He places one hand against Everett's cheek, pausing to look deep into his husband's eyes. He's looking for his future, but he can't yet see beyond his past.

"Did you really hit your brother?"

Everett smirks. "I did. He disrespected you."

Davis trembles, waves of desire moving through him. Everett backs him against the wall.

"That's kind of hot." He arches his back and Everett lifts him by his waist. He wraps his legs around Everett.

"Yeah? He went down with one punch."

"You defended me." Davis moans, giving Everett a devilish grin, his desire only becoming more intense.

"I'd do it again in a heartbeat."

Everett braces himself against the wall with one arm. He takes a moment to stare at Davis, to study his face. He sees the yearning in his eyes. They kiss, Everett's tongue lapping slow gentle strokes against his lips. When Davis moans again, Everett enters him, unwilling to make him wait any longer. Davis cries out; Everett slows down. He looks at Davis, who opens his eyes, who nods slowly. Then he kisses Davis again, pushing himself deeper. He is cautious, gentle, tender in a way he usually is not. And his eyes never move from Davis's face, which is why his heart stops when he sees tears welling in Davis's eyes; why he's already pulling himself out when Davis presses a palm against his chest.

Standing there, the water splattering against them, Davis speaks first. "I'm sorry." His eyes circle the drain.

"Did I do something? Did I hurt you?"

"No." Davis shakes his head, then steps to the side and out of the shower. "I just can't." He apologizes again, stepping around Everett to exit the bathroom.

Later, they lie next to each other in bed.

"It's okay," Everett says. He shifts onto his side. "It's probably too soon."

"That wasn't about you," Davis says. "You know that, right?"

Everett nods. "Come here." He pulls Davis close to him, gently rolling him onto his side, cocooning himself around him. He runs a hand up and down Davis's side. He wants to say something, but he doesn't have the words. Until he feels Davis's body start to tremble: He's crying.

"You regret not going."

Davis shakes his head. "I'm glad I didn't go. What I regret is being his kid."

"Davis—"

"My father died on our wedding day, Everett. I'm angry! He has no place in this marriage! But I keep feeling like he can see me now, see us. I can't get him out of my head."

TWO

The next morning, Everett has already left for the gym. Davis sits up in bed and wraps the comforter around himself. He stands, opens the bedroom door, and beckons Bam-Bam into the room. He watches as Bam-Bam bounds forward, bouncing onto the bed, and burrows into the blankets.

"Bam-Bam, can I show you something?"

Davis walks over to the closet and flips the light switch as he enters. Like the Montauk house, this apartment features a large walk-in, but it's even more luxurious. In the center there's an upholstered bench where he sometimes sits with coffee. Against the back wall is a standing full-length mirror. Davis has always wondered how these items came to be because when it comes to fashion, Everett keeps it simple. Fitted suits, turtlenecks, and button-downs in dark colors, jeans, tennis and running shoes, and a few pairs of boots. His side of the closet isn't even filled; so one glance, and anyone would know whose side was whose. But Davis, as he moves through years of clothes—shirts that he wore in auditions and slacks he's worn for concerts, the garment bags housing the jumpsuits he now exclusively performs in—feels as though his side of the closet isn't nearly as Davis as it could be, when Everett's side is so clearly Everett.

When he reaches the back of the closet, he kneels. There, the two boxes—the wedding jumpsuit and the wedding dress.

Davis is excited to get every picture from the wedding, as soon as they are ready. But truthfully, he's especially excited for the disposable camera photos from when he tried the dress on. He pushes aside the box containing the jumpsuit and opens the box containing the dress. When he runs a hand along the bust, he sighs. Something about it calms him. He stands, pulling the dress from the box. He unzips it, sticks his legs in, and pulls it up to his chest. It's strapless, but it holds, as he tries to zip it up all the way. When he knows it's secure, he walks out of the closet. Bam-Bam, sitting upright on the bed, seems to nod his head, before jumping down and trotting over to Davis. Davis walks back into the closet, Bam-Bam following him this time. He stands in front of the mirror. He gathers his braids on top of his head, mimicking a simple updo. The dress has a long slit in the fabric up the side. Davis finds it, shoves his knee through it, then his entire leg, almost to the hip bone.

Everett loves his legs; he would've loved this.

Davis looks himself up and down in the mirror, but he realizes the picture isn't complete. He rushes out of the closet and into the bathroom where he keeps several tubes of lipstick behind the mirror. He grabs one, the bold sensual red that he wore on his wedding day, and carefully applies it, his hand steady as ever. He turns his head to the left, then the right. Pretty as a picture. The Reverend's worst nightmare: his boy in a dress. He wonders if his father can see him now.

He smiles. "I'll give you Sunny Boy," he says. He looks at his lips, painted in a strong, bright, sensual red. He undoes the bun.

He shakes his head. His locs fall to the right side of his face, reaching halfway down his chest. He lowers his underwear—the black thong he'd worn under his jeans last night—pulling his feet free of it, then stands there completely naked underneath that dress. He lifts one arm, pressing the palm of his hand against the crown of his head. He leans into that arm and cocks his head to the side. He crosses his legs tight, tucking himself between his thighs. He flexes his already flat stomach, arches his back, and turns to the side.

Full hips and thighs, yet carrying the slender waist of a goddess, he feels unbelievably sexy for the first time since the wedding. He feels like himself. He sucks his cheeks, pursing his lips, then unzips the dress, still looking at himself in the mirror as he does it.

I could have it dyed, he thinks as he carefully folds it back into its box, and tucks the box back into the closet. *I should* have it dyed.

DAVIS CLIMBS BACK into the bed, allowing himself to fall into the plush feather-down pillows. He stretches, then curls his legs. He rolls around, sprawling in the bed in Everett's absence. He tries to take up as much space as possible, gradually urging Bam-Bam toward Everett's side of the bed. It happens by accident, his sudden arousal, his hand brushing his dick. But there it is, insistent. Just what he needs, he thinks, to get him back in sync with Everett. He opens the drawer in their bedside table, where he pulls out a jar of coconut oil. He dips his fingers into the jar, the cool solid melting on contact. He scoops it out and drizzles it on himself. At his movement, Bam-Bam starts, then jumps down from the bed. He trots to a corner in the room where he hides in one of his favorite spots behind an accent chair.

A surge of guilt moves through Davis. Since he's been with Everett, he only masturbates when he travels, leaving Everett back in New York. There's no need, and even though he knows Everett would only encourage him, he feels a bit like he's cheating. He finds it hard to maintain his focus, though he's determined to get off. He thinks of Everett—of his shoulders, his chest and arms, and how good he is with his hips. Davis is filled with longing; it's almost painful. He opens his eyes; streaks of yellow, orange, and pink sunlight stream through the windows, painting the walls. He thinks, again, of the heavens, and then of the Reverend. If the Reverend saw him last night, if the Reverend saw him in that dress moments ago, then it follows that he can see Davis now.

Yet Davis finds himself unencumbered. He keeps going, anticipation building every second. He's defiant in the Reverend's line of vision, determined to get what he wants. And when he does, he falls into the pillows, panting, wondering how he got through this solitary, arguably shameful experience when last night he couldn't get over the fact that the Reverend, now being in heaven, might have seen it all—every little thing Everett did to him, not only last night but on the eve of the wedding. The Reverend now knows, beyond certainty, how Everett takes control of him, makes him moan and shudder; the way Davis whispers Everett's name as though it's the last word he'll ever say, and how he sometimes calls Everett "Daddy."

Davis lays there for a moment, simmers down. Then he rises. He walks to the bathroom where he wipes himself off.

ONCE DAVIS HAS made a fresh pot of coffee, he returns to the bedroom. One of his favorite things to do on a lazy morning is drink his coffee in the shower. It was Everett who gave him the idea, Everett who once entered the shower with Davis in one hand, a fancy German stout in the other. Davis has no interest in beer of any kind, but he does enjoy a coffee or a glass of pinotage in the shower from time to time.

He stands tall, throwing his head back as the water washes over him, as the heat envelops him. He's been feeling a bit congested, as he often does this time of year. The shower is a place for relief, a place where he can fill his lungs to capacity, and when he does— whenever Davis takes the deepest of breaths—his grip on life tightens. He feels grounded, free, alive in the most literal sense! He remembers something the Reverend used to say: that as long as there is breath in his lungs, there is the chance to get right with God.

Davis hasn't thought of this thing the Reverend used to say in years.

After taking a few minutes to relax, he begins by washing his hair, massaging his scalp with a moisturizing shampoo, really working it into his roots. After he rinses, he does the same with a heavy-duty moisturizing conditioner, which he lets sit in his hair for seven minutes. Then he rubs a sugar scrub up and down his legs, his arms, and his torso. He stands directly under the water, allowing it to rinse out the conditioner and rinse the sugar from his body. Then he washes, all the while taking small sips from his coffee. It feels nice to pay attention to his body, to treat it well. He needs this.

When he steps out of the shower, he realizes that Everett is back home. He dries himself off, wraps a towel around his waist, and walks into the bedroom. "Good morning," he says lovingly, sweetly. He walks up behind Everett, who stands by the bed removing his shirt. Davis wraps his arms around him. "How was the gym?"

Everett seems a bit distracted. He takes a moment before he answers, then throws his phone onto the bed. "It was fine. Nothing special."

Davis sits on the edge of the bed. "Will you lotion my back?"

Everett climbs onto the bed, positioning himself behind Davis, who hands him the lotion. He dips two fingers into the pot, then spreads it over his hands. "What do you want to do for breakfast?"

Davis turns and glances back at Everett, who uses his forearm to push Davis's locs around his shoulder. He starts by rubbing the lotion all over Davis's back. "I was thinking it might be fun to cook for you. Pancakes?"

Everett is surprised. "You don't want to go out?"

Davis shakes his head. "I feel like nesting. So much has happened the last few weeks, and we really haven't gotten a lot of time together."

"Why don't we order in?"

"I mean, sure. I almost get the feeling you don't want me to cook for you."

Everett pauses, then kisses the top of Davis's head. He takes a deep breath, his tone gentle. "You are so talented at so many things . . ."

Davis laughs. "Fine, fine, fine, order from your precious diner! I see how it is." He shakes his head, playfully slapping Everett's thigh.

Everett moves his hands to Davis's lower back, where he starts to massage him. Davis squirms; Everett hears a sharp intake of breath. "That hurt?"

"A little."

Everett decreases his pressure.

He begins to feel Davis loosen when Davis's cellphone rings. It's Olivia.

"Hi," Davis says when he answers it, his voice dreamy, as though he's minutes from falling back asleep. Everett can't hear what Olivia says, but he feels Davis perk up. He watches as Davis nods, as he begins looking around the room.

THREE

As Olivia drives, she's struck by the lilting sound of her brother's voice, connected by Bluetooth to the speakers in her car. The effect is granted, entirely, by the quality of her speakers, but he sounds close, almost as though he actually sits in the car, riding in her passenger seat, the same way he did when he was a boy and he'd visit her on weekends.

She nods when he thanks her for handling the funeral. It takes her a minute to realize that the silence on the other end is him, because he can't see her nodding, can't see her acknowledging his gratitude. "You're welcome," she says. "I understand why you didn't want to come." And she does understand, though deep down, she wishes his love for her could have eclipsed the dysfunction of his relationship with the Reverend. Intellectually, she understands why it doesn't. Emotionally, she fears that her brother has found the limits of her empathy.

"I know it was a lot of work."

She nods again. "Yeah, it was a big service. Lots of Baptists to wrangle." She takes a moment, makes a right turn. "But anyway, I called because I've decided to sell the house. There's no need for it anymore. You're in New York, I have my own place, and it's so far out there in Chagrin Falls."

"Oh," Davis says. "I guess that makes sense." He pauses; Olivia suspects it's him who's nodding now, who has momentarily forgotten that they can't see each other.

"I'm not in any rush to do it," she says.

"Okay."

"There's a lot of stuff that's yours."

"Yeah."

She rolls her eyes. "Davis. You're going to need to come get it, sort through it. Toss it, donate it, figure out if there's anything you want to keep."

"Oh! You can just toss it. Torch it for all I care."

"Davis, everything from your childhood is in this house. You want me to just get rid of all of it?"

She waits. She hears some shuffling in the background. "Is that Everett? Hi, Everett!"

"Hey, Olivia. We're just over here figuring out breakfast."

Something about the bass in his voice stuns her over the phone. She blinks. "I won't keep you then, but let me ask you something right quick. Don't you think that Davis should take some time to look through his stuff?" She listens as he chuckles, relaxed, easygoing. "I mean, you've never even been to Cleveland, right? Never seen where he grew up, never been to the school he went to as a kid, you've never eaten at any of his favorite local restaurants, right?"

Everett chuckles again. They've only met once—at the wedding—and yet she can easily imagine the way he's nodding, his chin resting against his thumb. He was distinctive and had made an impression. "She's got a point, Davis."

"It would be nice to see you at home, sometime," she says.

"You're right," Davis says. She can practically hear him rolling his eyes.

"Like I said, I'm not in a rush, but I'd like to put the house on the market this summer. So maybe you can come home in the spring?"

"Okay," Davis says. "I'll figure it out."

"Awesome. Thank you, love you, bye!"

Olivia is unsure of how that went. It's true, she really does need Davis to come home and deal with all his shit. There are clothes and favorite books and school projects and photo albums. Surely there are things Davis has forgotten, things that if he just saw, he'd want to keep. But it's more than that. Olivia's on a mission. The Reverend's death has clarified some things for her. This relationship can be rehabilitated. She and Davis can be close again, and she wants that closeness; she needs it. Davis is the only family she's got, and there are things he's finally old enough, mature enough, to know.

Like the long-buried truth that, in the early days of their mother's pregnancy, when Davis was technically an embryo, no bigger than an apple seed, there were two pregnancies in Reverend Doctor John Freeman's house.

Or the fact that she'd intended to get an abortion before either of her parents knew anything about it, in part because her high school boyfriend, Ben, was white. This was something they shouldn't have had a problem with, given that it was their choice to buy a house in lily-white Chagrin Falls, but Olivia was smart enough to know her father didn't always have a close relationship to reason, especially where race was concerned, and especially where his daughter was concerned. Though the Reverend led a coalition of more than forty Baptist churches in the greater Cleveland area, the majority of them being white, he thought white boys were generally unruly. He regarded them like vultures. Their fathers, he'd felt, were rarely any better. A part of him—she'd long suspected and now knew—had relished his own distinction, his two graduate degrees, his doctorate from an Ivy League theology program, in a sea of white mediocrity. He led these men, was held in high esteem; his counsel was sought and, most often, obeyed.

A daughter pregnant at seventeen, a senior at the most exclusive girls' school in the city, was inappropriate, never mind her commitment to her own ambitions, her own future. For Olivia, the choice had been very clear, until it wasn't. She has no regrets, and no desire to become a mother—not now, not ever. All of this would be a massive revelation for Davis, one she's not sure he's ready to receive. She wants to feel him out, see where she can get with him, but it's going to take time to repair the relationship that once was.

The Reverend's death is a reminder of this, too: that everything— life, love, and the secrets we keep locked inside—is bound by a ticking clock, one way or another.

FOUR

Everett is at the office when he gets a frantic call from Davis. He checks his watch as he answers, putting Davis on speaker.

"I've got, like, three minutes; what's up?"

"Everett, I've . . . I've won an award."

"Baby! Congratulations!"

"It's called the Finley-Whitaker Career Grant. It's a really big deal." Davis speaks in a monotone, as though he's in shock. His energy is not entirely dissimilar from what it was at the wedding when he learned of the Reverend's death. Behind him, Everett hears the drone of a news channel.

"Tell me about it."

Davis takes a deep breath. "Every year this foundation selects ten to twelve recipients, all emerging classical musicians. The award is fifty thousand dollars, and we have to do a solo debut recital at Lincoln Center. It'll be reviewed, so I'll have to bring it—"

"You always do."

He hears Davis smiling through the phone. "I always thought my quartet might have a shot at it, but I never thought about it for me as an individual. A soloist."

"How did you find out about it?"

"My agent just called. The press release will go live after the new year, but it's all very secretive until then. Our recital dates are already picked out, but if you went to Lincoln Center to see a schedule of next year's artists, my date would just say TBD. Not even Finley-Whitaker Career Grant."

"So they just chose you?"

"Yeah. It happens this time of year. I have friends who've won it, you know. But it's never on the exact same day, and no one really knows how they make their selections. It just happens, and then all of a sudden, you're a star."

"That sounds incredible! Davis, we have to celebrate!"

"No, we can't! Not yet—it's top secret until the press release!"

"Let me at least take you to dinner. Just the two of us. You've been wanting to try that new place around the corner. What's it called?"

"Enoteca. Yeah, it's tiny. But insanely expensive."

"It's in the West Village. Everything is expensive."

"Okay, yeah, that could work."

"Leave it to me. I'll text you all the details."

"Okay! This will be a nice change of pace. Thank you!"

Everett rises behind his desk. "I love you. I'm proud of you."

As Everett hangs up the phone, he takes a moment to really consider all the work Davis has put into this moment. He practices endlessly, many hours every day. He and his friends geek out over Bach, Beethoven, and Brahms. This is a part of Davis that Everett admires, loves to brag about even, but doesn't share in, and doesn't really understand. He's always thought this was a good thing. Their work lives are completely separate—very different endeavors in very different fields surrounded by very different people. And Everett and Davis hold their careers in very different types of esteem. For Davis, music is part of his identity, a calling bestowed upon him from a higher being. In fact, until now, he's said he feels a little icky when referring to what he does as his "career." For Everett, his work in wealth management is a means to an end. He enjoys the work, enjoys making deals and winning; it taps into a part of him that he sometimes feels the world wants to tamp down—his aggression, his maleness, his endless desire to run with the big dogs.

It's important to him, but not important in the same way. It is not a constant force in his life, a thing he relies on for a sense of safety, or purpose. It doesn't see him through his challenges or heartbreaks. It's work.

They talked about it once, Everett readily admitting that if he didn't do this, he would do something else and be similarly content. Davis couldn't fathom what that felt like. "Music keeps me going," he'd said. "It's why I'm on this earth."

Davis also said, on many occasions, that he would be perfectly happy if teaching became his primary source of income. Everett can't even begin to fathom that.

LATER, AS THEY walk to the restaurant, Everett guiding Davis the few blocks with a hand on the small of his back, he finds himself enchanted. Davis, it seems, has gotten used to the idea of this prize. He's more himself than he's been in weeks.

He's always a bit experimental with his fashion. Tonight, he wears high-waisted gray houndstooth pants and a matching sweater with cold shoulder cutouts—a set, he'd said back at the apartment—made of thick wool, cinched with a black belt, and the same pair of black knee-high boots he'd worn to go bowling. His locs are gently gathered into a loose, messy bun. He's never worn an outfit like this, at least not since they've known each other, and Everett finds it, and his joy, incredibly sexy.

He suspects that tonight might just be the night.

When they're seated, Davis leans back, crossing one leg over the other. Everett has loved Davis's shoulders from the moment they met; he loves how they're on display tonight, his skin taut, glistening in the soft warm light from the cocoa butter and coconut oil he'd rubbed all over himself earlier that evening. He gives Davis a sly smile from across the table.

They chat, Everett telling Davis about his day, wanting only to hear more about the prize. The waiter comes, glances at them both, and addresses Davis.

"Good evening, miss, my name is Paolo and I'll be your server tonight."

Everett wonders, briefly, if it's the outfit or the makeup—Davis's face looks very similar to the way it looked at their wedding, the way it looked the other night when they were out bowling. He knows how much Davis hates his beard, lamenting the discomfort of the hair growing in. He seems happier with it covered up.

"Thank you," Davis says.

The waiter blushes. "My apologies, sir—"

"None necessary," Davis says. He smiles, his cheeks a little more pink than they were before.

The waiter finally turns his attention to Everett. "Would you like to hear about the specials?"

ONCE THEY'RE EATING, Everett listens to Davis—thinking, processing, scheming, about the prize.

"I've been on the phone with Clarissa all day. She can't do too much before the press release, though she can start some conversations and make sure I'm top of mind when the news hits. I'm going to start getting far more frequent invitations to solo with orchestras, from all over the world. To give recitals in amazing venues, to teach at prestigious festivals and programs. It's going to be a lot, but it's going to be so good!"

Davis looks giddy as he leans across the table, as he slides his hand into Everett's.

"How does this compare to that competition you won a few years ago? In Austria?"

Davis takes a deep breath. "That was a big deal, too. That got me a lot of what I've done in the last three years. But now, there's only one competition that's really a step up from this, and I haven't entered it. I'm going to have to now, and I'm going to have to place." Davis dims for a moment, intimidation setting in. "I'd kind of hoped to avoid it, honestly."

Everett strokes the top of his hand with his thumb. "You don't have to do anything. But also, I know you'll be amazing. You're already one of the best." He smiles as Davis smiles.

When their food comes, he asks more questions. "So you're going to be traveling a lot."

"We always knew that would happen eventually. I'd love for you to come with me, though, when you can."

Everett nods. "Like I did in Seattle."

Davis breaks his gaze, fingers his engagement ring. "Yeah."

"I'll see what I can do."

"Everett, I'm serious. I'm going to need you." Davis squeezes Everett's hand. "My mother was the one who wanted me to be a musician. But it's the Reverend who made it happen. He paid for all my lessons; he drove me to orchestra rehearsals; he was proud of my talent. This is his win, too. He's at the root of this part of my life. And that means that music is another thing that's inextricably tied to him."

Everett nods. In just a few seconds, Davis has added dimension to his musical career in a way Everett hadn't considered. It's like a twister, Davis's talent, traveling this way and that, taking what it can from every available source and stowing it away, somewhere inside him.

WHEN THEY ARRIVE back at the apartment, Davis gives Everett a lingering kiss in their bedroom—the kind of kiss that means that's all he's getting. "Will you walk Bam-Bam?"

Everett nods. He changes, quickly pulling on running shoes, gray sweatpants, and a Dartmouth sweatshirt to protect him against the frigid cold, though if anything, Everett needs to cool off.

A walk this late is always a quickie for Bam-Bam, but when they reach the lobby and Bam-Bam takes off running toward the West Side Highway, Everett is shocked. He quickly picks up his pace to match his dog's. He enjoys the surreptitious glances and bemused expressions from late night passersby at what he's got flopping around in his pants. A drunken twink gives a little nod of his head. Everett rolls his eyes and runs right past him, irritated despite the fact that this boy has no way of knowing he's married.

Everett knows he can have just about anyone he wants—man or woman, gay or straight, married or single—but the last few years have been different for him. There's only one person he actually wants—the one person he's suddenly having trouble having.

Carefully they cross the highway, running south along the water, nearing the pier. Bam-Bam begins to slow down, paws traversing a regular route, but never this late at night. Everett loves the West Village, loves this pocket of the city, relishes the way it feels like a charming little wonderland, something out of a vintage Americana film.

After his divorce, Everett had never intended to be married again, never wanted to share his life with another person in that way. As he and Bam-Bam run toward the water, he thinks of all the days when Davis broke through the barriers Everett successfully held in place for more than a decade: the anniversary dinner when he gave Davis a key to his place, the Thanksgiving when he introduced him to his family. The early summer's day when he moved Davis into his apartment; intended to be a temporary arrangement, it felt so natural they were quick to make it permanent. Everett had quietly added Davis to his bank accounts the following month, when it became clear to him that this was the formation their lives were going to take. All of these were things Everett had done in his previous marriage. All of these were things he'd had no interest in repeating, though many had tried over the years.

The thing is—the thing he clings to when he wonders if all of it is worth it, if Davis is worth it—is that out of nowhere, Everett saw a future, a long one, that featured another person, standing by his side, aging with him. He saw this when he met Davis, almost instantly. It wasn't planned, but there he was—Everett's partner, Everett's future, and, as he sometimes thinks quietly, his wife. Because he felt like Davis's husband, in a very traditional sense— much like his brother and his straight friends—long before they were married, long before he'd even proposed.

The feeling was immediate; it hit him like a lightning bolt, within minutes of seeing Davis. Everett had been standing by the bar with a friend when he saw Davis walk in, this tiny Black kid with golden skin that seemed to glisten, obviously new to the bar, if not to the city. He entered with a flourish that no one cared about, wearing high-waisted short shorts, denim with fringe hanging off them, and a crop top. He carried the kind of confidence that served as a red herring. Dumber men than Everett were fooled by it, and one such man walked right up to Davis, offered a drink, and stood mere centimeters from him. In seconds that man wrapped an arm around Davis, pressed him against the wall, began grinding against him. Everett never forgot the look that passed through Davis's eyes, only for a moment—the kind of urgent, raw fear that can't be covered up—when the man leaned down, close to his neck, and started whispering in his ear. It happened in a second, and then his face was subsumed by the man's height, his shoulders slender, but not nearly as slender as Davis's.

Everett never asked Davis what the man said to him, and Davis has never offered. Though they are both aware of it, this meeting— their actual first—isn't the meeting they talk about when someone asks how they met, though Everett always considers it when he tells the story of them.

How he watched as Davis tried to pull back from the man, tried to duck under his arms.

What still strikes Everett as odd is the number of people that stood in between them—at least thirty—and how none of them, not one, seemed to notice Davis when he walked in, or pay attention to the way that man cornered him. Everett quickly excused himself from his friends, grabbed his beer, made his way through the growing crowd, and when he reached them, he slid around the man and stood next to Davis. "Baby, you good?"

He'll never forget the relief that flooded Davis's eyes. He caught on immediately, faking recognition. "There you are." Davis stepped closer to Everett, who didn't take his eyes off the man, who looked between them inquiringly, as though asking for a ménage à trois, before putting his hands up and backing away. Everett watched him until he left the bar.

"Thank you," Davis said.

From there the memory becomes hazy. Everett knows they chatted for a few minutes, and he remembers very clearly not asking Davis for his number, not wanting to be the kind of guy who swoops in and saves the day, only to perpetuate the same aggression.

And he remembers that he spent months returning to the very same bar on the very same night, week after week, hoping to catch a glimpse, to see him again. Funny, he thinks as he runs by that bar, how they live only blocks from it now, and yet they've never dropped in for a drink.

Everett turns left at the corner. A few blocks, three more turns, and he'll be back home. Cooled off and ready to see Davis once more, he's filled with the same feeling that settled into him all those Thursday nights a few years back, when he waited patiently for that wisp of a boy to return to that bar: that Davis would one day, at some point, come back to him.

It's just a matter of time. They have to get through this; they will get through this. As he and Bam-Bam round the corner and approach Jane Street, Everett thinks that perhaps it's time to admit something he hasn't wanted to: He doesn't really understand what it is about his father's death that has driven Davis to such dramatics. They weren't speaking, hadn't really spoken in years. Davis had barely ever mentioned him. For so long his family was one big question mark to Everett. Davis ran off when he was eighteen, the minute he graduated high school. He ran to New York City, built himself a life and a career, and he did it in under a decade.

He made it so that he didn't need his father—at least, not in any material way.

But sometimes, especially in the last few weeks, especially as Davis reaches goals so lofty he'd never even set them for himself, as he seems to put more and more distance between the two of them, Everett is left wondering if Davis really needs him.

WHEN EVERETT LEAVES to walk Bam-Bam, Davis begins to realize how tired he is. He walks into the bathroom where he stands at the sink and begins to remove his makeup. He is emotionally exhausted by surprise, joy, gratitude. And yes, even grief. As he exfoliates his face, a thought begins to creep in: that perhaps he hasn't fully considered the complexity of what it was to be his father, to be the Reverend.

Once his face is cleared, he unclasps his belt, pulls his pants down, and his sweater up over his head. He'd needed a moment to himself that afternoon, had taken a walk around town, stepped into a little boutique where he'd found the sweater set, and something else: something lacy to wear tonight, for Everett. But he's too tired; this day has taken everything he has inside him, and at the moment he doesn't have much to begin with. He digs around in their chest of drawers for an old T-shirt, worn from years of being slept in, with the name of his beloved chamber music camp, a place where he'd spent six summers as a kid. As he pulls it over his head, he smells the years that T-shirt spent stowed away in a chest of drawers, that wooden mothy smell that comforts him, that pulls him into the past.

HE AND THE Reverend were in an old man's attic, a man who sold all manner of stringed instruments. The room smelled of wood, and of old age.

A storm was coming, Davis remembers this quite clearly: the sound of the wind, carrying the timbre of a disembodied voice ripping through the trees, a terror. The man lived and worked in his house, in a neighborhood called Lyndhurst on a winding road where the houses sat farther back, and there were no fences separating one yard from the next. The house sat on the corner of Belvoir and Eastman at the top of a steep hill. There was a large yard filled with many wide-trunked trees, all of them tall, and patches of flowers—yellow daisies and purple and blue irises. Clusters of pink begonias and even a few ferns; all of them lent the yard a vast feeling of lushness, and the light but lingering scent of a flower shop.

While the man walked toward a glass cabinet filled with child-size instruments, Davis stood next to the Reverend. He waited anxiously. He looked up and out through a window, a tiny octagonal thing that rattled like it might shatter from the sharpness of the rain and the strength of the wind. When they'd walked from the car to the back door of the man's house, Davis had thought he'd seen something—a spirit whipping through the trees and rustling between the fallen leaves. He was frightened of everything he saw—of the man, who was quite large, and his house and the spirit, and even the Reverend, who didn't seem to be in a very good mood. But Davis knew it was important to be there, gravely so. He'd grown enough that he needed a new viola.

The man, who was quite old, had come recommended to the Reverend by Davis's teacher, a woman who taught at the conservatory downtown. Davis had been taking lessons with her since he was four, after both he and Adina had been utterly enchanted by an older boy's violin solo one Sunday in church. When Adina pressed the boy's mother for information about who was teaching her son, and finally approached the teacher, she'd said quite simply, "I don't need any more violin students. But I do need violists, and so does every symphony in the world. If you want him to have a better chance of going far, have him play the viola."

So Davis played the viola; he never even touched the violin. Davis was a child who knew how to behave, who did as he was told. He was raised to be obedient, dignified; this seemed of the utmost importance in his family, and especially to the Reverend.

He was frightened in that room, by that man, and the darkness, and an odor that somehow made him understand that this was not a space accustomed to the noise and energy of a child, even though Davis had not been, and never would be, that sort of child—the type to run around wreaking havoc and embarrassing his father. Nonetheless he was a guest here, and he understood this, and he took it very seriously.

So he was extra quiet, and extra still.

He was reluctant to leave the Reverend's side, and John, sensing his son's fear, kept his hand on Davis's shoulder while they watched the man insert a key into the glass cabinet. It creaked when it opened, but the man pulled several instruments that had been hanging by their necks into his arms. He set them on their sides on a table that was almost as tall as Davis. Then he went back to the cabinet where he pulled several bows that had been hanging alongside the violas. He lined them up to the side of the instruments.

The man spoke to Davis and the Reverend as he did this, his back turned to them as he arranged the violas. He gave them cursory information about each instrument as he came to it—the year each one had been made, and the name of its maker. When he remembers this man now, Davis generally thinks he was a kind man who harbored no dangerous instinct. He was simply a salesman. He was old and white and tall, and he spoke with a strong Italian accent, and he lived in Cleveland where there was a long history of racial tension between Italians and Blacks. Davis now understands that any discomfort on the part of the Reverend was that he held no trust that the man would sell them a good instrument for a fair price. But he spoke to Davis kindly as he pulled the first viola from the table and chose a bow to go with it.

Davis positioned the new viola on his shoulder. He curled his left hand around its neck, his fingers floating above the fingerboard until he dropped them down onto the strings.

The man sat on the edge of the table. "Well? Play."

Davis played scales, but he played them from memory: three octaves, a C major and then a G major. He'd been having trouble with vibrato lately, but he vibrated the top note of both scales, and the sound soared straight into the wooden beams at the top of the room. By the time he put the instrument down, ready to ask for another, the man had jumped to his feet. He was nodding, pacing, and clapping enthusiastically. He had large, heavy hands, and the sound of it startled Davis, who jumped and put the viola down, and ran back toward the Reverend.

"No," the man said. "Come here."

"Go on," the Reverend said. He gave Davis a gentle push, proud of the way his son had impressed the man.

"I had no idea you were such a fine player."

Davis nodded, but said nothing more.

The Reverend spoke up. "His teacher says he's advancing very quickly. He's already mastering intermediate technical studies. Her words."

"Etudes?"

The Reverend nodded. "He's only been playing for two years. She says he has prodigious talent and that he needs the very best size-appropriate viola we can find. And she said you're the man to come to."

The man puffed out his chest. "I sell the best fine instruments for children in the region. It's hard to find really excellent stringed instruments for exceptional children, but they're out there. Who is his teacher?"

"Adrienne Elisha."

The man smiled. "Very good. Follow her to the ends of the earth, she'll get him where he's supposed to go."

The Reverend nodded, and the man turned his attention back to Davis, taking his hand.

"There's no need to be scared, my boy." Davis flinched; it went unnoticed by the man. "My name is Giovanni."

"Introduce yourself, son." The Reverend looked him in the eye.

"My name is Davis."

Giovanni shook his hand and led him to another cabinet in a corner of the room, farther away from the Reverend. He pulled another key from his pocket and opened the door. "Here is where I keep the better instruments—for players such as yourself. Most of these are going to be too big for you, but there's one that might work." Giovanni reached all the way up to the very top shelf and pulled down the first instrument, what looked to Davis like it might be the smallest of the bunch. "I've been waiting for the right player to show this one," he said. "Try it." Then he pulled another bow from a sleeve that hung from a hook on the side of the cabinet. "The bow is just as important as the instrument. Remember that."

Davis began with a scale. The sound of it shocked him; it blasted from the viola, and he thought of a rocket launching into space.

"No, no, no!"

Giovanni grabbed another viola and bow from the cabinet. "No more scales." He quickly tuned it and began to play a jolly melody that was familiar to Davis.

"I know that one!" Davis set the bow on the G string and started playing. He'd gotten through half the piece before Giovanni started clapping and walking in circles. He ran his hands through his hair and turned to the Reverend, astonished. "He knows Telemann? He knows Telemann!"

The Reverend chuckled. "I guess he knows Telemann. I have to confess: His mother was the one who really handled his music."

"Well, where is she? She should be here! He's a wonder!"

The Reverend looked down at the ground, before raising his eyes again to Giovanni. "She passed. A year ago."

Giovanni walked over to him, put a hand on his shoulder. The men were silent for a moment. Davis thought he might cheer them up, so he began playing the concerto again. "You must keep his studies up." Giovanni looked him in the eye. "For her. He's extremely talented." He turned back to Davis, walked toward him, and then slowly paced in circles. "Six years old! Telemann!" He shook his head.

After a few minutes, in which Davis played another movement of the same concerto, Giovanni smiled at him. "That's kid's stuff! Let's try something else." He picked up his viola and stared at him as he began to play a few measures of another medley, something slower, far more somber. "Do you know that piece?"

Davis, quiet, shook his head.

"Try it."

Davis walked closer to Giovanni. He squinted his eyes. "Can you play it one more time, sir?"

Giovanni played it again. He kept his eyes on Davis, whose gaze traveled between Giovanni's left and right hands. When he finished, Davis picked up his viola—for he'd known immediately that it would be his—and played the piece, much like Giovanni had.

Giovanni turned to the Reverend. "His ear is exquisite. Six years old." He said this almost in wonder, then turned back to Davis. "But wait. You didn't use any vibrato. This is Schubert—you must play with vibrato. It's very passionate, romantic music."

Davis gulped, then played it again.

"Your wrist is collapsing, just slightly." Giovanni stepped close to him and adjusted his wrist. "Keep it steady, and in line with the rest of your arm."

Davis played it again.

"Good boy. Your vibrato will get wider and faster as you get stronger, but wide is more important than fast on the viola, remember that!" He walked over to the Reverend. "Yes, very good. I think this viola will do very nicely for him, for the time being."

The Reverend looked alarmed. "The time being?"

Giovanni nodded. "Well, he's going to grow, and when that happens, he'll need a bigger one. And you'll visit me again, and you can trade it in for something even better. But this will do for now. His teacher will be pleased."

The Reverend cleared his throat. "I see."

Giovanni turned back to Davis. "You keep playing. Continue to get acquainted. Maybe think of a name for her. She's like a beautiful woman, no?" He led the Reverend out of the room and down the hall to another room.

Davis had learned to be very serious about scales, so he focused on those. He had memorized his three octave major scales months ago and was now memorizing the minor scales. He focused on the tips his teacher had given him for his left hand: making sure his fingers stood straight up and down on their fleshy tips, keeping his left arm and wrist straight, adjusting his left elbow every time he crossed strings so that he could reach the note with his pinky finger. He tried to concentrate—he loved everything about playing the viola, even his scales—but the beauty of the instrument kept distracting him. It was not like the one he'd had before. This one was a work of art. The wood was beautifully varnished. There were dark spots and golden spots and reddish spots, and it all blended together. The ebony fingerboard had a brown streak—barely visible, but it was there. And each tuning peg was adorned with a tiny gold button. He turned it over and looked at its backside—one single piece of wood that glittered like amber tiger stripes.

And its sound! It sounded like a real viola. Its power had surprised Davis when he first played the open C.

It was the most beautiful—and powerful—thing he'd ever owned.

When the Reverend came back into the room sometime later, he told Davis, kindly, to pack up. He watched closely as Davis put the viola in a case, wiped the rosin from the strings and then wiped down the whole instrument in gentle, sweeping motions, with a special rag Giovanni handed him.

The Reverend kneeled down close to Davis, who felt a great seriousness emanating from him.

"She's yours. Treat her kindly. She's beautiful, but she's old." He made eye contact with Davis, who nodded, ever somber about anything having to do with his music.

"Is it as old as you?"

He went back to loosening the bow hair.

The Reverend leaned closer, a rare smile crossing his lips. "Older." He chuckled. "And so is the bow."

Giovanni led them through the house once more, and when they reached the door, the Reverend shook his hand and took the viola, scooped it under one arm. With his other arm he picked up Davis. "It's pouring, so we'll make a run for it," he said.

When they reached the car, he opened the back door and placed Davis in the seat and buckled his seatbelt before sliding the viola into Davis's lap. "Hold tight, now."

The Reverend closed the door and climbed in the front seat. He turned the key in the ignition, and pressed buttons on the dashboard—for the heat and the window defroster—and he turned on the lights and shifted into gear, and they started moving. When they had turned out of the driveway and were several minutes along Belvoir, the Reverend looked into the rearview mirror.

"Son?"

"Yes?" Davis peered into the rearview mirror as well, to meet his father's eyes.

"Do well, or do not bother."

Davis nodded. "Thank you, Reverend." He gripped his viola even tighter.

"Thank the Lord. It's by his grace that I can even afford to buy you that thing."

Davis nodded, obedient as ever. Cold rain poured down upon

them, unruly wind had nearly picked up the Reverend's hat, and still Davis felt his father's love for him. He felt it in the way he had been scooped up and carried to the car in the midst of a storm. He felt it in the strength of his fingers when he buckled the seatbelt, tugging the straps to make sure they were tight enough. And he felt it in the simple fact that his father—the Reverend—had bought him something beautiful. With his arms still around the viola, Davis clasped his hands, closed his eyes, and said a thank-you prayer.

Davis relishes the late-night stillness of the world, the momentary feeling of solitude; even the moon is hidden behind clouds. All is quiet, all is peaceful. And then he hears Everett: his cough as he tosses the keys into the bowl in the foyer, his heavy feet clomping down the hallway on the other side of their bedroom door, Bam-Bam following behind him. Davis feels Everett's presence like a ray of light moving through his body, a life force. When Everett slides into the bed next to him, wrapping his arms around him, holding Davis close, he feels electrically charged. But when he reaches for his husband, he thinks only of darkness, and turns away. Davis drifts to sleep, thinking how lucky he is that Everett doesn't peel their bodies apart in order to sleep more comfortably.

FIVE

Three years before, on a humid Saturday afternoon in early August, Davis and Everett ran into each other, literally bumped into each other, in Central Park. Everett walking Bam-Bam, Davis running after a Frisbee he was never going to catch and falling into him.

"I know you," Everett had said as he pulled Davis to his feet. "The gym?"

"I don't go to the gym," Davis said.

"Gym Bar, then."

Davis shook his head. "No. The Chamber Music Society?"

Everett snorted his laughter. "Definitely not."

They ditched their friends, fingertips brushing as they walked through Central Park, Everett naming venues and places and parties, and even people they might have had in common.

"Let's get food," Everett said. "I'm hungry. You're hungry." They'd found a little café in Hell's Kitchen, laughed and joked through happy hour, feet continuously bumping into each other under the tiny table for two. They weren't far from Davis's apartment, he learned as he was wrapping up with the check.

"You're a college senior who has your own apartment?" Everett had been impressed as they sauntered up close to Lincoln Center.

"Trust me, it's nothing impressive. It's one of those old Upper West Side tenement buildings. I'm incredibly lucky to have my own bathroom." Davis, contemplative, had looked away then, across the street at a bar.

"Stop for a drink?" Everett asked.

"No. Come home with me. I have booze; you like gin martinis?"

Everett nodded. He'd never been with someone who seemed so singsong, so childlike, and yet so precocious. Davis pulled him into a kiss then. A few feet away, a group of teenage girls sharing fast food started whooping and whistling.

Davis blushed. "Come on," he said, pulling Everett along. Everett placed his right hand on the small of Davis's back. Like that, they walked.

"I'd never have been able to rent my own apartment when I was a college senior."

"You would've if you'd had to." Davis had kept his eyes straight ahead, as if he was unsure of where they were going. They enjoyed the sounds of the city as they moved—the horns honking, the voices laughing, the clatter of footsteps as they were passed by a large group of tourists taking pictures.

They walked for twenty minutes. Davis led the way hurriedly up to apartment 15G, turned his key in two separate locks, and gave the door a nudge with his shoulder. When they entered, Davis pointed Everett to the bathroom, then the bedroom while he went to the kitchen to make the drinks. The room was shockingly bright, yellow sunlight pouring in through a crack in the blue linen curtains.

"Feel free to turn on the AC. There's a remote on the bedside table!"

Everett kicked off his shoes, tucking them close to the bedroom door. He turned on the AC, then considered taking off his shirt. He didn't want to be aggressive. Davis seemed delicate; better to let him take the lead.

When he came in with the drinks, he set them down on the bed-side table, then walked right up to Everett and slid his hands be-hind Everett's neck. Standing on his tiptoes, he pulled him into a soft, gentle kiss. "You're a good guy, Everett. I can tell."

Everett felt a bit miscast; his most recent ex had screamed at him that he was a scoundrel. "How can you tell?" He lowered his hands and cupped Davis's ass: denim booty shorts, fringe lining the bot-tom. He knew exactly who this was.

"I figured it out. We met a year ago, right?"

"Pieces," they said in unison.

"Some guy had me cornered. I believe you came to my rescue."

Everett smiled, kissing Davis back, and guided him toward the bed. "I believe I did."

Davis winked, ever the flirt. "A girl likes that from time to time, you know. Being rescued."

Everett laughed. "I aim to please." He continued to kiss Davis, gently pushing him back onto his bed. A diagonal beam of light flut-tered against his skin.

"I want you naked." He climbed on top of Davis then, and kissed him all over his face, his neck, down his body. He pulled Davis's shirt up and over his head, his hair, tossing it to the floor. Every-where he put his hands, he found skin soft as butter and smelling of honey. When he commented, Davis nodded and said, "Smells good?"

"Feels even better." Everett's every touch, whether gentle or firm, brought with it some new kind of sound from Davis, and after several minutes in which all clothes were tossed aside, Everett un-derstood he needed to be sedate about the whole thing.

They were kissing, Davis's head against the pillow, his locs splayed in the shape of a Japanese fan. Everett was perched above him, his hands flat against the mattress next to Davis's shoulders. Davis pulled his lips away, placed an open palm against Everett's chest, a look of concern flashing across his face. Everett stared at him.

"You're nervous," he said after a moment.

"No," Davis said, though he nodded, his head bobbing up and down. When Everett said nothing, Davis looked toward the window before turning back to him. He mumbled a confession. "I wasn't going to say anything, but this is . . . kind of my first time."

"Should I stop?"

They stared at each other. Everett heard, twice, the second hand of the wall clock.

"No," Davis said. "Please don't stop."

Afterward Everett leaned upright, his back against the headboard, his arm around Davis's shoulders. He couldn't remember the last time he'd been with a virgin; once he'd turned thirty, he'd forgotten they existed. With his middle finger Everett traced hundreds of tiny circles in the smooth skin of Davis's shoulder. Under the sunlight that was beginning to fade, the last of Davis's boyhood had revealed itself to Everett and vanished. Davis slept against him now, a relaxed and satisfied smile newly visible.

AN HOUR LATER they woke, moving with the quiet intimacy of two already living as one. Everett stood on one side of the bed, in the spot that he understood, somehow, was his. Davis, who had opened the curtains, stood on the other side by the window. Manhattan, swathed in pinks, purples, and reds of dusk, smiled over them, and staring at Davis, Everett was mesmerized—Davis's honey-colored skin seemed to glow as he bent to put on a pair of boxer shorts. Everett pulled his undershirt over his head. Davis moved toward him, then behind him, slipping his feet into a pair of mud brown flip-flops.

"Hungry?" Davis asked. Without waiting for an answer, he turned and walked out of the room. The smacking of his sandals against the soles of his feet echoed as he walked to the kitchen. Everett followed, shaking his head.

"I have to go," Everett said. He stood in the entrance, leaning with his forearm against the top of the doorframe. The kitchen was microscopic. There was no counter space to speak of. Davis bent in front of the refrigerator, pulling out blocks of cheese, a pack of prosciutto, and a jar of pitless olives. He placed them on the kitchen table, really a rectangular hall table that was no more than a foot in width, and stood against the wall. There were three transparent plastic placemats, decorated with images of sunflowers.

"No you don't," Davis said. He remained stooped, his head practically in the refrigerator.

"I do," Everett stepped into the kitchen, feeling like a giant. "Bam-Bam." He put his finger to his chin, thinking, then gently put his hands around Davis's waist. Davis stood, then turned toward Everett. "Who?"

"My dog. I have to go home to feed and walk my dog." Everett smiled sheepishly.

"Oh," Davis said. "I love dogs." He stood up and closed the refrigerator. "You named your dog Bam-Bam?" He wrinkled his brow.

"Hey, I think it's cute!" Everett laughed, then glanced down at his feet.

Davis gestured toward the table. "At least let me send you home with some cheese." He paused again. "Camembert? Aged Gouda?"

Everett smiled, then took a step closer to Davis. He shook his head. When Davis started to protest, Everett quietly shushed him. "If you send me home with cheese my dog will almost definitely get into it. You wouldn't want poor Bam-Bam to shit all over my apartment, would you?" He kissed the top of Davis's head. Davis turned around, opened the refrigerator again, and returned the cheese, meat, and olives. When he was done, Everett stepped out of the kitchen, was about to say goodbye, when a new idea occurred to him. "Come back to my place. Meet him. Spend the night."

It was as simple as that, an invitation, his hand extended behind him, Davis grabbing it, nodding, slipping past him, somehow leading the way to a destination he had no knowledge of.

Everett found it charming.

Six

The holidays arrive.

Everett guides their car gently into the driveway of his family's home in Darien, Connecticut, his right hand resting on the stick shift as it always does. Between the two of them, he is the driver; Davis refuses to learn how to drive stick, having tried exactly once, and having burst into tears when the car stalled in the middle of rush hour on Tenth Avenue. Davis listens to the crunch of the snow under the tires, his forehead leaning against the window. Their drive had been slow and silent, stop-and-go traffic the result of icy accidents and rubbernecking East Coasters.

"You'd think they'd never seen a fucking car accident before," Davis said earlier, before stepping out of the car when they stopped for coffee. He slammed the door and stood on the sidewalk, hands on hips, back to Everett who stood, waiting wordlessly, until Davis wiped away his tears and walked by his side into the coffee shop. How boyish Davis looked, wearing loose-fitting jeans, a puke green hoodie, and a pair of black Vans that Everett has never seen before. It's been up and down with Davis since the wedding, and Everett can chart his emotions through his clothing. As they waited for their drinks, arms brushing up against each other, both their faces buried in their phones, Everett found himself tamping down his irritation. This was how their marriage was now. Their world was encased in a giant eggshell, one that sprouted a new crack and would shatter any day now. At any time, the littlest, most mundane thing could set Davis off, casting a shadow over that face, muting his boisterous laugh, and dulling those glistening eyes.

Davis looked angry, and the weight of that anger aged him. It reverberated through their home. Even Bam-Bam felt it—Everett was sure of this—because as much as a dog could tiptoe around their home in an effort to go unnoticed, Bam-Bam did.

And now, as Everett parks and shuts the engine off, he turns to look at Davis for the first time since they got back in the car. He pauses, then reaches out, placing his thumb and forefinger around his husband's jaw and turning it until they are face-to-face. There is something electric in their touch, still—Everett feels heat moving from his body into Davis. "Are you okay? You ready?"

Davis blinks as though he's been woken from a deep sleep. He rubs his arms up and down, feigning a smile. "I'm fine." He nods. "I need a shower and a little nap." Everett holds his hand on his face, silence engulfing them for another moment, until the front door of the house opens and his family spills out onto the porch, bringing with them that same chaotic energy. Everett narrows his eyes, peers through the window, waves as they stare, then leans close to Davis for a chaste little kiss. He knows which direction all that energy will be directed.

"Out you go," he says, opening his door as Davis opens his. Davis feels himself flipping through the air, can almost hear the splash when the family crashes into him. Christopher reaches him first and sweeps him up into a fatherly hug, clapping him hard on the back. Davis glances behind him as Christopher lifts him off his feet; he sees Everett quietly open the trunk and start pulling out bags while he is flooded with all that Caldwell energy.

He feels passed around, objectified in a way: the men squeezing him tight, moving him amongst themselves—almost like a football, a plaything—their hands clapping his back, their voices shouting their love. The women hug him, too, Charlotte's and Courtney's hands grazing his back, their energy contagious but tranquil. After a few minutes of assuring everyone that he's okay, that he's happy to be there, that all he needs is a shower and a nap, he notices Everett standing in a pile of their suitcases raising his arms.

"Hello? Bueller? Bueller?"

Davis and the rest of the Caldwell family turn their attention to Everett. Davis remains on the porch, momentarily enchanted by the joy that radiates through his husband's face as his family rushes down to him, bombarding him with hugs and kisses—though none of them, not even Christopher or Connor, can lift Everett from the ground. They look like a nineties Campbell's soup commercial, before they have the soup. After a moment, Davis shivers, the wind ripping through him. "Come on, Bam-Bam."

He opens the door, yellow and bright as the summer sun on an otherwise white house, and walks in. It isn't until he shuts the door behind him and kicks his shoes off that he notices Caleb, standing by the window, hands in his pockets, watching the outdoor fray.

"Hi, Caleb. Merry Christmas."

Caleb takes a step toward Davis. "Hi. I'm, um, sorry. About your father."

LATER, IN EVERETT'S childhood bedroom, Davis bends over his open suitcase, unfolding sweaters and skinny jeans and leggings, and thick winter socks that Everett made him pack because the house is big and drafty.

"Do I have to talk to them about the Reverend?"

Davis pulls a giant, sparkly, reindeer-ridden sweater with puffed short sleeves from his suitcase and hangs it in the closet. Everett has reminded him that they are expected to dress in ugly sweaters for Christmas Eve. "Not if you don't want to," Everett says as he stuffs a handful of boxer briefs into a drawer. He grabs several pairs of socks next. "They're just interested. They won't push." He sighs, then turns to Davis. "I've instructed them not to push."

Davis stares at him, his face expressionless.

"I'll remind them not to push. Again."

Satisfied, Davis turns away from Everett, setting his makeup bag on top of an antique chest of drawers. "I'm tired," he says. "Why am I so tired all the time?"

Everett sits on the bed and opens his arms. After a moment, Davis sits, too, and scoots himself over to Everett until he can curl up against him. He closes his eyes when he feels Everett's lips against the top of his head. Bam-Bam steps close to the bed, resting his snout against Davis's thigh. "They love you."

"I know that."

"Sometimes I think they love you more than they love me."

"Ha!" Davis smiles. His fingers play with one of his locs. "They're just worried about me, Everett."

"Yes."

"You're worried about me."

". . . should I be worried about you, Davis?"

Davis shrugs. "I don't know what's wrong with me. I'm sorry."

Everett nods. "You have nothing to be sorry for. Grief is physical, too."

"I know that." Davis turns, his face furious. "Don't you think I know that?" He reverts, calm once more. "Sorry. I don't feel like myself, is all." He rubs his calves together, forlorn.

Everett wants to ask him who, exactly, does he feel like. "Why don't you take a nap? Don't worry about cocktails, just come down for dinner at seven." He wraps his arms tighter around Davis, who then unwraps himself and stands. He looks at Everett silently for a moment.

Then he gestures for Everett to move. "Get up! So I can pull back the covers." Davis tries to laugh, covering his rudeness.

Everett stands, looks at Davis, then returns to his suitcase—

there are still sweaters to unpack. Behind him, he listens as Davis takes off his pants and pulls the hoodie over his head. He glances at Davis standing there in his underwear, long-lost smile nowhere to be found, skin looking sallow and dry.

This is not the person he married. He's honestly not sure if Davis has ever worn a pair of Vans—or gone this long without slathering himself in lotion.

"Stay with me, Everett? Just for a few minutes."

Davis slides into the bed, pulling the sheets and quilt up to his chin. "It's kind of exciting to be in your childhood bedroom." He smiles at Everett then, a glimmer of sunlight from the window gleaming in his eyes, a lightness emanating through him. Everett pulls back the covers and slides in. He lays on his side as Davis backs into him, snuggling against his chest.

"Listen. You don't have to talk about anything you don't want to talk about. Let me handle everything. I know how overwhelming they can be." Everett feels Davis breathing in and out against him. A wisp of air escapes Davis's lips, as his head relaxes against Everett.

Whatever is going on in there—and Everett wants to know, is trying to understand—Davis has found a few moments of peace and quiet.

He's tempted to text his family that they'll both be staying upstairs until further notice, until he realizes that right now, at this moment, he would rather be downstairs with them, huddled around the kitchen island, laughing and drinking and catching up. He would rather be with his father and Connor, and he misses his mother's laugh.

And he needs, at some point, to get a few moments alone with Caleb—though Everett isn't sorry for hitting him at the wedding, and he doesn't know what he'll say when the time comes.

Everett quietly removes the covers and rises from the bed. He puts away his few remaining clothes, zips his suitcase, and hides it in the closet, Davis asleep the entire time. Everett closes the door silently, carefully creeping down the stairs where the din of his family rises.

WHILE THE REST of the family is gathered in the kitchen, Caleb sits on the couch, draped in a blanket, reading. Everett wants to walk past him, tries to walk past him, but can't do it without lightly smacking him on the head.

"Fuck off," Caleb says, without batting an eye. Everett stops, turns to Caleb. After a moment, Caleb sighs, closes the book, and lays it on the couch next to him, which Everett takes as an invitation. He walks over and sits on the opposite end of the couch. He leans back, spreads his legs, rests his arm along the top. Once he's comfortable, he looks at Caleb. "Didn't know you could actually read."

Caleb smirks. "How's your wife?" Caleb raises both his arms in defeat when Everett lunges. "I'm sorry, I'm sorry, it was a joke."

"I don't even know why I try with you," Everett says. He steps back, returns to his seat, pulls out his phone.

"Try with me? When have you ever tried with me?" Caleb's laugh is quick and bitter cold. "Listen, Everett—"

"What's your issue with Davis?"

Caleb shakes his head. He looks at the floor, then the window, then the family portrait that hangs over the mantel. "No issue, man. I'm sorry, really."

Everett nods. "His dad just died."

"I know. I'm an asshole."

Everett smiles in spite of himself, of his anger. "Yeah, you are."

"Did you tell him what I said?"

Everett shakes his head.

"Good." Caleb taps his foot against the floor.

"Caleb, can I ask you a question? Who'd you vote for?"

Caleb laughs. He thumbs a loose thread on his sweater. "Clinton."

"But you—"

"I was fucked up, Everett. I was just really angry, really messed up about someone."

"A girl?"

Caleb nods. "Something like that."

"Who was it?" For a moment, Everett looks directly into his little brother's eyes, who doesn't answer the question. "Listen, you can't talk about my . . . about Davis like that."

Caleb crosses his heart. "Never again."

Everett stands. "I might kill you. I'm kidding, but I'm not kidding."

Caleb stands. They shake hands, and Everett pulls his brother into a quick hug.

Caleb steps back, clears his throat, puts his hands on his hips. "Everett, can I just say one more thing?"

"Of course."

"You used to make fun of people like Davis. You were pretty brutal."

Everett nods. "When I was a dumb kid, yeah."

"Does he know that?"

Everett lies. "We've talked about it."

Caleb stares at him for a moment. "No, you haven't, but that's not the point. The point is, you've changed. You had space to grow."

By now Everett wants to join everyone else in the kitchen. "I'd like to think so."

Caleb takes a step closer to his brother. "Just make sure Davis has that same space." He presses his hand to Everett's shoulder and steps around him, leading him into the kitchen.

This is part of Everett's problem with Caleb. He somehow always ends up feeling outsmarted by Caleb, even when the topic is someone, or something, in Everett's life that has little to no bearing on Caleb. It's also what he loves about Caleb.

Everett, shaking his head, follows him into the kitchen, where Courtney hands him a red wineglass.

He holds it in front of Charlotte, who dutifully gives a generous pour. "Is Davis joining us?"

Everett sips his wine. "After a shower and a nap. He'll be down in time for dinner." He sets the wineglass down. "So everybody keep the volume down! Don't be so loud!" Their eyes linger on one another, his mother's question silently asked and left unanswered.

Christopher looks between Everett and Caleb. Everett nods, then Christopher nods. Moments later, Everett's phone buzzes with a text from his father. *Thank you. He's trying.* Everett looks again at Christopher, smiles, nods again. Out of the corner of his eye, Everett sees Courtney watching them both. "What?" he says.

She shrugs, takes a giant gulp of her wine, and sets it down. She grabs Connor's hand and pulls him out of the kitchen.

"I'm going back to my book," Caleb says. He looks at his mom. "I'll just be out there." He jerks his thumb toward the family room.

Once he leaves, Christopher looks at Everett. "Now we can speak honestly. How is he, son? Really?"

Everett sips his wine and gazes toward the staircase thinking that perhaps he should've stayed upstairs with Davis after all. Then he looks again at his parents. He thinks about the life his parents built—this house, and his brothers, and Davis and Courtney. The child, entirely theoretical at this point, that Connor and Courtney are hoping to have. He thinks of the noise and chaos, their busy, joyful childhoods—all the sports and all the homework, the graduations and the holidays. All the times he wanted his parents to himself, wanted everyone and everything else to disappear.

He's grateful for these few moments. He thinks of how Davis will never again get a moment alone with the Reverend. He thinks of how Davis hasn't had a moment alone with the Reverend in nearly a decade. Everett looks at his father, then his mother. He wants to say something more, but he struggles to find the right words. "He's not doing well."

Christopher stares at him "Of course he's not."

"He doesn't really want to talk about it."

"I picked up on that, so I'm asking you." Christopher rises, walking over to the bar and grabbing a bottle of scotch. Sometimes Everett thinks of a bull when he thinks of his father, of the way Christopher is when something's amiss in the life of one of his children—or, in this case, one of his children's partners. Everett is filled with warmth for the way his family accepts and loves Davis.

"Time for the good stuff," Christopher says. He opens a cupboard, pulling two tumblers down in one hand and setting them on the countertop. He offers them both a generous pour, then pulls down a third tumbler and looks at his wife.

"No, thanks," Charlotte says with barely a glance. She wipes down the oven and tosses the sponge aside. "I'll head out and pick up the pizza."

Christopher takes a seat across from his son. They clink their glasses, for a moment sipping in unison. Everett observes his father—the way his long, fat fingers hold the glass, the way he tilts his head back and closes his eyes as the scotch slides down his throat. The way he sighs when he sets the glass down, satisfied. Everett looks at the liquid in his glass. He notices the grain in the wood. He looks forward to being where his father is. "Davis won't let me touch him."

He glances up, his father's dark eyes intense, unyielding. Small and round and brown, like sharp little lasers pointing at his heart. Waiting, at attention, ready to be launched any minute, assured of puncturing their target. Everett has always felt this way about how his father looks at him. Somehow diminished, perhaps not quite a fully grown, now fully married, man.

"What do you mean he won't let you touch him?" Christopher coughs and wipes the back of his hand across his mouth. He takes another sip and sets the tumbler down with a heavy, serious thud.

"Is this weird, Dad?" Everett glances across the room through the doorway that leads to the living room and the staircase. "For us to talk like this?"

"Why would it be weird?" Christopher doesn't flinch from his oldest son's gaze.

"Because we've never—"

"Look," Christopher says, compassionate in intent, bullish in tone. "You can talk to me about anything, you know that."

Everett says nothing, silently wondering if, in fact, he does know that.

"You were always so independent, Everett. To be honest, I never felt like you really needed me. I used to tell people that it was Connor who made me a father, and Caleb that made me a good father. You kind of just . . . came out this way."

Everett blinks. "I never knew that."

Christopher lifts his glass, tipping his drink to his son. "Talk to me. Let me be your dad. You could use one right now; anyone can see that."

"Okay." Everett pauses, nodding and rising from the table. He walks around the room, ensuring their privacy. He closes the door that links them to the living room, then grabs the scotch and when he sits, he pours.

"What I'm trying to tell you is that Davis won't let me touch him. My husband . . . won't let me touch him." Everett turns away from his father, looking through the window. "I miss him."

Christopher furrows his brow, then nods, solemn. "I see."

Everett laughs. "Can you handle this?"

Christopher takes another sip. "I'm good. I've got this." He leans back and stretches an arm across the back of the stool next to his. "Well, son, your mother and I—"

Everett shakes his head. "Nope. Never mind—because I can't handle that."

Christopher motions like he's zipping his mouth shut. "How long has he been . . . withholding?"

Everett looks down at his feet. "Since the wedding."

"You mean, since his father died."

Everett nods. "Yeah. He's really hurting, and I don't know what to do about it." Both men pause; both men sip. Everett feels his father's eyes on him as he looks out of the window.

"It's a hard thing, losing a parent."

"I know."

"You haven't experienced it yet."

"I know that, too."

"It changes you," Christopher says. "That kind of loss, especially when it's unexpected . . . everything is a little off after that. For a long time." Christopher slides his hand around his tumbler. "Everything feels just a little bit askew."

"Yeah, but it wasn't like you and me, Dad. Davis didn't even talk to his father." Everett takes a quick sip. "He called his father 'the Reverend.'"

"He what?"

"Yeah! That's what I'm saying! That man made Davis and Olivia call him 'Reverend' when they addressed him." Anger courses through Everett. He stands, hands on hips, eyes on feet, pacing around the island. "They weren't speaking. Davis had cut him out of his life."

Christopher nods, looks into his drink. He swirls the glass. "I knew they weren't close; I guess I never thought about the depth of it."

Everett stops pacing. "Neither did I." He pauses, looking again at the closed door. "Davis never really talked much about his family. I was happy to just absorb him into ours, and not have to deal with a difficult father." His forefinger runs along the brim of his tumbler. "I guess I should've asked." Everett sits. He closes his eyes, rolls his head back. He sighs. "I'm a dick."

Christopher shakes his head. "He might not have wanted you to ask. I know his generation is all about their feelings, but Davis has always been an individual."

"Dad."

"Give it time, son. Eventually, his world will sort itself out. Right now, he's trying to be his father's boy, and that's clearly not an easy thing. He'll come back to you."

Everett squints his eyes. "How do you know?"

"Because," Christopher says, his eyes focused on his oldest son, his mainmast, his boy who went thirty-nine years without needing him. "I've seen the way he looks at you." Pride heats Christopher's belly as he looks at Everett, the kind of man any father would want his boy to become. "Son, the Reverend is his past." Christopher points to Everett. "But you are his future."

THIS IS A family that sings.

"You know Donner and Dancer and Prancer and Vixen . . ."

Davis listens as he descends the staircase wearing black tights under the ugly Christmas sweater, and indoor knee-high house shoes. He smiles, coy, flirtatious, at Everett; the entire family gestures at him on the word *vixen*. Davis wants to fall into the embrace of this family—into their joy and their energy—each bolstered by the simple fact of being together. He stifles the impulse to turn and scamper up the stairs, to hide in Everett's childhood bedroom. Everett's family is not why Davis married him, and yet, it is so much of what he wanted, he reminds himself.

He is quick to come down the last three stairs, to let Everett pull him into the family circle, to kiss and linger on his lips, to breathe him in and find his place among these people. He doesn't sing (though he can!), but he whispers the words as Christopher hands him a mug filled with eggnog. He notices the way the family gathers round the roaring fire, the way every person seems to be touching someone else at all times. They're all connected. He thinks of one of those icebreaker games he'd played in freshman orientation: the human knot, where everyone entangles their limbs and must somehow unfold themselves and one another into a circle without unclasping their hands. This family fastens around you in times of strife, and Davis knows he's lucky to be part of it.

He leans into Everett's chest, feeling Everett's arm slide around him. Everett's hand tightens around his waist, thumb brushing against the elastic of his underwear. Davis scans the room, as each member of the family glances at him, joy and sympathy pouring from their eyes. There's something about being looked at with such sympathy and sadness while being the only Black person in the room that eats at Davis from the inside.

But he feels lucky to be part of this family. It is a blessing to feel the weight of Everett's arm anchoring him in the tsunami that is the Caldwell clan. Davis takes a large gulp of the eggnog, finding solace in the sharp way it warms him as it goes down.

Some thirty minutes and much fanfare later, they're seated around the dining room table, greasy pizza slices dripping all over paper plates, two bottles of red wine on each end of the table. Everett's hand rests on Davis's knee, though it feels to Davis like Everett barely looks in his direction. It intimidates Davis, the ease with which Everett slides into place with his family—no conflict, no complicated history to set aside for the sake of getting through the holiday. Even Caleb, who'd remained indoors when they arrived, abstaining from the circus of their welcome, is in animated conversation with his brothers and father about the Knicks.

It isn't until dessert is served—the wine accompanied by another helping of eggnog—that Christopher directs his attention to Davis, clearing his throat. "And congratulations to you, son, for this Finley-Whitaker award. A grant, isn't it?"

Davis smiles, feeling bashful. He looks down at his unfinished slice of pizza. Everett squeezes his knee, then kisses him on the cheek. "C'mon," he says. "I told them all about it, but you're a Caldwell now. They want to hear it from you."

When Davis looks up, he's astonished to see each of them, every Caldwell, holding a glass aloft, waiting for him to join. Charlotte slides over a glass, and he holds it up, signaling the clinking, the table erupting in light applause. "Basically, it's a fifty-thousand-dollar grant intended to support the career development of talented emerging instrumentalists who are building a career as a soloist."

"As opposed to playing in a symphony."

Davis smiles at Everett. "Exactly." He looks around the table. "The winners are usually already making a name for themselves, but this honor kind of cements their status among the next great classical musicians."

"Since it was announced, it seems like the entire world is trying to book Davis. It's a real game changer."

Davis nods. "Major orchestras and recital opportunities, all over the world. I'm already basically booked for the next two years, and there's going to be a solo album as well."

"An album!" Christopher exclaims, breaking his stern expression for a moment as he tips an imaginary hat toward Davis and takes a sip of his drink. "Well, we're all extremely proud of you, Everett especially. He called us immediately after you found out about it."

"Really?" Davis puts a hand on top of Everett's hand. "I had no idea."

"Of course, baby." Everett leans close, puckering his lips. They kiss, then everyone raises their glass.

"To Davis!"

"To Finley-Whitaker," Davis says and winks.

When they die down, Christopher looks at Davis again, his expression softening. "I imagine the Reverend would be prouder of you than even any of us could be."

"Dad." Everett shoots a warning look at his father.

Davis squeezes Everett's hand while looking down at his plate. "Perhaps."

"Given all that he invested in your success."

"Dad!"

But Christopher plows on, ignoring his son. "How are you holding up, son?"

Something about the way he says *son* this time doesn't quite sit right with Davis. He looks at Everett, who looks back at him. "You don't have to answer that."

Davis blinks, smiles, then takes a deep breath. He looks around the room, their eyes all peering at him, waiting. "I'm fine. I'm absolutely fine." He squeezes Everett's hand again, willing his gratitude to come through. "Your son is such a support. He's the only thing I need."

Christopher doesn't break eye contact with Davis. He just nods, taking another sip. Then he leans in, his stare growing ever more intense. "Listen, son. I know what it feels like to lose a parent. It's destabilizing; it feels like the entire world is just the slightest bit off-kilter, and nobody sees it but you. And the only people who truly understand it are those who've lost the same person you've lost."

Davis gazes hard into his drink, unable to look at Christopher, who continues speaking.

"It feels that way. It feels very singular, but it's not true. I know what you're going through. My wife," he says, gesturing at Charlotte, "knows what you're going through, because we've been through it. And eventually, we all go through it. Everett will, and so will everyone at this table, God willing."

Anger flares through Davis instantaneously, but he tamps it down, and does his best to steady his voice.

"But, Christopher, like I said, I'm not going through anything. I'm thriving. You all just toasted me!" He laughs, strained, trying to look anywhere but into the six pairs of eyes looking back at him.

Christopher shakes his head, seemingly unaware of the way Everett looks at him, before turning to Davis. "You're not thriving. How could anyone be thriving in the wake of a loss like that?"

"With all due respect, Christopher, you don't know how I'm doing, and I'd like to—"

"I know you're pulling away from Everett."

"Dad."

But Christopher continues. "I know you're not letting him—"

"Dad!" Everett stands up and takes a step toward his father. Davis drops his fork against his plate and looks up, hard, at Christopher.

"Excuse me?" Then he turns to Everett. "What did he mean by that?"

Silence descends upon the Caldwell home. Only Davis moves, looking back and forth between his husband and father-in-law. Everett refuses to face him; Christopher looks down at his plate, ashamed.

Davis understands. He gently places his fork on the plate and rises.

"Davis—"

Davis puts up a hand, silencing Everett. He grabs his drink and walks away from the table. When he reaches the door to the living room, the foyer, he pauses like he wants to turn around and say something. Then he thinks better of it and storms from the room.

Once they hear the bedroom door close, chaos erupts. Charlotte throws a garlic knot at her husband. "What the hell is wrong with you, going after Davis like that?"

Everett looks at his father, anger and disappointment commingling all over his face. "Really? How could you do that?"

"You mean how could I tell the truth?"

Everett looks his father up and down. "Wow, okay. I never should've trusted you with this."

He leaves the table, quickening his long strides, then taking the stairs two at a time. Christopher, Charlotte, and the rest of the family listen, bodies jolting with the sound of his bedroom door slamming into its frame.

EVERETT'S NEVER SEEN so much movement from Davis. His suitcase lies open on the bed as he runs around throwing clothes and toiletries into it, entirely devoid of the careful packing he'd done the previous night. For a moment Everett stands in silence, waiting, his back against the door.

"Davis—"

"I can't believe you told him!"

"I shouldn't have."

"Damn straight." Davis throws a dress into the suitcase, looks up, and brushes a few locs from his face. "I can't even look at you right now!"

"I'm sorry."

"What were you thinking?"

Everett takes a step forward; Davis takes a step back. "I wasn't."

Davis is near tears, his voice shaky. "Our sex life is none of your father's business!"

Everett looks at his feet. "I know."

When he looks up, Davis has moved back to the closet. "I can't stay here." In his rush, he drops several hangers on the ground. "Were you trying to humiliate me? Are you that angry with me?"

Everett shakes his head, rushing over to Davis. He grabs Davis's hands. "No, of course not. Of course not!" He tries to lead Davis to the bed, but Davis doesn't want to budge.

"No."

"Davis."

"No!" Davis shakes his head. "You don't get to just drag me over to the bed."

"Fine." Everett picks him up, throws him over his shoulder, and places him down on the edge of the bed, his voice firm, resolute. "Sit down."

Davis sits, then scoots back against the headboard, farther away from Everett. He picks at a hangnail on his thumb. When he finally speaks, his voice is quiet, shaky. "I told you I didn't want to come here. I told you I wasn't ready to be surrounded by your family consuming copious amounts of alcohol! I told you all of that."

"I know."

"You promised it would be okay."

"I fucked up. Big-time. But, Davis—"

Davis continues. "Yes, you fucked up. And then, your father—he just kept going, and you didn't stop him! At first, I just figured you'd had a few drinks, you weren't quite keeping up. And I was fine. But it never occurred to me that you would complain to your father about our sex life!"

"I didn't complain."

"What did you say? Who all did you tell?" Davis slaps his palm against his forehead. "Oh God, do they all know we're not having sex?"

"It's not like that. My dad and I had a moment alone, and he asked how you were doing. He's just concerned; he wanted to help. And I told him not to say anything!"

"You know, Everett, the best way to make sure someone doesn't say something they're not supposed to say is to refrain from telling them the thing they shouldn't say!"

"I know." Everett sighs, and tries to scoot closer, but Davis just pulls his knees up to his chest and leans back against the head-board. "Don't you dare touch me."

"Davis, he just wanted to give me some fatherly advice."

"Like what? How to put up with the frigid bitch you married?"

"Listen. I overshared. He overstepped. I never thought he would do something like that. But, Davis, in his own strange way, he was trying to help. You haven't exactly . . . dealt with all of this." Everett tries to approach Davis again, who, this time, doesn't move away from him. Everett slides next to him, slips his arm around his shoulders. "You're not fine. We both know that. He just wanted you to know that you can talk to him."

Davis turns, looking at Everett, scrutinizing him. "Are there any boundaries in this family?"

Everett smiles and pauses for a moment. "I think we both know the answer to that." He kisses the top of Davis's head. "I'm so sorry.

I said I'd protect you from them, and instead I offered you up like today's hot topic." He pulls Davis even closer. "Forgive me."

"That didn't sound like a question."

Everett tongues Davis's ear, then whispers, "That's because I know you will, in time." He turns Davis's face toward him and, tenderly, kisses him. "Now, do you want to leave?"

Davis looks him in the eye, thinking.

"It's okay if you do. We can leave."

Davis nods. "I'm sorry; I know it's the holidays. But I just don't think I can be around them after that."

"Then we'll leave." Everett moves to stand, when Davis puts a hand on his arm.

"It's late, and we've both been drinking. Why don't we get some sleep and leave in the morning?"

Davis starts undressing and slides under the covers. He holds the comforter up for Everett, who follows suit. He lies on his back, beckoning Davis into his arms. When Davis turns away, scooting to the other end of the bed, Everett feels a sharp pang in his stomach. Every night they've been together, Davis has always fallen asleep—safe—in his arms.

"I'm sorry," he says again. He leans over, kissing Davis's cheek, lingering, before returning to his side of the bed, turning off the light, and sleeping flat on his back, arm extended should Davis choose to roll over to him in his slumber.

MORNING COMES, THE sun peeking through blinds, warming their sleeping bodies through the comforter.

Everett rises first. As he opens the front door, Bam-Bam bounding into the front yard and crouching near the flower bed, he intends to run five miles when he bumps into his father, also about to run, bent over to tie his running shoes. "Everett!" he says, clapping him on the back, as though the previous night didn't happen and everything is fine between them.

"Morning, Dad." Everett keeps his words curt. Just as Christopher is about to speak, Everett jumps in while bouncing down the stairs so he can pick up Bam-Bam's mess. "Dad, we're, um . . . we're going to take off after my run." He puts a hand on his father's shoulder, calls Bam-Bam, and gestures for him to go back inside. Then he descends the steps to the driveway.

"Now hold on, wait a minute. It's Christmas Eve," Christopher says, following him. "You're leaving, just because of that?"

Everett turns around. "Are you fucking kidding me, Dad?"

"Watch yourself."

"No, you watch yourself! How could you have done that to me last night? To Davis?"

Christopher's face is pained. "I really didn't mean anything by it, son."

"I explicitly told you not to ask Davis about his father. I explicitly said that!"

"Look, it just came out, Everett. I didn't even mean to say anything."

"It wasn't your place to confront him! Dad, if Davis doesn't want to tell you how he's feeling about his father's death, he doesn't have to tell you. It's that simple—all you had to do was say nothing."

Christopher sighs, puts his hands on his hips. "I know that, son. I crossed a line."

"I don't think you do! You were so far past the line I don't think you can see where the line is."

"I just wanted to help, son. That's all."

"That's funny, Dad. You wanted to help mend my sex life with my husband? You, of all people?"

Christopher steps back. "What do you mean, me, 'of all people'?"

Everett laughs. "Come on, Dad." He turns away from Christopher and starts running.

Christopher runs to catch up to him. "Everett!"

For several minutes father pursues son, keeping close but unable to close the gap. When Everett is forced to stop at an intersection, his father finally reaches him.

Panting, Christopher points behind him in the direction of the house. "What did you mean back there?"

Everett looks around—at the traffic waiting for the light to change, the pedestrian walking slowly in the crosswalk, the local businesses opening up—and leans close to his father. "You weren't exactly thrilled when I told you I was bi."

"That was a long time ago, Everett! I've changed a lot since then."

"I've never forgotten how you reacted when I told you and Mom to start calling me Everett."

"Because your name is Carter! We gave you that name, son, your mother and I. It was important to us, and you just threw it away!"

"It wasn't about you, Dad!"

Christopher scoffs. "You made that perfectly clear."

Everett, suddenly winded, sits on the sidewalk.

"What are you doing? Son, are you okay?"

Everett puts his head in the palms of his hands. He rubs his temples for a few seconds, and then he looks up. "You kept us from him, Dad. He was dying, and you kept us from him."

"What do you—"

Then Christopher's heart sinks. He crouches, then sits on the curb next to his son. "Everett, in those days we didn't know—"

"Bullshit. You knew we weren't in any danger. Mom knew that, doctors knew that by then."

"I guess you know all the answers, then."

"Well you certainly don't."

Everett begins to stand, but Christopher puts a hand on his leg, stopping him. "You knew I was keeping you from your uncle?"

Everett nods. "Connor and I knew. We weren't idiots, Dad."

"I see." Christopher pauses, looks around, picks up a stick, and digs a small hole in the dirt next to him. "There's no excuse for that. I see that now."

"And then you never talked about him. Mom did, sometimes."

"But only when I wasn't around."

Everett nods, puffs his cheeks, then sends the air out of his lips.

"Do you know what it would have meant for me to have had him in my life back then?"

"You knew all the way back then? That you were . . . bisexual?"

Everett nods. "I didn't know the words for it, but I knew."

Christopher takes a deep breath. "I don't know what to say."

"You never liked him. He was Mom's twin brother, and you never liked him."

Christopher looks at his son. "That's not fair."

"But it's the truth. So can you blame me? And can you blame Davis? It's like a stench, and Davis—let me tell you—he can smell a droplet of it a mile away."

"Everett, it wasn't always so black and white. Let me tell you something, son. Sometimes you aren't the man that you want to be. Sometimes you fail."

Everett stands and extends a hand to his father, pulling him to his feet. "Yeah, I know that, Dad. Last night I failed as a husband when I confided in you."

EVERETT AND DAVIS carry their bags down the stairs as quietly as possible, hoping to sneak away without waking anyone, when Christopher walks through the door. "You two move quickly," he says. He steps aside, holding the door open.

"Davis, why don't you wait here while I get the car loaded and warmed up?" Everett nods at his father as he walks by, his words to Davis more command than suggestion. Davis, still embarrassed about the previous night's revelations, averts his eyes from his father-in-law.

He watches Everett exit the house, negotiating the porch and the stairs with their bags. He watches Christopher follow Everett as he tries to implore his son not to leave on account of his error. In an instant Davis's heart melts for this man he's dragging away from his family on Christmas Eve. Everett is angry with his father; this much is clear. And despite Everett's insistence that leaving will be the best thing for them, that Davis was right and they never should have driven up for the holidays in the first place, he feels guilty. He fears he's well on his way to becoming a wedge between Everett and his family. He wonders how long it will take for resentment to build, for the idea to creep into Everett's mind that perhaps he's made a mistake; perhaps he's staked his love on the wrong person.

Davis watches as Everett sets their suitcases by the trunk, goes and sits in the driver's seat where he starts the car and turns up the heat. Then he begins shoving suitcases into the trunk. Christopher stands there wanting to help. Physically, Everett is animated, but Davis can't hear a word he says. At some point Christopher tries to help him, but Everett puts up a hand, blocking him from touching any suitcase. Once everything is loaded, Everett grabs an ice scraper from under the driver's seat, but whatever Christopher says stops him in his tracks. He raises his voice enough that Davis can now hear him, though he can't distinguish Everett's words. He feels a bit voyeuristic, like maybe he should turn away, when Caleb steps up behind him.

"Leaving already?"

Of the two brothers, Caleb's voice is actually the closest to Everett's in tone. For a moment Davis thinks it is Everett standing behind him. He turns around, then narrows his eyes.

"Caleb," he says.

Caleb steps back. "Davis."

In that moment, Davis realizes something. "I think that's the first time you've ever said my name out loud. To me, at least."

Caleb looks toward the stairs. "That's impossible."

Davis nods. "Not once, in nearly three years." He turns around, glances through the window. Everett and Christopher are completely caught up in their confrontation. He turns back to Caleb. "You don't like me very much."

Caleb continues looking at the stairs. "That's not true."

"What did you say about me at the wedding?"

"I'm sorry about that. I didn't mean it, and I'm not going to repeat it."

Davis is unsure of what else to say. He glances outside again. "Seems like they might be a while. I need coffee." He steps around Caleb and walks through the living room, then the dining room, until he reaches the kitchen, Caleb mere steps behind him. A fresh pot's just been made. Everett, probably. He smiles, feels a flutter in his chest. Quietly, he rummages through the cabinets. "I know Charlotte has to-go cups with lids somewhere, a whole pack of them. She told me so last night."

Caleb nods, thinking, speaking slowly. "Last night."

Davis turns around, suddenly shouting. "I mean, who does that?" He points toward the front of the house. "That man actually fixed his face at the dinner table to call me out for not giving his son enough p—" Davis stops for a moment, rubs his forehead, stomps a foot. He takes a deep breath and lowers his voice. "In what world? In what world is that even remotely okay?"

Caleb looks at Davis. "Yeah. That was . . . painful. Just watching it unfold." He wiggles his fingers, makes a face. "Yikes."

"Oh, it was, was it? It was painful for you?" Davis tips his head to the side. "But you don't like me, Caleb."

Caleb shakes his head. "Again . . . not true." He grabs a to-go cup for Davis and a ceramic mug for himself. He fills them both with coffee, and hands Davis a pint of half-and-half from the fridge. "Here. I went out and bought this for you because I know you only drink coffee with half-and-half, and even though Mom knows it, too, she forgot to get some for you." He comes within inches of Davis's face, sets it down with a thud. "I like you fine." They stare at each other. "Stop running. Just tell the truth." Caleb takes a breath, then a step back. "That's what I'm trying to do."

For a moment Davis stops breathing. "Come on, Caleb. You know I don't run."

Caleb continues staring at him, offers a laugh, and takes a sip of his coffee. "What was it you called us after your first visit? Caucasian running fools?"

Davis smiles. "And you are. There I was having a good time with my morning coffee and donut and every single one of you popped your head in and asked me to go on a run." Davis shakes his head. "At seven A.M., I just want to enjoy my donut in peace."

Caleb nods. "Fair." Then he turns on his heel and leaves, the door to the dining room swinging in his wake. As suddenly as he left, he's back, standing by the door. "You're afraid I don't think you're good enough for Everett, for this family"—he pauses, wiping his sleeve across his face—"when the truth is that none of us are good enough for you. Not yet, anyway." Caleb jerks his thumb toward the front of the house and shrugs. They both hear Everett bounding toward the kitchen. "He will be, though."

Davis watches as he leaves, and seconds later Everett walks through the same walkway. He's puzzled. After everything from the last twenty-four hours, it's Caleb—of all people—whose casual regard has somehow pulled him into this family in a way that makes sense, in a way that Davis can adapt to.

SEVEN

Their departure is the polar opposite of their arrival. There are no goodbye hugs, no family gathering on the porch. Everett was wordless as he walked through the house, found Davis in the kitchen, and brought him outside. He opened Davis's door for him, then slammed it shut before opening the rear door so Bam-Bam could jump into the car. Then he sat in the driver's seat and started the ignition.

He's silent, eyes staring out the windshield as he pulls out of the driveway and through the traffic lights of Darien. But the warmth of his hand resting on Davis's knee belies his silence, and Davis trusts that Everett is not angry—or at least not angry with him, that it is simply early and they have some hours to go. Davis sighs and turns his gaze to the passenger window, just as he did on their drive to Darien the day before.

He observes as they pass large, dignified brick houses, their walls like barricades protecting their inhabitants. He thinks again of the house he hasn't visited in more than seven years, how he used to hope he and Everett would eventually move to the suburbs. Since the Reverend passed, though, he has no interest in any dwelling other than their apartment on Jane Street. How easy it is, he thinks, to get lost in the illusion that a beautiful house is the best place to grow up, the best place to settle down, the most fertile soil for planting roots.

He thinks, also, of the last time he saw Olivia: Christopher was behind the wheel, having been determined to be in the best shape to get them safely to the nearest airport after the wedding. Davis had been looking at Olivia from behind because she'd sat in the passenger seat, ear practically glued to her phone, so he and Everett could sit together in the back. Everett had done what he always does, pulled Davis close, into the middle seat, Olivia's rental car like a speed demon released from the gates of hell trying to get them into the city, to JFK or LaGuardia, even Newark would do.

The car was a beautiful, dark SUV with heated leather seats and a tinted glass roof. The kind of sturdy luxury vehicle in which you feel you can go to war, stake your claim upon the battlefield, and survive. Davis remembers the silence of this ride, the perfectly smooth paved roads, the tinted windows through which he saw a clear sky filled with stars. In that moment he'd been reminded of the size of the world, how small and insignificant he really was. He was reminded that for all the peace that surrounded him right then, in other parts of the world, people were not at rest. In Moscow the streets were filled; in Tokyo businesses were open. Somewhere in the world it was Sunday morning, and congregants were headed to church, looking to worship, looking to praise the Almighty, looking for fellowship in one another's company. He felt keenly aware that his little wedding—indeed, his little self—was nothing more than a speck, a relic of the past that was already in the rearview mirror.

He thinks of how he'd looked away, how Olivia had audibly gasped at some detail of how an unlucky soul had stumbled upon the accident, had found the Reverend's body, her hand flying to her mouth to mute her outburst. He remembers how Everett had grabbed her shoulder from behind, was giving her a strong squeeze when Davis peeked out from behind his palms, saw her nod, saw her acknowledge Everett's touch.

In that moment, he'd never felt more fearful, and he'd never been so cold, despite the heat blasting from the air ducts and the seat warmers turned on high. He'd wanted to close his eyes, to return to that morning, when he'd risen before the sun, his entire life ahead of him. Instead, he kept refreshing various airline apps, and Everett, too, trying to find seats on a plane that would get them home as quickly as possible.

When they arrived at the airport, Davis pulled Everett aside while Olivia went to the ticket counter. It was in the bathroom where he kneeled in a closed stall in front of the toilet, his husband behind him rubbing and soothing his back and holding his hair out of the way, when it occurred to Davis that his father hadn't been in his life for the better part of a decade and why should death be his invitation to do so now.

He coughed, still on his knees, and then he held a hand up to Everett. "Tell her to wait. Tell her not to buy the tickets."

Everett helped him to his feet. Davis rinsed his mouth, wiped his face, popped a mint, and ran back to his sister. He remembers, like it happened yesterday, telling her not to buy him a ticket, not to buy one for Everett. He remembers staring into her eyes, holding both her hands in his, and he remembers how she remembered, how she covered her lips in surprise—perhaps at her own thoughtlessness, perhaps at the realization that she was on her own as far as it came to celebrating their father—how she went limp after she hugged her baby brother, how she went back to the counter and purchased her ticket, and never looked back, never said goodbye. How he texted her endlessly to one response, and only one time: *It's handled.*

Davis is lost in a reverie of shoulda coulda woulda when Everett pulls the car into the exit lane just a few miles south of Boston, bringing him back to reality. "I'm taking you on a detour. That okay?"

Davis understands that Everett isn't really asking, but nods his head, anyway. He continues staring out the window, and slides his hand on top of Everett's, which hasn't moved from his knee since they started driving.

"I didn't think to stop for flowers. I should've brought flowers," Everett says as they walk among the graves over a dirt path. Their walk is tender, hand in hand, Everett leading the way in case Davis stumbles over a rock or tree root.

"Well, you weren't planning to bring me to a graveyard . . . right?"

Everett nods. "We won't stay long; I know you're cold."

"I'm fine," Davis says.

They walk for a few minutes, Everett stopping at a grave now and then, walking up to a tombstone, shaking his head and saying, "It must be just a bit farther." When they reach the grave they're looking for, they stand quietly for a few minutes, Davis peeking at Everett, copying his every move—clasping his hands in front of him, bowing his head.

After a few minutes, Davis reads the inscription on the tombstone.

EVERETT ROBERT CAREY
OCTOBER 12, 1951–JUNE 26, 1991
DEVOTED FRIEND, LOVING UNCLE AND BROTHER

"Who is this?" he says.

"My uncle." He pauses, Davis nods and steps closer to the tombstone. He watches as Davis wraps his arms around himself. He turns to Everett. "Three first names, I love that. You've never mentioned him."

Everett steps forward. "My middle name, yes. I never told you why I go by that name, but I do it to honor him. Connor and I, and Caleb—even though he was really little—loved him so much. He and my Mom were—"

"Twins."

Everett nods. "Yes. My father tolerated him because they were so close, but he never really connected to Uncle Everett because he was gay." Everett shoves both his hands in his pockets and takes another step closer to Davis. "When he was dying, my mother wanted to care for him, but my father didn't want him around us because he was worried about someone catching it. He banned my uncle from our home."

"Oh my God."

"I know. My mother took him to the Montauk house for the summer and cared for him all by herself." He steps closer to Davis again. "My uncle didn't allow the disease to take its course. He wanted to die on his own terms, so one day, while Mom was cooking, he fell to the ground from a window on the second floor."

"Oh my God."

Everett steps closer again and takes Davis's hands in his. "It happened in the room Caleb was in. My dad threw him in there after . . ."

". . . after what he said about me."

Everett nods.

"I didn't want him around you, but my father wanted him nearby because he was so high. He put Caleb in that room. That's why Mom lost it."

Davis is awestruck, his voice nearly silent. "It was the room where her twin killed himself." He holds Everett's hands, his thumb lovingly caressing his veins and hair and knuckles.

"That's why she was freaking out when you came upstairs. He wasn't responding when she knocked on the door."

Davis nods. "God, she must've been terrified. How could your dad put him in that room?"

Everett shakes his head. "That's what I'm saying. I kind of see him in a different light now . . ." Everett trails off. Davis stares at the tears welling in Everett's eyes.

"I needed him. I needed my uncle. And my father kept him from me."

"Of course you needed him."

"After my divorce, I started going by Everett. I think it's time I changed my name legally. I'm tired of telling people, 'My name is Carter, but I go by my middle name, Everett.'"

Davis steps closer to Everett, puts his hands around his neck, and gently, soothingly kisses his husband's lips. "I only know you as Everett. My Everett."

"My father isn't the man I thought he was. And I've known that for a long time, but I think I couldn't face it until now."

"You know what's funny? Neither was mine. All these years I thought all the distance had helped me figure him out. But nope!" Davis turns around, leaning back against his husband.

Everett kisses his neck. "Even now. He's not the man I want to be."

"You aren't him, Everett."

"I've been . . . resentful. Of you."

Davis looks at his feet. "I know."

"You do?"

"I mean, I figured . . . I'd be angry. I *am* angry with myself."

Everett shakes his head. "You shouldn't be."

"I know that in theory." Davis looks up at Everett. "But knowing and feeling are two different things. For instance: I know that you know—in your head—that I'm strong enough to be there for you. But I also suspect that you are so busy being strong for me that it doesn't really occur to you to lean on me in all the ways I lean on you. You don't feel that from me." Davis blinks. "And that's my bad. Because you should feel that from me."

"Davis, I . . ."

But Davis holds a finger up to his lips, shushing Everett. "I should give you a few minutes alone with him."

Everett nods. Davis steps back, allowing his hands to trail down Everett's chest, before he turns to make his way back to their car. As he walks, he considers something new: He knows Everett doesn't know everything about him, but it's never occurred to him that he doesn't know all there is to know about Everett, that both of them bring their full pasts to this marriage, and Everett, in fact, has a longer and more expansive past. He's always admired that about Everett, even looked up to him in a way. He smiles as he approaches the car, fiddling with his wedding ring, spinning it around his finger. This kind of vulnerability from Everett is uncharted territory; it makes Davis love him even more.

EIGHT

By the time Everett sees Olivia again, they are well into March, Davis's recital at Lincoln Center is just days away. Olivia, true to her word, comes to the city so she can attend his debut. "So, how is he, Everett?"

Everett takes Olivia's hand in his. They sit together on a bench on the High Line, directly over Fourteenth Street, each with a steaming cup of coffee. "I'm starting to worry. He's avoiding my calls."

"Yeah, I know." Everett looks her in the eye. "To be honest, I think it's pretty wild that he hasn't been back to Cleveland during all of this."

"I know," Olivia says, as she sips her coffee. She holds the cup close to her face. "I'm pissed. I feel like I've been dealing with all this shit by myself." She bites her lip. "And after we'd just gotten ourselves back into a better place, too."

"I think he misses you, Olivia."

"Ha! Well, that's something, isn't it?"

"I tried to get him to fly to Cleveland, to be with you during the funeral. I really did."

"Were you going to come, too?"

"I would've, but when he considered it, he never wanted me there. Honestly, I probably would've come anyway."

Olivia blinks, then looks away. "That doesn't surprise me. It's almost like he has these two different lives that he keeps separate. But yours is the real life, and ours is like . . . I don't know, translucent, or something."

Everett nods. "But, Olivia, his relationship with your dad was very different from yours."

"I'm aware of that, Everett."

Everett puts his hands up in surrender. "Sorry, I didn't mean to—"

"No, no, no. I'm sorry I jumped down your throat. I just . . . I'm the one who's been caught in the middle all these years. All because of a spanking." She sighs.

"A spanking? That's what all this is about?"

Olivia shrugs. "I don't know, Everett. Sometimes I think it's a bit of a cover. Like he just wanted to run away into this different life and he used one drunken mistake by our father to fuel him." She pauses, steps on a twig with her shoe. "I think he wanted to come to the wedding."

"The Reverend?"

"I think he wanted to give you both his blessing and he was heading to the wedding to do so that night."

"How do you know that?"

"Well, I don't know for sure. But he's wanted to close the gap between him and Davis for years."

Everett stands, wanting to stretch his legs. "You want to walk for a bit?" He offers Olivia his hand, helps her to her feet. "I tried to get Davis to invite him."

"Oh, I know. He told me."

Everett kicks a pebble down the path. "He was still angry."

"Was? Is, I'm guessing."

"I think it's more complicated than that."

"How can it not be? I just didn't know he was mad at me."

"I don't think he's mad at you."

Olivia stops in the middle of the walkway. "He could've been mine, Everett."

Everett gestures for her—for both of them—to move to the side, out of the way. "What do you mean?"

Olivia makes a face and spreads her arms. "Davis. He could have been my son. I started having sex around the same time that my parents were trying to conceive him. Of course, I didn't know they were trying at the time. But my boyfriend, Ben, got me pregnant."

"I had no idea. Does Davis know that?"

She shakes her head. "Don't worry, he's not mine. You're not uncovering some *Desperate Housewives* foolishness. It's just that the Reverend wanted me to have the baby and raise it or give it up for adoption. He wanted me to get a job downtown. And my mother wanted me to have an abortion, and I wanted to please her, and also the idea of giving birth was terrifying, and also I never wanted to be a mother, so here I am. I had an abortion."

Everett turns, standing next to her. "Do you ever regret it?"

She shakes her head. "Not for a second. I may not have been ready to make the decision on my own, but it was the right call. She knew me well enough to know that down the line, I would agree. But the Reverend? It took him a long time to even forgive my having sex, let alone getting rid of his potential grandchild."

"I'm not sure I fully understand the connection."

Olivia blinks, smiles, looks out at the city. Then she nods. "I think you should talk to Davis, then."

"He's kind of shutting me out."

She nods again. "He does that."

It's Everett's turn to pause, to think, to glance away from Olivia, then look her in the eye. "You should tell Davis. I think knowing this might help him. It might bring you closer."

"In what way?"

"I think maybe he feels very alone in the family. He doesn't know you had a similar . . . tension with your father. Around sex, that you also earned his disapproval. It might help him open back up to you. And to me."

"Yeah, well, he can join the damn club."

"Olivia."

"I'm serious, Everett. I'm pissed, too! I had to do everything by myself. Identify the body, plan the services, be gracious in the face of all those church folks who came from all over, and answer all the questions about Davis and his whereabouts. I was alone through all of that."

Everett nods. "I know."

"And not just that. The Reverend had been getting older. Who would've had to care for him, had he gotten sick? Davis isn't the only one with a life." She slams her coffee down on a railing so hard it topples over the edge and falls to the street. "Shit!"

And then they're laughing as they duck below the bannister so as not to be seen. Laughing, hugging, trying to catch their breath.

Once they gather their composure, Everett helps Olivia back to her feet. "I think he would want to know that you're feeling this way. I really do." They continue walking. "Davis is going to have feelings about us showing up at dinner together."

Olivia smiles. "I was just thinking the same thing. Should we stagger it a bit?"

Everett thinks for a moment, finger pressed against his chin, brow furrowed. "No," he says. "He and I are married. You and I are family now. We both love him, and he loves us. This"—he gestures between the two of them—"is a good thing."

JUST BEYOND THE door of the restaurant, they spot one another, Davis coming from one direction, his husband and sister coming from another. He sees that Everett's arm is around Olivia, in a jovial way, and she smiles up at him, too.

He hugs her first, of course; he hasn't seen her since the airport.

They linger, and she pats him warmly on the back when he steps away and into Everett's arms.

Seated now, Davis looks around the restaurant. It's small, the floors and tables made of dark wood. They are seated in a back room. When Everett suggested this place, Davis had to look it up. Though it's only a block from their apartment, it's easy to miss; Davis must've walked by it a thousand times and never noticed it.

When the waiter comes, rattling off specials, they listen attentively. Once he finishes, Everett orders a bottle of red wine for the table.

"And a Hendrick's martini, dry, up with a twist, to start," Davis adds. He looks at Everett and Olivia quickly, and then says, "Make that three."

It's then that Olivia leans forward, clasping her hands. "So, how are you, baby brother?"

The restaurant is oddly quiet as Davis stares into his sister's eyes, considering how best to respond. He thinks back to the way he'd felt put on the spot when Christopher asked him the same question. Then he thinks back to the nights he spent living in his sister's guest room, curled on her bed, a lost and scared teenager, and how she'd fed him apples and peanut butter and gotten him off to school, and the relentless way she kept asking and asking—*What happened? What happened between you two?*—and the way he fessed up to only what the Reverend also fessed up to.

"Not great." He notices then, the flicker of a look from Olivia to Everett, though Everett stares down at his menu, unflinching in his concentration. They had clearly met up early to discuss him.

Davis looks at his plate, fiddles with his flatware. He deserves that, honestly.

Olivia maintains eye contact. "It really sucks. Feels like a different world without him, doesn't it?"

"I never expected that," Davis says. "I thought—"

The waiter arrives, quickly setting the martinis down, nary a spill.

Once he disappears, all three of them clink glasses. Olivia looks expectantly at her brother once more. "You were saying?"

Davis bends forward. Under the table, he rests his forearms against his thighs, clasping his hands. He takes a deep breath, not entirely sure of the words that will come out.

"I think I thought I would be fine. That I might feel better, lighter. Freer—with him gone."

Olivia takes a deep breath, then nods, about to interject, but Davis continues. "That makes me awful, doesn't it. I'm awful."

Both Everett and Olivia shake their heads.

"No, baby," he says.

"Absolutely not," she says. She slides a hand across the table. Davis shifts and brings his arm up to the table and grasps hers. "Say more."

Davis looks at Everett, who by this time has moved his chair closer to Davis and swings his arm up and over so it rests on the back. He nods his encouragement.

"Sometimes," he begins, looking up again, "I just feel so hormonal." He looks at them. After a moment, Olivia says, "Go on."

"Well, my emotions are all over the place. One minute I'm happy, the next I'm miserable. I'm tired all the time, and I have a really hard time concentrating. I don't know. I don't feel like myself—at all." Davis looks between them. "I'm just . . . off. Bereft, maybe."

Already, he has revealed far more than Everett expected, far more than he has verbalized in the privacy of their home.

Davis feels himself trembling; he places a hand on his stomach in an attempt to settle it. "The thing is . . ." He looks around them, as though sharing his innermost secrets. "They had me when they were older, Mom and Dad. So, yeah, we weren't expecting him to die now. But it's not like I didn't know the Reverend was going to go sooner or later. And sometimes I thought about it. I wondered what it would be like for me when he was gone."

His voice has transformed itself, from something meek into an eager whisper. Everett sees a light in Davis's eyes; he knows there's more for him to say, more that wants to get out.

Davis takes a sip of his martini, delicately dabs his lips with his napkin, and spreads it in his lap.

"For so long . . ." he says, though he pauses then. He clutches Olivia's hand then he lowers his voice. "For so long I waited for this moment, wondering how I would feel. I really thought the answer was going to be relief. Freedom." He lets go of Olivia's hand, holding up both of his, defeated. "But it's not."

"How *do* you feel?" His sister sips her martini, leaning as close as she can without tipping her chair forward into the table.

"Like I never got closure."

Olivia sits back in her seat. "You should've come to the funeral. You should've said goodbye."

"Goodbye? Olivia, I said goodbye seven years ago. I said goodbye when . . ."

Everett looks up from the menu then. "When what?"

Olivia and Davis both glance in his direction, her lips forming a tight, thin line.

"Nothing, never mind," Davis says as he looks away, glancing out the window. He smiles when he feels Everett's hand rubbing his shoulder, tightening briefly at the nape of his neck.

Olivia shakes her head and says again, "You should've come to his funeral."

"I didn't need to say goodbye. I still don't."

"For me, then. You should've come for me."

Davis sets down his drink, his expression quizzical. "For you?"

"For me. You should have gotten on that plane and come home with me and helped me plan that funeral. Do you know how hard that was for me?"

Davis closes his eyes, holds his forehead in his hands.

"You didn't think about me at all. And I have always—always!—been there for you. I am always thinking of you!"

Davis opens his eyes. "I sent you money."

"I didn't need your money! I'm a doctor for God's sake!"

"Olivia," Everett says.

"It's okay," Davis says. "She's right."

"Even if you didn't want to come for you, you should've come to support me."

"Why didn't you say anything?"

"I don't know." She eyes the waiter, approaching from behind Davis and Everett. "It should've been obvious."

Everett turns toward the waiter, signaling that they need a few more minutes.

She continues. "You're the only family I have. No aunts and uncles, no cousins."

"I don't know what to say to that."

"Of course you don't." Olivia gulps down the rest of her martini and stands. "You're ungrateful."

"I was a child!"

"Wait," Everett says, rising to his feet. "Olivia . . ."

"Don't you get it, Davis?" She stuffs her arms into her coat sleeves, pulling it over her shoulders. "Our father was extending an olive branch."

"Our *father*? Since when did you start calling him that?"

Olivia blinks. "He was trying to apologize."

"'Hallowed be thy name,' right, Olivia?"

She looks down at the table, rapping her fingers against the edge. Then she looks up, eyes narrowed into slits. "Why do you think he was driving east?"

She turns to Everett. "It was nice getting coffee with you."

She turns around; Davis speechless, still seated as she walks away from the table. Everett remains standing where he is, arm extended in Olivia's direction, as she exits the restaurant.

"Let her go," Davis says.

Nine

Typically, when he makes it to one of Davis's performances, Everett stands among the shadows in the rear of the recital hall. He towers over the entire audience, watching patiently until the moment Davis walks confidently onto the stage, heels resounding against hardwood, hand wrapped around the neck of his viola, bow already tightened in the other hand.

It's almost a routine, the way Everett watches as Davis takes his place by the piano or in front of the orchestra. He waits for the brief moment when Davis peers out into the audience, over their heads, squinting until he finds Everett. In the biggest concert halls, the lights over the audience are already dimmed, and Everett knows that Davis can only make out his figure—the shape of his hair, the width of his shoulders. No light spared to see the details of his face, though Everett knows that Davis can fill in those details with his eyes closed. Even without eye contact, the brief connection feels intimate, a split second of electricity moving between them before Davis turns his attention to his instrument, tunes, and begins performing.

It's simply an opportunity for Everett to give Davis some extra support, and yet he thinks of it as one of the routine practices of their shared life. It's a recurring moment of vulnerability for Davis, and Everett can be there, can show up for him in a literal way—be the man that Davis wants and needs. Although he still hasn't said much to Everett about his father in the months since the Reverend passed, Everett has come to understand more about how the man rarely showed up for his son, consumed as he was by the constant call of his faith. As far apart as they are in these concert halls, as much as it highlights the difference in their skills and interests, in these moments, their intimacy is as palpable to Everett as it is in the bedroom.

Tonight's recital is one of the most important performances of Davis's young career. The culmination of winning the Finley-Whitaker Career Grant earlier this year, this recital is Davis's official solo debut at Lincoln Center. The recital hall is standing room only, but Everett, his parents, Caleb, Connor, and Courtney are comfortably resting in seats reserved for the winner's family in the second row. Olivia has left town, returning home early. Weeks ago, Davis brought Everett to the Rose Studio and pointed out the specific seat where he wanted him, where he said he needed him to be.

"Here." He'd pointed at the seat Everett occupies now, then he rushed onto the stage and approximated where he would stand. "Jimin will be playing piano over here, and I," he said as he shuffled closer to the stage, "will be standing right about here." He stood in place, mimicked playing for a moment, nodded, then turned to Everett. "I need to be able to see you at any moment. Even if I'm mid-measure, I need to be able to turn my head and see you looking back at me. Please." He pointed again. "Sit there." He'd looked small and scared standing up there on that stage—his eyes big and seemingly, as they often were of late, on the verge of tears. And there was a new weight, Everett had noticed, to the way he moved, the way he held himself, like at any moment he might collapse under it.

Underneath the chatter of an eager audience, Everett feels the second hand of his watch tick tick tick, moving past eight P.M. The lights flicker and the audience quiets. All of a sudden, every sound, every cough, every candy wrapper covertly opened, every anxiously tapping foot, is another sound in a litany of noises that must settle themselves when Davis emerges. Charlotte rests a hand on Everett's arm, leans close, whispering, "I'm so nervous for him." She grabs his hand and squeezes it, then settles back into her chair.

Everett nods, though he's not nervous in the slightest. All of Davis's attention has gone into preparing for this recital. He keeps his eyes on the stage as the lights dim, and a disembodied generic male voice plays over the sound system asking everyone to silence their phones and refrain from photography. It tells them the recital is expected to go eighty-nine minutes exactly, including a ten-minute intermission. After a moment, the lights dim even further.

A dark moment of silence, then several orbs of light appear, forming a path from the side of the stage to a spotlight in the center. The piano, though shrouded in darkness, is visible to the first few rows. A door at the side of the stage, previously invisible to Everett and the audience at large, opens silently. Out comes Davis, perhaps a bit slower than normal, but walking with purpose nonetheless. He looks stunning, his hair styled in the same loose updo from their wedding, his sparkling, wide-legged, red jumpsuit glittering in the sheen of the stage lights.

The applause is loud and long, the audience enthusiastic at this already-acclaimed new arrival on the global classical music scene. Davis smiles, then bows, his eyes momentarily catching Everett's, who opens himself, allowing the nervous energy that only he sees to flow from Davis and wash completely over him. He wants the old Davis, the happy-go-lucky girlish boy for whom the world always seems to align itself. Davis deserves this moment, has earned this glory.

As Davis straightens, he gives Everett a brief smile before taking in the rest of the audience. Then he turns, angling his feet toward the audience and the scroll of his instrument toward the opposite wall. He's taught Everett about this before, how important it is for a violist's f-holes to point straight out to the audience for maximum sound production.

"People think the way a musician moves when we perform is just us getting swept away in the music, but for the viola, it's actually part of our technique," he'd explained to Everett on one of their early dates. Everett, who still barely grasps the difference between a violin and a viola, thinks of this moment every time he watches Davis perform, every time he loses himself in Davis's passion.

After pausing to assume the correct position on the fingerboard, Davis gently places the bow on the string.

From silence, he draws the bow downward on the C string.

On the next note, his ring finger vibrates before he moves the bow upward and shifts down the string into a low melody. The music is filled with questions, hills and valleys, the viola rich, resonant, lush. Sound envelops Everett; he thinks of heat blasting from a wood-burning oven. He thinks of dark chocolate melting against his tongue; Davis's soft, pliable fingers caressing his ears.

A pin could drop in the recital hall and Davis's note would be the only sound heard; the pianist waits patiently as Davis grows his volume, his urgency, until he returns to the original A, beginning anew. This time the pianist joins him, playing soft gentle chords that seem to prop Davis up, compelling him to amplify, his fingers climbing up the instrument in scales, in arpeggios, moving his bow faster and faster until the viola sings, reaching the rafters, before Davis pulls the bow from the string in a flourish of movement—joyful or desperate, Everett can't yet tell. But for a moment he closes his eyes, sits back, revels in the music his husband makes.

Davis has announced himself—here he is!—and Everett glances all around him at the audience. Rapt, all of them, every single one; the world has taken notice.

FOLLOWING THE PERFORMANCE, the foundation hosts a brief reception for donors, season ticket holders, and the press. A receiving line, bushels of flowers. Afterward, there will be a late private dinner—Everett has arranged something special.

As they walk to the restaurant, Everett falls behind the group, ready to let Davis do his thing, when there Davis is, walking next to him, close to him. He bites his lip, looks up at Everett.

"What?" Everett laughs, puts an arm around Davis's waist. "You can't possibly still be nervous." He leans in close, brushing his lips across Davis's ear. "It's over. You did it. You were brilliant. I can't believe how brilliant you were." He stands tall, watching the smile spread across Davis's face, shy and modest, sure, but also sure of himself.

"I was brilliant?"

"You really were. Maybe the best I've heard you." He grabs Davis's hand, prepared for him to slip away, to mingle up front with the others, but he doesn't. Davis settles in, allows Everett to be next to him, close to him. For a moment, he leans his head against Everett's arm as they sidle down the street, their pace unhurried despite the cold.

"You okay for dinner? Not too tired?"

"I think I could stay up all night! I could do that entire recital again!"

He drops Everett's hand, steps in front of him, and turns around, clasping his hands in front of his face. "I did it!" he squeals. He jumps up and down several times in place. It fills Everett, to see him so unabashed in his joy. Then Davis laughs and falls in step next to Everett again.

"I could listen to you play like that all night."

They arrive, walking through the general dining room and down the stairs. From the bottom of the stairs, they move through a tight hallway until they reach a room, a private wine cellar. Davis steps in, wondering why he is suddenly leading their little processional, not realizing that everyone has fallen back to allow him to make his entrance. They're dining in a private wine cellar, ancient bottles stacked floor to ceiling surrounding them. His friends, his best friends, are seated in different places at the exquisitely appointed table. There are place cards for seating with names spelled out in ethereal script, spring flowers and leaves decorating the table, and everywhere, bottles of red wine emptied into carafes with placards naming the varietal, the year, the region. He steps forward, and around him, everyone begins to clap and cheer.

He turns to Everett. "Because I haven't had enough fancy dinners celebrating me this year." He wraps his arms around Everett's neck, drawing their faces close together. "Thank you," he whispers. When Everett kisses him, their lips are deep, locked together, tongues briefly roaming freely. More cheering. They break apart, smiling, looking away from each other, Everett sending Davis to entertain his fans with a quick and quiet, "I love you," Davis's hand lingering in his for a moment before he walks up to the table.

Maybe tonight, Everett thinks.

Christopher stands next to Everett, puts an arm around his son's shoulders. Everett tenses but remains where he is. They are here; they are trying. He turns to look at his father.

"Your mother and I are glad to be here, Everett. What a treat that was."

"I'm glad you're here, too. And I know Davis is."

"We'd never heard him play. Of course, you've told us how talented he is for so long, but . . . I mean, really, son. That was extraordinary." Christopher claps his son on the back before stepping away with Charlotte to look for his seat.

For hours they sit in that wine cellar, guests and friends slow to leave, reluctant to exit the evening, until finally it's just the family: Davis, Everett, Christopher and Charlotte, Connor and Courtney, and Caleb.

Charlotte turns to Davis. "Davis, darling, where's Olivia? I was so looking forward to chatting with her again."

Everett and Davis share a look as Everett pours more wine into Davis's glass. "She couldn't make it. You know how it is, someone somewhere is always having a baby."

Charlotte makes a face. "Oh phooey! There are other OB-GYNs. This is Lincoln Center! You're her brother; this is your debut!"

Davis nods. "Yes, but there aren't other Olivia Freemans." He shrugs. "She's one of the very best."

"Well, so are you! You proved that tonight."

"A family of high achievers, Charlotte! You can't blame a girl for saving a life." Christopher raises his glass. "To Olivia!"

Davis and Everett clink their glasses, sharing another look.

By now the seven of them have condensed, all sitting across from one another at the center of the long table. Everett, affably chatting with his brothers, glances quickly between Davis and his parents. He stretches his arm across the back of Davis's chair and takes another bite of his dessert.

Charlotte looks down at her plate, then back at Davis, squinting her eyes. "How did you get into playing the viola? It's kind of a random instrument, no?"

Davis smiles, a little twinkle in his eye. He leans back in the chair, and Everett's arm moves from the top of the chair to Davis's shoulders. "I get that question a lot. And it's a story. My mother was a jazz singer." He pauses.

"Go on, dear." Charlotte nods.

"She got me started playing the viola really early. I'd heard a violin solo in church, but my teacher was the one who suggested I play the viola. She said I'd have a lot more opportunity if I played the viola. After she died, the Reverend kept me playing."

"The Cleveland Orchestra is one of the most renowned orchestras in the world," Everett pipes up, drawing his brothers' attention to Davis, who nods.

"So anyway, we go to this instrument shop one day because my teacher said I needed a better instrument. It's after school, autumn, already dark outside, and thunderstorming. This old man takes us in the side entrance of his house, and up to his attic. I remember being frightened of the dark, and of the way his house smelled. The room is warm, with deep red carpet, and lined along all four walls are stringed instruments, of all sizes. He had lined up several violas for me to play. They were . . . fine. But as soon as I was done, he got really excited about my playing, and then he showed me a special viola. It was French, from the nineteenth century. It truly was a 'fine' viola, suitable for an advancing student. They're hard to find in little kid sizes, so that made it extra special. That's when I knew I was good, and that I couldn't imagine my life without it."

"So you really started on the viola," Charlotte says.

"I really started on the viola," Davis says, and smiles at her. "And once I did, I never wanted to play the violin. Even though the repertoire is more expansive and there are so many violin concertos I absolutely love. The Barber—God I wish that piece had been written for viola. But the viola has an inherent design flaw that makes it unique, that . . . makes it human—inasmuch as an instrument can be human." He chuckles.

"Say more," Connor says.

Davis looks around, seeing that he holds court. Under the table, he crosses one leg over his knee, bouncing his right foot, brushing it against Everett's leg. "Obviously these instruments have a lowest note and a highest note, right?" Everyone nods. "So we call that an acoustic range. And there's a correlation between the size and dimension of these instruments and their acoustic range. A full-size violin and a full-size cello are the ideal size and dimension for their acoustic range. However, the viola is not. When I was just starting out, I learned very early on that there was no standard- or full-size viola. You just had to find the one that fit your body. When I got to high school, I had grown and we were shopping for a new viola, and one of the shop owners we went to explained why the viola didn't have one full-size that I could work toward like the violin does: The ideal size for the viola's acoustic range is twenty-one inches along the back." He looks around; the entire Caldwell family is staring at him blankly. "Meaning that it would be impossible to play. For anyone, any human. At least up here." He gestures, miming playing his viola on his shoulder. "So everyone just plays the biggest one they can, but most people top out at a sixteen and a half."

"How big is yours?"

"Mine is a sixteen and one-eighth. So what this design flaw means is that the viola has trouble producing the same amount of sound and resonating with the same ferocity and power as the violin and the cello. It's slower to respond, sound-wise. It's temperamental; it needs some coaxing. A gentle hand."

"Sounds like someone I know," Everett says. He takes one of Davis's hands, holds it to his mouth, kisses it gently. The table collectively groans.

"People assume the technique for playing the viola and the violin is the same but it's not at all. It's very different; the viola is bigger and heavier, the strings are thicker, it's slower to respond—as I said—and so it requires a different approach, physically. There are places on most violas where the player will have a hard time getting a clean resonant note out of the instrument. And when I work with students, I can usually tell by their playing if they started on viola or if they started on violin and then switched over at some point. Just by how they play, how they produce sound."

"So you're saying part of why you love the viola is because it has natural, insurmountable flaws. Lucky me," Everett says, leaning closer to Davis, who smiles shyly, takes a sip of his wine, and continues.

Davis, for a moment, is somewhere else, entirely absent. "I'm saying I identify with that aspect of the viola—the built-in flaw, the very real limitations to the body in which I navigate the world every day. We're the same, myself and my viola."

"Limitations? In what way?" Charlotte asks, leaning practically over the table.

It startles him, the way she says it, pulling him from a reverie. "Oh, you know—I'd like to be taller, lose five pounds, things like that." He shrugs. "Physically, I'm better suited for the violin—I'm short, I have small hands, but here we are."

"Well, it seems to have worked out for you, anyway," she says with a smile.

"Because of this issue, for centuries various luthiers have experimented with different shapes for the viola. There's this Japanese maker in Philly who makes these instruments where the bottom is really wide, and then the shoulders, essentially, have cutouts so the player can more easily lift their arm up and around it when they need to shift into higher positions. He's just one more well-known example, and you see his violas in many major orchestras. But that maker I went to in eighth grade had done something innovative with the bass bar inside the instrument to make up for the deficit. And the viola I bought from him really had a lot of power. The thing is, whereas for the other instruments everyone is chasing the sound of those three-hundred-year-old violins from Cremona, luthiers who make violas are always looking forward, always trying to figure out a new way to capitalize on the acoustic range while keeping the instrument physically playable. It's an ongoing challenge. And that's what really fascinates me—that constant push for evolution."

"Wow. I'd never think about that kind of thing." Christopher looks at Charlotte, then back at Davis. "And what about you? Do you have one of those Japanese violas with the fat bottom?"

Davis blushes. "No, though I tried one in college. I own a viola made by a wonderful contemporary maker, also from Philadelphia. I love it dearly; it'll serve me well for the rest of my life. But"—he leans close, looking mischievous, holding his finger in front of his lips as though to shush everyone—"I'm cheating on it. It's not the viola you heard tonight."

"Get ready for this," Everett says.

"Earlier this year, I was loaned a Lorenzo Storioni from 1785, by the Reuters-Koenig Foundation. It's all gone so well that they are considering allowing me to keep playing it on loan." Davis is wide-eyed, somber. "I should find out any day now."

"This is because you won the award?"

Davis nods. "I mean, you don't have to be famous to play a fine instrument on loan, you just have to be good." He leans closer to Christopher. "But it helps! So yes—it was loaned to me for a concerto performance and it's been amazing. The colors I can achieve on it." He looks around at the family, almost ready to tear up. "It's exquisite."

"Well, can you buy it?"

Davis laughs. "Heavens, no. It's not for sale. And it would be so expensive, and the bow is even more expensive. They all are when they come from that era."

Connor looks confused. "But if they loan it to you, can they take it away?"

"Yes, they can."

"Does that happen?"

"All the time. They just take them away and loan them to another player, or maybe the owner sells them. Unless they give me a lifetime loan, I won't be playing it forever. Ten years if I'm lucky. It's like a marriage that you know is going to end. It becomes an extension of you. That Storioni is already an extension of me." Davis bites his lip, looks at Everett, energy suddenly gone. Charlotte glances between them, then at her husband. She watches Davis reach for Everett's hand.

"Well," Davis says, "sorry to talk your ears off. I'm just . . . so easily excitable right now." He smiles again, the light in his eyes diminished, but not entirely gone.

Connor and Courtney look at each other and start reaching for their things. "We should be going, we have a long ride down to Brooklyn at this hour. Caleb, do you want to ride with us?"

He jumps up, nodding, glancing now and then at Davis.

Charlotte and Christopher look at each other, Charlotte stifling a yawn. "Us, too. I mean, we're close to the hotel, but it is getting late."

"And I'm sure you two can use some time alone," Christopher

says, putting his drink down. Charlotte tips her wineglass at Everett
and Davis. She rises, Christopher grabbing and unfurling her coat,
holding it open behind her. They move with flawless synchronicity,
as though this practice is really a long-rehearsed dance.

Davis and Everett stand at once, taking turns hugging everyone,
wishing them safe travel home. Davis watches as Everett claps his
father on the back in that heavy way men do to show intimacy.
When they leave, Everett sits back down.

"Everett?" Davis tilts his head toward the door.

"Not yet." Out of nowhere a chilled bottle of champagne arrives.
Everett gestures for Davis to sit.

Davis glances at his watch. "I'm tired. Aren't they closing soon,
anyway?"

"We still have some time. Sit down. Get comfortable."

Davis sits. Everett scoots his chair close to him, so close their
legs nearly touch. Wordlessly, Davis lifts his legs and plops them
into Everett's lap. "This comfortable?"

He smiles, closing his eyes as Everett begins gently rubbing his
legs. "This is just the beginning."

Everett undoes Davis's strappy heels, gently pulling them loose
from his feet, which are perfectly manicured. They fall to the
ground as he starts massaging Davis's toes, then the balls of his feet,
then the arches. Davis catches his breath, jerks his feet away from
Everett, before slowly sliding them across his thighs once more.

"Hey—that thing you said about your body," Everett says.

Davis nods.

"You know your body is perfect. Perfectly you."

Davis blushes again. "I know, I know." He fully reclines against
the back of his chair, his head dangling off it, eyes closed, voice like
a whistle moving through a light spring breeze. "Thank you," he
says.

"Always."

Everett slowly works his way up from Davis's tiny ankles, fingers
digging deep into his muscular calves. It's as pleasing to him as it is

for Davis; he loves how smooth and moist and rich Davis's skin is, now that he's starting to take care of himself again. He's recently taken to shaving his legs, a new practice for him. Everett had forgotten how much he enjoyed that aspect of sleeping with women— their bodies carrying a warm, comforting softness, elusive for even the most effete of men. And yet Davis, altogether different from any other man Everett's ever been with, has brought that warm comfort to him in much the same way.

"Come here," he says, moving his lips along Davis's legs to coax him closer. Davis sits up; in one swift motion, Everett pulls him over until he's sitting in his lap, and then they're kissing furiously. Everett's body comes alive, desire coursing through him with the strength of the blood of Christ. He can move mountains, set the world on fire. He picks up Davis easily—Davis who clings to him, whose lips and legs are open, ready and waiting, blood thrumming— and places him gently on the table. Everett steps back for a moment, staring at his husband, this pretty young thing looking up at him with big doe eyes and the softest, plushest lips. He cups Davis's face in his hands, and gently kisses him, his tongue probing like a light-footed visitor, before sliding a hand around Davis's waist, and marching his fingers up Davis's exposed back. At the nape of his neck are the buttons that hold the top of the jumpsuit together. Everett isn't a clumsy man; he undoes the two buttons with ease, all while burying his lips in Davis's neck. The top falls to Davis's waist, exposing his chest.

"Everett, we're in public." Davis is breathless when he says this.

"I already paid the check. We have the room to ourselves until closing." Everett's vision is clouded by his desire.

They kiss again, for several moments, until Davis breaks the kiss, once more breathless. "Take me home."

Everett grabs the champagne, wraps Davis, who hadn't thought to bring a coat to the concert hall that afternoon when it was unseasonably warm, in his coat, and guides him up the stairs and out of the restaurant into a car that's already waiting.

"Magic," Davis says.

"Good planning." Everett laughs as he opens the door and gestures for Davis to enter. The ride to Jane Street seems quick, but neither of them can confirm because they spend it making out like teenagers who've just left the prom.

In the elevator Everett presses Davis back against the wall. He takes both his arms and pulls them toward the ceiling, pinning them together. He loves the way Davis looks up at him; it's the first time he's seen Davis aroused, titillated, since the wedding. It hasn't been easy for Everett not to take Davis's vanishing libido personally.

When the elevator opens, they spill passionately into their apartment, Davis placing his viola on the bench that sits in the foyer by the door, and then pulling Everett by his tie toward the bedroom. Wordlessly, Everett picks him up and carries him the rest of the way, Davis giggling, before placing him down on his feet. Davis walks toward the bed.

"Nope. I want you over there." Everett guides Davis across the room until his back is against the windows that run floor to ceiling. He's rough, pushing Davis as he turns him around, so his belly rests against the thick glass. Davis looks tiny, dainty, delicate, but his sexual appetite is anything but. Everett growls, giving him a little spank, and stands back, allowing his eyes to explore every inch of Davis's body. Everett sees, very clearly, how much he is wanted by his husband. Davis's skin, moisturized to high heaven, glistens in the beam of their bedroom's recessed lighting. His tight, round, perky little ass stretches the fabric of the jumpsuit just enough to be sexy without being vulgar.

Since he'd been sitting in the front of the recital hall, Everett had missed the opportunity to take in the inevitable surprise from the audience when Davis walked out onto the stage: surprise for his youth, his Blackness, his attire, his sheer beauty. Everett loves to see the men who perk up at the sight of Davis, loves the game of determining whether their curiosity comes from desire or disgust, or most often, some entanglement of the two. He enjoys the bewilderment in their eyes when, during the reception, he walks up to Davis and slips an arm around his waist. And yet tonight Everett enjoyed sitting so close to the stage, placed so squarely in Davis's inner orbit. He'd almost felt like he was participating in the concert, faithfully performing his task of never looking away, of making sure his face was always available for the grounding familiarity Davis needed to push him through to the end. It was the first time he sat at attention in a different way, the first time he wasn't on edge, waiting for someone to huff their disapproval or suppress a laugh. It was the first time he didn't stand with his fists balled at one of Davis's concerts, silent and brooding, ready to handle the wrong kind of attention.

Everett undoes the top button and watches the jumpsuit fall to the ground, draping over Davis's feet. When Davis begins to step out of his heels, Everett stops him. "I want you in them." And then Everett is pressed against him, his own shoes kicked aside, erection growing quickly as he runs his hands up and down Davis's body, his lips and tongue and teeth gently taking turns kissing and licking and nibbling his neck, hands grabbing and fingers pinching and palms slapping any available flesh harder and harder yet. Davis is the instrument now, making all kinds of noises, fingertips pressed hard against the glass by the time Everett drops to his knees, beginning to use his tongue to open him up, to loosen and lubricate him. He will enter slowly; he will make love; he will prove himself again and again, for as long as Davis needs, until Davis sings like he made that viola sing. Everett buries his face deeper, slapping him hard enough to leave a momentary handprint and a patch of red skin. With his tongue he probes so deep that Davis's cries are muffled until he is sufficiently wet, and Everett rises, unsheathing himself, the size of his body enveloping Davis against the window. Suddenly Davis pushes himself back from the glass, colliding against Everett. He turns to look Everett in the eye, a question, perhaps an accusation, splattered across his face as he shrinks back against the window, Everett's arms on either side of him. "I told you to stop."

"What?" Everett's heart falls to his feet. Stop, when he's never been more ready?

But the look Davis gives him—surprise, then fear, then hurt—is one Everett's never seen him give. Davis steps back, supported by the window once more, and puts a hand up. He speaks slower, now, almost gasping for air. "I told you to stop."

All is silent, dark; the city lights seem to have dimmed. Everett backs away and Davis walks over to his side of the bed, where he sits and swings his legs up onto the white comforter, curling back against the pillows. Everett follows and sits at the edge of the bed, feet firmly planted in the rug, his back to Davis. "I'm sorry." He listens to Davis gulp as he pulls his knees to his chest and wraps his arms around them. In silence once more, Everett turns to look at his husband.

Davis stammers when he tries to speak. "I . . ." He shakes his head, choking back tears, mumbling, his words difficult to parse. "I know you . . ." Davis puts his hand on his chest, staring at Everett, trying to calm himself. "I'm sorry," he finally says.

"It's okay." A crack spreads through Everett's heart like a vase, just for having caused any pain, any fear; just for having momentarily forgotten himself. He scoots closer on the bed until they face each other. He brings his hand to Davis's cheek. "It's okay," he says again, brushing his thumb right above Davis's damp cheekbone, wiping away tears.

Davis feels ashamed of himself now. He whispers. "I wanted to, I really did."

"I know."

"I'm not ready, I guess. He's in my head. It's like he's right here, watching us."

"It's okay." Silently they both slip under the covers. Everett lies on his back and lifts his arm up, waiting for Davis to nestle against his side, cheek to chest, sniffling like a sickly child. "I don't know what came over me," Everett says.

Davis slides his arm across Everett's stomach, giving him a little kiss. "It's okay." He shushes Everett, who gently draws his fingers through Davis's locs, every so often turning and planting a soft kiss at the crown of his head. Like this they remain, passing the night.

MORNING COMES.

Davis, in a giant T-shirt, stands in the kitchen holding a steaming mug of coffee, when Everett comes up behind him and slides his arms around him. He sweetly kisses Davis's neck, nuzzling him when Davis's phone rings. Davis leans back into Everett, closing his eyes as his agent speaks, rapidly telling him of the soloist who canceled in Cleveland that morning for the following weekend.

"Some family emergency, I don't know what," Everett hears through the phone. "Do you want the gig? Two performances of the Walton with the Cleveland Orchestra—Friday and Saturday over the weekend."

When Davis is silent, Everett listens as his agent says, "Yes, the answer is yes. You need to say yes."

Davis nods. "Okay." When he hangs up, he turns around, eyes fearful.

"You're going to Cleveland."

"I'm going to Cleveland."

"You've always said you're one of theirs."

Davis nods again. "But the question is, do they feel that way?"

"They came to you." Then, "You're going to have to call your sister."

"I will call her; I will see her. But I'm not going to that house."

BOOK THREE

ONE

Davis settles in behind the wheel of his rental car. It's been years since he's sat in the driver's seat. He takes a deep breath, starts the engine, and for a moment sits there with his eyes closed. He listens to the quiet hum of the motor, feels its gentle rumble under his feet. Then he pulls the car out of the space, through the lot, and into the street. His hands laze against the warm leather of the steering wheel as he merges onto I-71. It's Sunday, late afternoon, and the highway is bare. It took no more than ten minutes to get from the terminal to the rental car desk, but the car assigned to him had been given to someone else, so he was upgraded to a luxury vehicle. He adjusts his sunglasses and smiles, thinking of Everett's driving posture: fully relaxed against the back of the seat, his legs spread, one hand—sometimes just a couple fingers—pressed against the steering wheel.

Not only has it been years since Davis has driven, but as he maneuvers the car along the highway, he's struck by how much the city has changed. The houses look different, refreshed, perhaps newly painted in brighter colors. The trees look greener, more lush. The highway has been repaved, in fact entirely reconstructed and moved somehow, and yet Davis seems to know his way by muscle memory. He knows when to shift from one lane to another, when to turn a block early to avoid a busy intersection, how to use back roads to shave a few minutes from his trip. It comes back easy, as if by instinct, as though he remembers this place as home. As he drives, he's lulled into a sort of comfort, a feeling enticed by the familiarity of his surroundings. He hasn't done this before—the prodigal son thing, returning to a home he'd once fled—and yet he feels as though he's done this all before, every step. It unsettles him. He feels a chill; his shoulders tense, the hairs at the nape of his neck stand on end.

Davis quickly glances at his side-view mirror before merging into a new lane to avoid an exit he doesn't want to take. Seconds later, passing that exit, he begins to cross a bridge. As he drives, he looks out at the horizon, past Lake Erie, at the cityscape. There's beauty here, and it feels like a discovery, like he's seeing it for the very first time. He presses a button on the steering wheel, speaks a command into his phone: "Call Everett."

He's crossed the bridge and entered downtown Cleveland when Everett picks up the phone on the fourth ring. "I wish you were here." He speaks before Everett even has a chance to say hello. He pauses, letting Everett's deep chuckle wash over him the way it would if they were together, if Everett were holding him close, his ear pressed against Everett's chest.

"I take it you've landed."

"They upgraded my rental car. I'm fancy now." Davis hears Everett laugh alongside the ice machine grumbling in the background.

"What kind of car did you end up with?"

"I think it's a Mercedes—"

"You think?" Davis can sense him smiling through the phone.

"Okay, I wasn't paying attention to that part! But get this— I pressed a button to turn it on! I didn't need the key."

"Baby, our car starts with a button, too. You'd know that if you drove it once in a while."

Davis shakes his head. "In New York City? No, thanks; I'm good."
He relaxes a bit, sitting back in the seat. He moves one hand to the
gear shift. "Everett, I don't know if I can do this."

"Do what? The concert?"

"Be here."

"How're you feeling right now?"

Davis sighs. "Fine, I guess. I don't know, I just got here."

"What are you afraid of?"

Davis glances in the rearview mirror, then switches lanes so he
can make an exit, though he's supposed to stay on the highway for
several more exits to get to the inn where he's staying.

"I don't know." He shakes his head. "I'm just afraid." He pauses.
"It's like I can feel him. He's atmospheric."

Davis pulls onto the exit ramp, begins to slow the car in prepara-
tion for a stop sign that's one hundred feet ahead.

"*Recalculating! Recalculating!*"

"Davis? Did you make a wrong turn?"

Davis silences the navigation system.

"Davis?"

"Sorry! I'm fine." Davis continues fiddling with the display when
he stops the car.

"Do you want me to fly out early?" Everett asks. "I can work a
few days from there, or take some days off."

"Maybe," Davis says. Then, "No, you're busy, you have meetings.
I'm being ridiculous. I'm fine, everything's fine." He tries to sound
more joyful. "What're you doing?"

Everett sighs. "Connor and Caleb are coming over to watch the
game, but I can cancel that and find a flight. There's probably still
enough time for me to get to you tonight."

"No, no, no. I just need to grow up and snap out of it."

"If you say so."

"I do. I say so." Then, "You're a good husband. I just miss you."
Davis turns, drives a few feet, then pulls the car over to the side of
the road. "Your brothers are coming over?"

"Yeah, the Knicks are playing. I'm chilling some beer, about to order food."

"I thought Caleb wasn't drinking."

"He's not, but he doesn't want it to be a thing so I've actually got some non-alcoholic beer for him. I tasted one; it's not bad."

At this, Davis's heart jumps. He actually wishes he could be there, wishes he could see Everett with his brothers. He loves watching them together—their energy, their joy, even when things are tough between them, can be addictive in its own right.

"You're also a good big brother, Everett."

On the other end, he knows Everett is nodding, has seen the growth in the relationship between Caleb and Everett, and Everett's seriousness in helping his younger brother.

"It's nice," Everett had said a few weeks ago when they were walking to dinner, the distance between them palpable. He'd turned and looked at Davis then. "He wants to be helped." The memory punctures Davis in his chest. He bites his tongue to distract himself from the sensations roiling inside him.

"I should go," he says. "I'll be okay," he repeats.

Everett pauses on the other end, as if replaying his words, dissecting them for the truth. "I love you," he says. "Drive safe." Everett's voice is pressing, insistent, and for a moment it's as though he's in the car with Davis, his hand resting on top of Davis's on the gear shift.

"I love you, too. Have fun."

After hanging up, Davis sits back, fully resting against the seat. Then he turns, looking all around him. There are few cars on the road, just upscale strip malls with huge, nearly barren parking lots on either side of him. Deciding that it's safe, he closes his eyes, grips the steering wheel with both hands, and screams as loud as he possibly can. Then he calmly shifts the car into drive and pulls back onto the road.

HE MANEUVERS EASILY through the suburbs of greater Cleveland: first Beachwood, then Pepper Pike. He passes two hospitals, schools and playgrounds, corporate complexes and more shopping centers; coffee shops and a vegan, gluten-free bakery. By the time he reaches Gates Mills, the landscape has become decidedly suburban, big houses with semicircle driveways alongside mid-century split-levels and Cape Cod–style cottages set back from the road. Davis drives past a college campus, his car dipping into tiny valleys and climbing tiny hills, the smoothness of the roads transporting him, as though he's moving through some kind of candy-coated fever dream.

This route isn't new for Davis, but it is compelling. He feels the pull of his past, felt it on the freeway, was powerless against the urge to switch lanes, to drive along the exit ramp, to stop by the side of the road and scream. And he feels it now, as the speed limits climb higher and higher, as he drives farther and farther from the city, and from his intended destination where a reservation for a suite in a small inn awaits him. He makes a few more turns, slows for a few more intersections, and finds himself driving along a county road that he knows very well. He knows it so well that he remembers which dips he can take at which speeds, which will cause his ears to pop. Muscle memory tells him when to slow down, when to engage his turn signal and make a right, through the wrought iron gate that never closes, onto a long and winding maple-, pine-, and fir-laden driveway. He slows until he's driving under the speed limit meant for reckless teenage boys, his eyes on the treetops that line the horizon ahead.

It's not until he reaches a small intersection from which he can turn one of three directions that he sees how the campus has changed. The entrance of the school looks the same: almost hidden on the other side of a driving circle, a place where harried parents drop their high schoolers off, where the branded school buses park after shuttling boys from the inner city, or the less-privileged suburbs.

Davis remembers being the only Black boy in his class who didn't come from the city of Cleveland, or one of those suburbs. He'd been raised in Chagrin Falls, practically a stone's throw away from the campus.

The school has undergone a cosmetic transformation. The original building, the school's third campus in its hundred-plus-year life, remained intact and solid, like the pit of a rotted peach. Around it—behind it, to its right and its left—is a taller, far more recent building, a behemoth, Davis thinks, with two terraces that extend around the entire thing, and what look to be floor-to-ceiling windows. At one end is a tall rotunda.

Davis drives ahead, then turns, intending to park in the circle, but instead he drives around it, then turns right. It's a few minutes through the woods to the school's loading dock, and a few more minutes out to the athletic fields. The campus is hundreds of acres; Davis remembers wandering the woods alone in his free periods, reveling in the quiet of this tiny little pocket of the world. He remembers, more specifically, how these trails—the same trails used by the cross-country team—became his safe space, the only space where he felt he could get away from the boys who tormented him.

The Reverend had wanted him at this school from day one, as early as kindergarten, and Davis had applied and been accepted. They'd visited the school, and Adina had admitted it was very impressive, clearly a home for bright boys. But she would not be sending her son there. When Davis was in high school, he had once complained to Olivia, and she'd remembered how Adina had always said he didn't belong in that school. *It's no place for Davis,* she'd said. Even then Davis's mother had understood him better than anyone else.

"She was worried the boys at that school would either bully you or rebuild you in their image," Olivia had said. So he'd stayed in public school long past his mother's death, until the Reverend could no longer abide his son as he was. He sent Davis with the best of intentions—an elite education, for sure. But they lived in a really nice part of town; he was going to get a great education either way. Davis remembers the Reverend sitting him down in the eighth grade, informing him that he wouldn't be returning to public school.

"You're becoming a man," he'd said. "And you need a school that will invest in you becoming the finest man you can be."

Davis shakes his head at the memory, squeezes his eyes shut, then opens them hurriedly. When he reaches the end of the road, he parks. He stays in his car, staring out at the football field, and the clubhouse, and the observatory. He remembers lacing up his boots in freshman year biology, venturing into the woods with his classmates, learning how to tap the trees for sap, and exploring the fish hatchery. But these fleeting moments are where the joyous memories end.

As he starts the car again, turns around, and drives back along the road to the school's main entrance; as he reaches the stop sign and glances in his rearview mirror at the glamorous new building, throwing up a hand and waving goodbye, just as it looks like the sun is about to set, he remembers what became of his time inside that building, a place that felt like a prison in disguise.

Davis exits the school's driveway, taking back roads until he reaches Chagrin Boulevard, the major nearby thruway. As he drives, he remembers the houses of some of his schoolmates. He remembers finding himself at a few parties senior year, a drink in hand, some boy having invited him only to corner him.

Grade-A DSLs.

Better than my girlfriend.

How many times had some boy followed him into the bathroom or the locker room (what was he even doing back there?) or an empty stairwell, trapped him, and kissed him—never sweetly, never asking. More often that kiss was a prelude to what they really demanded. The threat was in the hardened edges of their voices, and in the silent space—the words they didn't say.

He wonders what, if anything, the Reverend knew about his time at that school, and what he might know now. He wonders what his mother might've seen, peering down at him the way he likes to think she must've been.

Davis learned, rather quickly, about his lips. They were different from those of most of the boys in his school: thicker, fuller, wetter. They held a natural pout. And soon enough, he learned the power they offered him. They had the power to protect him, to keep him from becoming a punching bag, if for no other reason than word got around about what they could do. Those boys were curious; no one wanted their dick sucked by a boy with a messed-up face.

So, too, he eventually understood the leverage he held over those boys—the illicit desire he represented, the release he granted. Like them, he held power in the words he didn't say. Davis swallowed their secrets, buried them as far down as they would go—the same as he did with the desire he knew he wasn't allowed to carry.

WHEN DAVIS PULLS into the driveway of his childhood house, he's almost astonished. The drive was automatic, as though the car steered on autopilot. He has no memory of how he got here, only knows that he is here, though in some ways it bears little resemblance to the house it once was.

As he rolls slowly up the gravel driveway and parks the car, there's an added weight to his breathing. He stands and gets out of the car, his legs heavy, slow to lift. He walks around the car, leans back against the door. The house momentarily transforms before his eyes: the rose garden thriving; the sunflowers tall, the brightest yellow. The gravel is pure white and gray and periwinkle blue, and beaming in the remaining sunlight. The paint is clean, the shutters free of pollen. Davis is reminded of how fastidious the Reverend was about keeping the house clean, particularly the outside. That seems to have fallen away. The paint is faded, the flowerpots lining the front porch are rusted. It seems the house is devoid of any living thing, both inside and out. Vines grow up one side, moss the other.

He wonders how much of this is because the Reverend is no longer there to care for the house and how much of it predates his death.

Davis remembers the Reverend, awake at the crack of dawn every other Saturday, using a Weedwacker to keep those bushes in line. He pictures the heavy gloves the Reverend wore to protect his hands, and how he never, not once, asked Davis to do the task himself. It occurs to him then that he was never asked, nor expected, to maintain anything in the house other than his bedroom. He never shoveled snow; he never raked leaves or cleared the gutters.

And I never once thanked him for doing all of that.

Davis shakes his head.

Rather than enter through the front door, Davis is compelled to walk around the house, to really take in the land. He walks to the right. The first thing he notices are the overgrown bushes that line the house, so tall, so unkempt that they block the natural light from penetrating into the living room. He keeps walking around to the back of the house where he finds a patio, a new addition, complete with wrought iron furniture. He imagines the Reverend purchasing the set, intending to entertain, coming home after a long day at the office, pouring a drink or glass of iced tea, and sitting in those chairs himself, never once inviting anyone over to sit with him—except, on occasion, Olivia.

Davis staggers for a moment. He's struck by an intense loneliness; it nearly bowls him over. He feels the Reverend's loneliness as though it is his own. *I'm sorry,* he says, the words like a spiritual balm, filling him.

The sun begins to set. Everything as far as the eye can see is draped in pink and yellow. One thing that hasn't changed is the beauty of Chagrin Falls—the colorful light that envelops the landscape. Davis thinks of Everett, of Everett's arms wrapped around him, beer in hand, lips brushing his ears, whispering something as they marvel at the colors streaking the sky.

After a moment, he continues walking through the yard, dry grass crunching under his feet. He comes across the gazebo: faded wood, overgrown with vines, a floor covered in tiny red berries. With every step, Davis feels Jake's hand at his back, Jake's arm around his shoulders. He thinks of the last night he walked this grass, breathed this air, laid eyes on this gazebo.

He sees the picnic basket filled with all kinds of cheese: soft and semisoft, aged and wine soaked and dipped in truffles. He can still taste the crisp green apples he'd sliced, the parmesan crisps, the crackers, the mustard, and the raspberry preserves. Jake had offered to pilfer a bottle of wine from his parents' cellar, but Davis declined, settling instead for two bottles of fancy French lemonade. He really should've been practicing for the final round of his college auditions, but it was a special occasion. They'd been a couple— semisecret, semi-out—for three months.

He can still hear the way Jake knocked so easily against the sliding glass doors, then waltzed into the Reverend's house, and the way Jake so easily picked up the picnic basket and told Davis to lead the way. He remembers thick, heavy raindrops, Jake's hair flattened against his forehead, his white T-shirt soaked through and clinging to his chest. He remembers Jake's self-satisfied smile as he caught Davis staring at his nipples, as he slid his hands around Davis's waist. He remembers red lips and fruity tongues and the taste of those apples, that cheese, that fizzy lemonade. Then Jake, and the weight of Jake on top of him; Jake's arms holding him down, Jake's hands spreading his legs as he licked his fingers, as he gently pushed inside; the edge of his fingernail like a blade, ripping Davis apart from the inside out; Jake pushing Davis down to his knees, his face nuzzling Jake's crotch, his hands undoing Jake's belt; Jake's hand palming the back of his head; what a feeling it was to finally taste Jake in this way, to consume the most tender and precious parts of him, to make him feel so damn good.

Davis remembers what it felt like when Jake asked for more; remembers whispering *yes,* his consent like a furtive contract; he remembers the heat, the pain, the pressure, then the desperation of having Jake inside him, finding his rhythm, Davis panting as he found his pleasure. He can still smell Jake's hand covering his mouth when he cried out; he can still taste Jake's finger between his lips; he remembers the relief of Jake pulling out; of him sitting on the bench, lifting Davis and setting him down on his lap. He remembers the feeling of Jake's hands, strong and soft, tender and rough, knowing exactly how to touch him—as though they were practiced at making love. He remembers how they stared into each other's eyes, how Jake's face shape-shifted into something both ugly and beautiful when he came. He remembers lying on the floor of the gazebo, his face resting on Jake's rising and falling chest, his breath a satin scarf brushing Davis's cheek as the sky darkened while they drifted in and out of gentle slumber.

It was some time before they rose, before they walked back to the house in laughter, in love, holding hands, every part of Davis's body alive in a new way. He remembers seeing the Reverend watching them approach from inside the house, from behind the sliding glass doors; he remembers Jake stepping in front of him, moving toward the house, deciding for them both. The Reverend opened the door; Jake stood tall, taller than the Reverend, shoulders back and chest out, deep voice rumbling like quiet thunder; hand extended, an olive branch. The Reverend looked away from his son, ushered them both indoors. He set his drink on the table, then ran upstairs for blankets. Davis remembers how Jake reached across the table to hold his hand; he remembers how they listened to the fat raindrops slapping the house, the thunderclaps rolling throughout Chagrin Falls. He still feels the moment their hands unclasped, practically jumping at the sound of the Reverend thumping down the stairs, at his eyes moving between the two of them. He remembers how three scalding cups of tea failed to warm three bodies, how the rain slowed, how the Reverend escorted Jake to the front door, refusing to say a word. He remembers how Jake turned around, looked back at him, made a move to hug him but was stopped, blocked by the Reverend's arm. Davis remembers his own silence, the way he mouthed the words *go go go;* Jake's eyes were steady on him as he walked out, as the door closed behind him.

Here Davis no longer trusts the entirety of his recollection, but certain details have imprinted themselves on him:

Being body-slammed against the desk in the office; the Reverend's hand slapping his buttocks as hard as the rain slapped the house; the sound of the Reverend's belt moving through the loops on his pants; the sound of the leather flying through the air; its *thwack* as it landed against raw skin; Davis crying, and crying out for his mother; Jake on the other side of the front door, his fists banging against it, barely audible against the Reverend's pulpit voice, asking again and again, *You think God gave you a pussy, don't you?* The Reverend, so tall, his voice booming, reverberating throughout the house. *You're no better than your sister!*

Davis remembers silencing himself, going limp, the door eventually going still, only the sound of leather hitting flesh, and the pungent odor of blood and urine mixing, dripping down his leg.

TWO

"I'm going to have to get tested, and that's all there is to it. She's young and fertile, so I must be the problem," Connor says. Everett studies his brother's body language—leaning forward, hanging his head as though ashamed, staring at his feet during a commercial break.

A crest of feeling moves through Everett. He knows what it is to be a man unable to do what a man is supposed to do, or at the very least, what one expects of himself. He rests a hand on Connor's shoulder. Connor holds his head in his hands.

"How long have you been trying?"

"A year and a half." Everett watches as Connor shakes his head, as Caleb leans in from the other side, resting his hand on the other shoulder.

"No matter what, you're not the problem," Caleb says. Everett watches as he makes and maintains eye contact with Connor, as he nods, as Connor nods back, then sets his face.

"People go through this all the time," Everett says. "At least you're going to get some information. Once you have information, you have options."

"When we got married, I told Courtney I'd give her whatever she wanted." He laughs. "Who knew this would be the hardest fucking thing?"

"You will," Caleb says. "You'll give her everything you wanted to give her."

"And you're going to be a great dad," Everett says. After a moment, Connor sits back, eyes on the game once more. Then he turns to Everett. "How about you? Where are you and Davis on the subject of kids?"

Everett laughs, takes a sip of his whiskey. "Definitely not anytime soon. To be honest, I think we could both go either way. And since there's no chance of an accident, I think there's a good chance it won't happen."

Connor nods. "So it's down to me." Then he points to Caleb. "And this fucker who's been high for how many years?"

Caleb relaxes back into the couch, grins, and throws up two peace signs. "Don't hate." He glances at his left hand, then shakes his head. "Damn." He sits up again, looks at Everett. "I cut myself earlier and I'm bleeding again."

Everett nods, then points toward his and Davis's room. "Go into our bedroom and you'll find a first-aid kit in Davis's bedside table. It's the one closer to the window."

Caleb chuckles. "Don't worry, I promise not to say anything if I stumble across your lube and sex toys."

"You can say whatever you want, asswipe!" He turns to Connor. "That fuckin' kid. You two sure you want one? 'Cause sometimes they turn into jerks."

Connor makes a face, points his thumb over his head. "Kids these days."

For a few minutes they watch the game, whooping when their team scores. Everett doesn't even notice when Caleb returns, quietly taking his seat on the couch, sipping his non-alcoholic beer and watching intently. At the next commercial break, he leans back, crosses his arms, and looks at Everett, his face pensive, his eyes curious.

"What?" Everett says. He smirks. "What'd you see?"

"Nothing," Caleb says. He clears his throat, turns his attention back to the game.

When it's over, after Everett has waited until they're on the elevator, he walks into the bedroom. He thinks back to Caleb, to the way Caleb seemed to quiet down after grabbing the Band-Aid. He stands in the center of the room, surveying it, when he notices that the drawer to Davis's bedside table is still open. He walks over, pulls it open farther. On top of the first-aid kit are several photos that look like they were developed at a pharmacy. He picks them up.

The photos show Davis in a strapless wedding gown, posing all around the master suite of the Montauk house. Smiling, throwing his head back in laughter. Each one is stamped in the corner with their wedding date. In one photo, his leg dangles seductively through a high slit. Even through the medium of photographs, his face is inviting, daring Everett to take him, to make him his.

As beautiful as he'd looked that day, he looks absolutely stunning in these photos, his joy and lightness overflowing. Everett rubs the top photo with his thumb. He wants to hold Davis, to stroke his cheek, to tell him he's beautiful and wanted and loved, that he could've worn this dress if it's what he'd wanted to wear, and that it's all going to be okay; that they are going to be okay.

Everett texts Caleb. *Thank you.*

He pulls his suitcase from the closet. Then he calls his father. "Dad? I need you to come pick up Bam-Bam."

THREE

D avis runs from his parked car into the lobby of Olivia's building. Same building, renovated, but Olivia owns a penthouse now. Davis glances at the man sitting at the front desk; for a moment he slows his walk until he realizes why the face looks familiar. It's Charlie, the same man from so many years before.

Charlie breaks into a smile, recognizing him, standing to embrace him. Davis smiles and tries to be kind about it, but he's in a hurry.

"Olivia Freeman, PH2E," he shouts over his back. From the corner of his eye he sees Charlie nod, sit, and call up to his sister, right as Davis steps into the elevator. When the doors open, much like with his and Everett's apartment, he is suddenly in her apartment. She stands in her pajamas, hair tied up in a bonnet, wearing glasses. For a moment they stare at each other, until she puts an arm around him and pulls him farther into the apartment.

"Shoes off," she says. He looks her up and down as he kicks his shoes off, as he follows her into the kitchen, as he leans against the countertop while she boils water for tea. He opens his mouth to speak but struggles to figure out what to say.

He decides to ease his way in. "You were asleep."

She nods. "It's fine. You're here."

"It's really not that late."

"I have a long shift tomorrow."

"Right."

"I'll be at one of your performances though." She hands him a mug and tiny strainer with tea leaves in it.

"Lipton would've been fine."

"Not in my house."

Davis wraps his hands around the mug as Olivia pours steaming water over the tiny strainer. He takes a deep breath, the minty aroma filling his nostrils and clearing his lungs. He opens his mouth to speak, thinks better of it, closes his mouth, and purses his lips. Then he hops up onto a stool behind her kitchen island. She stands at the stove, squeezing honey into her mug. When she finishes, she looks up at him. "Want some?"

She takes a sip of her own tea, smelling of zesty lemon.

"The Reverend—Dad . . ." he says, trying the word out on his tongue, on his lips. It's not natural, or easy. He pulls the strainer out of his mug and sets it on a napkin on the counter. He tries a different tactic, his eyes still on the steaming water.

"That night when I showed up on your doorstep, I didn't tell you the whole truth. He didn't spank me. He beat me. He was brutal, like a monster, and I know he was drunk, and I know that was out of the ordinary, but that's the truth. That's how it happened. He said horrible things to me, and on one hand, it felt like he'd become someone else, someone I didn't know and had never seen. But it also felt like him—like I had given some base instinct in him the reason it needed to let loose, to fly. Each time he hit me, I felt years of anger. When I picture it in my head I think of a hornet's nest, just opened up, flying everywhere, hurting anything that it comes across."

"You didn't have any marks on you; I would've seen them."

"They weren't where you could see them. For years I've wondered if I was being dramatic, a princess—because this only ever happened one time. And he was a conservative man, and the truth is that I wasn't doing nothing. He walked in on me and my boy-friend. He saw something he shouldn't have seen."

"That doesn't justify—"

"I know, but that's not the point I'm trying to make." Davis hops down from the stool, grabs his mug, and moves toward the couch in the living room. Olivia follows him. "Olivia, I'm stuck. I've been stuck since he died. And then tonight, when I went to the house, I remembered something I'd forgotten: As he was beating me, he said that I was no better than you." Davis looks at Olivia, who takes a deep breath, glances out the window.

"You went to the house?"

"I don't have a key, so I just kind of walked around the outside." He sips his tea. "What did he mean when he said that I was no bet-ter than you?"

Olivia looks at him for a moment, studies his face. She looks at his chin, how it remains completely clean-shaven. His lips, pressed together in a single thin, straight line. His eyes, filled with questions and curiosity. She wonders if he can see her shame—not at her behavior, nor her decision, but at her secrecy, at her willingness to turn away from her past, and the consequences of her past enacted on an innocent party.

She gets up and walks back to the kitchen. She returns with a bottle of wine and a corkscrew. "We're going to need something stronger."

She uncorks the wine, takes a whiff, and brings the bottle to her lips. She takes a sip, then passes it to Davis.

"Is it Ben's?"

Olivia hears the question as though the Reverend is still there, pacing the other room, unloading on his wife. She had been banished to her room, could only listen to the remnants of her parents' conversation, their disembodied voices floating like spirits through the house. And yet she knew them so well that she'd been able to conjure all of it, like a film she'd directed, in her head. Her mother stood by the sink, absentmindedly and repeatedly rinsing her hands with dish soap and drying them on a damp towel.

"Is it Ben's?" The Reverend had repeated himself, raising his voice.

"Of course it is." Adina was losing patience, tired of tamping down her instinct to be curt.

The Reverend looked at his wife straight across the island. "You know these white boys. They think they own everything. I've seen them watching her, circling her." He paused, and Olivia heard him take a few steps. "Look at me, Adina."

"She wasn't raped, John, if that's what you're getting at. They've been sexually active for months now."

"Months? How could you not know about this?"

Olivia still hears her mother's deep inhalation and the steel in her voice. "Because she didn't tell me."

"Surely there were signs."

"And what if there were, John? What did you want me to do? Sew the girl's vagina shut?"

"Talk to her!"

Olivia remembers how he'd exploded so loudly that she'd backed away from the vent. She'd wanted to get in bed, to wrap herself in thoughts of Ben, but she was not a child; she might, in fact, have to bring a child into this world. This was not the time to turn away from something that scared her. She pressed her ear as close to the vent as possible.

"She's going to have to get a job. I suppose I could find her something in the office building. They're always looking for a good receptionist. Or we could look around town—no, no, no, I don't want all our neighbors seeing her like that. At least downtown she'll be anonymous. Tomorrow I'll call the building manager." Olivia's heart sank at these words, but more hurtful than the prospect of her ruined future was the way he spoke about her. The Reverend had always adored her.

She heard her mother set something down on the counter. When she spoke her voice was firm. "No, John."

But the Reverend didn't seem to have heard her. "She can take classes part-time at Tri-C or Cleveland State. Eventually she'll get a degree and then—" He paused. Olivia imagined that he'd been talking at her mother—as opposed to talking *to* her—looking elsewhere, perhaps still pacing, moving away from her, until he registered what she'd said. She imagined that he stopped, turned around. "Did you say no to me? Because I thought I heard you say 'no,' but that can't be right. You don't say no, not to me."

Olivia thinks often of her mother's voice in that moment, of the nerve she must've felt. To this day it boosts her, gives her what she sometimes needs to get through her day. "Yes, John, I did." Then she looked at him again, her calm having returned. She shook her head. "I'm sorry, baby, but it's not going down like that."

"Excuse me?"

"You want that girl's life ruined? Zip, zilch, zero, just like that? You've lost your mind."

Olivia heard a chair creak. The Reverend had taken a seat. "Woman, have you lost yours? What are you saying?"

"You know what I'm saying, John. And you know I'm right." Then another chair creaked; Adina was seated, too. Olivia imagined them staring each other down, neither moving, neither drinking, astonishment carved in each of their faces at the other's probable lunacy.

"Not in my house."

Adina sneered. "It isn't just *your* house, John."

"Isn't it? Who pays the mortgage?"

Olivia didn't know what happened in the silence that followed, but she knew the Reverend crossed a line and apologized.

"I'm sorry," he said. "But it's murder."

"It's what she wants."

Olivia could tell her mother had risen to leave.

"I may not ever get over this."

Olivia heard her mother place her glass in the sink, heard her rinse her hands and dry them one last time. From farther away, she then said, "This situation is not yours to get over, John."

Olivia listened as her mother's footsteps receded, paused, then returned. "One more thing: Olivia never even wanted me to tell you. Please don't make me regret the fact that I did."

When she turned around again, Olivia heard him ask—perhaps in shock, or more likely disdain, "Who are you?" Then he rose, and he, too, left the kitchen.

She listened as her father climbed the stairs, as he gently closed their bedroom door so as not to wake their sleeping daughter.

"She's my mother," Olivia said quietly. She rose and climbed into her bed.

Spring was upon them, the snow melting and the creek water rising. Winter was slowly being swept away, and life was coming.

"HOLY SHIT," DAVIS says. He takes another sip from the wine bottle, then wipes the dribble from his chin with his sleeve. He passes it to his sister. "What did you do?"

Olivia takes a large gulp. "I had an abortion."

Davis leans across the table and grabs his sister's hand. "And now you bring babies into the world."

Olivia rolls her eyes. "The irony isn't lost on me."

"Who else knows?"

She shrugs. "The doctor who did it. Mom brought me to New York. And Ben." Then, for the first time since she told her story, she looks away from Davis. "And Everett."

Davis's eyes widen; he almost jumps up from the couch. "Everett? You told him before you told me?"

Olivia nods. "I told him about it when I was in New York . . . before I left town in a huff. It just kind of came out." She pauses, closes her eyes, then speaks from silence. "I'm sorry about that. Leaving the way I did."

Davis looks at the ground, shakes his head, extends his arm for the bottle of wine. "I see."

"He was sweet, Davis." Olivia looks her brother in the eye. "You can tell him things."

"I know," he says. He takes a long sip. Then holds the bottle out in front of him, tapping it at the bottom. "We're running low."

Olivia darts up, grabbing another bottle.

"I kind of love this," she says. "You and me."

Davis grins at her, then glances at the time. "Actually, I should go. I haven't checked in to my hotel."

"You've been drinking. Stay over. Check in tomorrow morning."

Davis nods, picks up his phone, and calls the inn. When he puts it down, Olivia hands him the bottle.

"I'm so sorry, Davis. I'm sorry for all the things I didn't know. I'm sorry that my own indiscretions influenced how the Reverend saw you."

"How he saw me? How did he see me?"

For a moment Olivia looks uncomfortable. She crosses her legs on the couch, tugs at one of her socks. "Davis, I think you know." She looks him directly in the eye. "He loved you so much but he had a hard time—for a long time. You felt it then, and you feel it now. He died with a lot of regrets—some about me, but especially about you. That's why he needed to see you. That's why he was driving to the wedding." She scoots closer to him on the couch, puts a hand on his knee. "Before you go back to New York City, go by the house and go inside."

Davis rolls his eyes. "I know, I know, I need to go through my things before you sell it."

"It's not that. I mean, yes—please do that. But there were some things that he had on him, things that were recovered, one that's addressed to you. I hadn't noticed it until just a few days ago."

"What is it?"

"An envelope. I have no idea what's inside it, though. Maybe a gift?" Olivia walks over to her bedroom where Davis hears a drawer open. She returns with a key to the house.

FOUR

t's still dark when Everett makes his way to the street with his
suitcase. He slides easily into the backseat of the black car, its door
waiting open. He wants to rest his head on the drive to the airport
but instead he looks up the inn where he and Davis will be staying.
He looks at Google images—quaint—then calls to make sure his
name is on the reservation.

"You're coming on Thursday, right?" The attendant tries, and
fails, to hide a yawn.

"Change of plans," he says. "I'll be there in a few hours. Can you
not tell my husband? I'm surprising him."

When he hangs up, he closes his eyes for a minute, leans his head
back. Before he knows it the driver is slowing to a stop in front of a
door at the appropriate airport terminal. He wakes with a start,
clears his throat, jumps up and out of the car. He's got plenty of
time and the airport isn't all that busy, but he moves with an urgency and quickness that surges through his body, that feels as
though it can't be contained. Of course he's excited to see Davis,
but it's more than that. In some way, Everett feels as though he
knows Davis in a different way now. He feels as though his eyes

have been opened, as though all of a sudden he sees and understands details he'd never before been aware of. Security is a breeze, as is the flight, and once they land, he's off to the inn.

As Davis drives away from his sister's apartment, through Cleveland on smooth winding roads filled with large maple trees beginning to bloom, he thinks longingly of how picturesque this place is. He knows it was the Reverend's job that brought them to Cleveland in the first place, his appointment as the executive minister of their local Baptist association the only reason they would've left Philadelphia, and he knows that all of this happened before he was born, but somehow, Davis recognizes the love that went into that decision. The planning, the foresight, the life this Black man who'd come from near poverty would be able to afford his family. Choosing where to live in this city, and then choosing to live all the way out there in Chagrin Falls, where they had some privacy, some distance from the demands of the Reverend's job. He feels something akin to gratitude, and he wishes he could turn the car around and keep driving back to the house where he was raised.

When Davis arrives at the inn, he's even more enamored with the place than he was when he'd looked it up. It's a converted Tudor mansion in the heart of University Circle, close to downtown. Like the houses he'd passed in the outer suburbs, it features a driveway that encircles a statue. Honeysuckle and ivy climb the front of the building, and he walks under a trellis to reach the front door. It's heavy, and a strong gust of wind means that it takes several tries to get it open wide enough for him to walk through. There's little time to rest, to think, though he would like to lie down on the bed and call Everett. But he has to warm up and then practice. This afternoon is his first rehearsal with one of the world's most beloved symphonies. He needs to bring his A-game.

He unpacks his clothes and toiletries, and then decides to make coffee and settle in before heading to Severance Hall to rehearse.

It's still early, and he's not needed until one P.M., so he can take a little time to recharge before he arrives at the concert hall, and still have a couple hours to spare for a proper warm-up. No one will fault him for bringing the sheet music onstage for the first rehearsal if he decides he needs it.

Davis undresses, glancing around the room as he does. It's filled with sunlight from several windows and looks upon trees and the roofs of similarly large houses. He listens to the birds chirping, and every so often, the slam of a car door, or the bark of an excited dog. He misses Bam-Bam, who would surely be lounging in the center of the brightest, warmest beam of sunlight were he present. When the coffee maker sputters to completion, Davis fixes his cup and turns on the shower. He might as well relax.

After thirty minutes he steps out of the still steaming shower feeling refreshed, like a new person. He rubs himself down with lotion, careful to cover every inch of skin. He squirts some argan oil into the palms of his hands and runs it through his locs. He moisturizes his face, taking the time to really press his fingertips into his skin. He shaves every day, and since today is an important rehearsal, he decides to wear a little makeup. He dots the foundation on his chin, his cheeks, his nose, and his forehead. Then he brushes it in. With every swipe, every bit of beard shadow that's suddenly hidden, he feels more himself, more tethered to the world in which he lives. He feels more in his body, more in his spirit; less like a phantom floating through time and space and grief, looking for home, searching for realness.

He shimmies into a pair of black skinny jeans and a black turtleneck that features one long sleeve, and another exposing his shoulder, fabric hanging over the upper arm. He pulls his locs up into a messy bun. Then he steps into his knee-high boots. He looks himself up and down in the mirror, then adds a matte red lip for a bit of pop. When he'd checked in that morning, the front desk attendant had glanced at him as he searched for his reservation in the system and called him *ma'am*. It had taken him quite a few seconds before he looked up, spotted the stubble, realized his mistake, and corrected himself.

Except that moment hadn't felt like a mistake to Davis. He hates feeling like he has to correct people, like he has to specify that he's a man. He closes his eyes. He thinks of Everett, of Olivia. Of the Reverend. Of the life he's built and the person he's been.

In recent years, he's stopped correcting people. Waiters approaching the table from behind, seeing only his locs and his stature; random passengers, usually men on airplanes, offering to help him lift his bag into the overhead compartment, glancing at him and not noticing his stubble, or his chest that's flat in the space where breasts would be. It feels feminist to eschew the correction, to clarify—in his own quiet way—that it's not an insult to be assumed a woman. Or at least, he's not insulted. He wants to believe— and has told people—that it's because he doesn't see women as less than men, that he doesn't feel insulted by his lifelong proximity to femininity. This is what he believes, what he occasionally proclaims. But the quieter truth is that in these instances, in these quick flashes of insight on the part of random strangers, he feels seen. It's as though his inner life runs in circles in a deep dark cellar, and every so often runs through a beaming ray of light, rendering him visible and highly transparent.

All of this feels true for Davis, and yet it also feels insufficient.

He looks himself up and down one more time, grabs his viola, and walks out of the hotel to his car. He maps a route to the local coffee shop the desk attendant recommended, then to the concert hall. As he opens the door and sits in the driver's seat, knowing that he's traveling a grand total of seven minutes, he reminds himself that at the end of the week, he'll have performed as a soloist with the Cleveland Orchestra. It's a thrill to be here, to do what he's doing.

"Like ships passing in the night."

"I'm sorry?" Everett smiles at the front desk attendant who checks him in, who hands him his key.

"You just missed him. Your husband?"

Everett sucks in air. "I did, did I?" He looks around at the stylish lobby, a pleasant blend of modern design with down-home Middle America suburban charm.

The attendant nods. "You can probably catch him! I directed him to this coffee shop, right here." The attendant pulls a brochure from a drawer behind the desk, grabs a pen, and circles the address.

"Thanks," Everett says. "I think I'll hang out here, maybe go for a run."

He heads upstairs, finds the room, unlocks the door. Immediately, he feels Davis's presence in the room. He smells his products, sees his towel tossed to the ground in uncharacteristic fashion. There's a half-drunk mug of coffee on the bedside table.

Everett lifts his suitcase onto the bed and begins to unpack. He opens the closet and pulls out enough hangers for his button-down shirts and a few blazers. He arranges each one on its appropriate hanger and then carefully places his items behind Davis's, when he sees that Davis's garment bag is unzipped. There are two hangers in there, but the only item he can see is the black jumpsuit from Davis's recital. He wonders what Davis will wear for the other performance, but he decides not to look—he wants to be surprised, too. He pushes the garment bag to the side, making room for his items.

Davis pulls up to Severance Hall at ten a.m. sharp, three hours before he's needed for rehearsal. Having grown up performing with the local youth orchestra, he knows the route from the underbelly of the parking garage to the main entrance of the concert hall. When he enters the building, the security guard at the front desk is surprised.

"I'm this week's soloist. I'm here early, to warm up and get settled in before rehearsing."

He pulls out his ID, but the security guard shakes her head. "Let
me call the office."

A few minutes later, an assistant runs, breathless, into the main
lobby. "I'm so sorry, we weren't expecting you so early!"

She beams up at him, her eyes filled with questions.

"I just wanted to practice some on my own, and I didn't want to
disturb the other guests at the inn."

"Of course, of course! I'll show you the way!"

"You know, if you're busy, I know my way around here. I'm an
alum of the youth orchestra."

She nods, starts walking, then gestures for him to follow her.
"Oh, it's no problem, no problem at all!" Davis can tell she's a recent
graduate of the local conservatory. Her angular haircut is parted
down the middle and dyed pink.

"You look fabulous, by the way. Cleveland needs you."

Davis smiles and nods, but remains quiet, following her into the
bowels of the building. He would've been irretrievably lost had he
tried to find his way himself. She opens a door, turns on the light,
and pokes around for a moment. "Okay, there's the humidifier, and
the heat in case your fingers are cold. The pianos were all tuned last
week so that should be good! They're planning to start rehearsing
the orchestral part of the concerto at noon, but you won't be needed
until one. If you like, I could bring you up a few minutes early,
maybe twelve forty-five, so you can get a taste of the direction the
conductor is moving in . . ."

She looks at him, and he nods. "That would be great."

"Awesome! Can I get you anything while you're warming up?"

"I would love a bottle of water, if possible. Cold cold cold."

"You got it."

She nods and runs off. Davis is warming up again by the time she
returns, knocking quietly on the door, then opening it without wait-

ing for his okay. She opens the door ever so slightly and pushes her arm through, resting the water bottle on a chair next to his viola case. "You sound great!" She gives him a thumbs-up, then slips a piece of paper into his case. "If you need anything else, just shoot me a text or call!" She steps out into the hallway.

"I do sound great," Davis says under his breath, but he smiles nonetheless. He does sound great, his viola warm and vibrating with ease. The acoustics in the practice room belie its slightly run-down appearance. He plays one more scale, one more arpeggio, then the opening lines of the concerto he's here to perform. He focuses on the opening phrase, pulling his bow slowly across the string, trying to get the warmest, fullest sound possible, while still playing relatively softly. He moves quickly through the most diffi-cult sections, paying attention to his left hand for agility and his right arm for tension. He plays more aggressively to see if his strings will slip out of tune, but they remain steady. In what feels like no time, the assistant knocks on the door, ready to escort him up to the rehearsal hall. When they enter, the assistant walks him up to the front of the auditorium, then fades into the background. He un-packs his viola from the case, then takes a seat. They are about halfway through the third movement. The conductor turns around and smiles at Davis, while the musicians continue to play. Once they've finished, and she's made a few remarks, she calls Davis onto the stage, where they shake hands. The musicians have a few min-utes to mill around, to stretch and use the bathroom and once they return, the conductor introduces him. Together, they speak a bit about the concerto, and then they begin the rehearsal. Davis tunes to the concertmaster's A, then goes silent, waiting for the conduc-tor's signal for the musicians to begin. The opening of the concerto is somber, melodic, rather brooding in parts. Davis thinks back to when he was first learning the piece, when he was in high school. He thinks of the endless hours of practicing, and how the Reverend never complained about the noise, with this piece in particular, which was his first of the three big viola concertos, and the only one he learned before going to Juilliard.

He thinks of the many nights spent in this very concert hall, his father by his side watching this very orchestra, with many of these very same musicians performing then, and rehearsing behind him now. He's one of theirs. It's too much, it feels like too much. With the orchestra behind him, Davis allows the tears he's held for the last few minutes to fall freely.

AFTER REHEARSAL, SOME of the younger musicians invite him for a drink.

"I can't tonight, but I'd love to later in the week—maybe when my husband arrives." He thinks back to Olivia, to her plea that he take one last look around the house. "Tonight, I'm going home." It's nice to be back home, calming in a way. But also, it's even nicer to be a visitor, to know that there's a new home, a chosen home with a chosen man waiting for him at the other end of this week.

They nod, clapping again at the beauty and tone of his playing, the authority with which he took the rehearsal stage of one of the most prestigious orchestras in the world.

"Your authenticity," says the musical director, clasping her hands, blond curls brushing her shoulders as she wipes away tears. "The colors, the sheer emotion. The fact that you were crying at that opening, which . . . I don't know how any violist doesn't cry when they play that line! Magnificent!"

She takes his hands in hers, shakes them, and walks away. Davis is escorted to the main entrance of the building. He takes a call from his manager, who checks in about the accommodations and gives him instructions for his radio appearance later that week. Once he's sitting, he pulls out his phone, checking for calls or texts from Everett. When he sees none, he takes a deep breath and starts the engine.

EVERETT JOGS EASILY up the steps at the entrance to Severance Hall. He checks his watch; he's arrived with fifteen minutes to spare. When he reaches the security desk, he inquires about the rehearsal.

The security guard shakes her head. "It's over," she says.

"It's over? What?"

She nods. "Who're you looking for?"

He closes his eyes, his frustration palpable. "My husband. Davis Caldwell?"

She opens a packet of gum, popping a piece into her mouth. "The soloist."

"Yes, the soloist."

"He left. Sorry, honey." She shakes her head sadly, smacking her gum.

"I don't suppose you know where he's off to?"

She shakes her head again, then points behind him. "They're with the orchestra, they might know." She waves over a few young-looking musicians. "He's looking for the soloist." Then she shoos them all away from her desk.

Everett extends a hand. "I'm looking for my husband, Davis. Do any of you know where he was headed after rehearsal?"

The musicians look between one another; a man about Davis's age with a cello strapped to his back steps forward. "We invited him out for a drink but he said maybe later, once you'd arrived. I thought you were coming later in the week." The cellist looks at one of the other musicians.

"Yeah, he seemed to think you were coming later."

"I'm trying to surprise him but we keep missing each other."

He waits as the musicians look between one another again. A young woman steps forward. "He said something about going home. So you can probably try the inn." She looks him up and down. "Are you bringing him anything?"

Everett's confused by her question. "What do you mean?"

"Well, if you're going for a surprise, you can't show up empty-handed, can you?"

When he doesn't say anything, she points to the right. "There's a florist two blocks east. Beautiful white irises."

Everett smiles, a bit taken aback. "Thank you. And good luck this weekend. I'll be in the front row!"

He runs off, and as he's exiting the building it occurs to him that Davis might not have been referring to the inn when he'd said home to these musicians earlier. He texts Olivia. She writes back immediately with the address, and he calls a car.

As Everett rides through Cleveland, he's shocked at first by how grand everything seems. Every house appears larger than the one before, every road wide and smooth and paved with jet black tar. His driver is talkative, delivering one long monologue, and after a few minutes, Everett is sure he can stealthily tune him out. He focuses instead on the growing feeling in his belly. He's eaten very little today, but it's more than that. His leg is restless, his fingers tapping against the seat beside him. He peers through the window at the trees now whipping past him; the farther out of the city they get, the higher the speed limits climb.

Everett had been home, in New York, with Davis barely two days ago. And yet he can tell that something is afoot, something is not as it used to be. He tries not to get ahead of himself, but given how distant Davis has been, and how this day has played out, Everett can't help but notice the pit in his stomach.

FIVE

Why hasn't Everett called him?

As Davis enters the town of Chagrin Falls, now only minutes from his father's house, he can't stop thinking about the fact that he hasn't had any contact with his husband all day. He doesn't think he's ever waited more than an hour for Everett to call or text him back. As he drives along Main Street, once again looking at the falls, the Popcorn Shop, and Shirley's Gourmet Ice Cream Parlor, it occurs to him that Everett would be really charmed by this town, that he'd love to go running here.

Davis himself loves the hills and valleys, the trees and river, and the way the light slants through the leaves and reflects against the water. He knows this place, and as he drives, he realizes he loves it. And yet he wishes Everett was here—his secure hand, his steady confidence, because life in New York City has made Davis a more anxious person. Though he's beginning to understand that perhaps love carries with it a healthy dose of anxiety. He worries that Everett will get sick of this, of him, of his tears and his resistance, and the way he aches for a father he ran so far to get away from.

He fears that in his own way, Everett is running from him.

Most of all, Davis worries he's ruined the one thing he's wanted all his life, above all other things, and that he's done so before it even got off the ground—all because he allowed fear to take hold. Fear of his father, the Reverend, of what the man might see. He's beginning to realize that his father had seen it all from day one.

As Davis pulls into the driveway, he thinks back to the chaos of their wedding night, when Everett ushered him through the airport in the wake of the Reverend's sudden death in the mountains of the Pennsylvania Turnpike, a freeway the Reverend might never have traveled that night if Davis hadn't been marrying Everett.

Had he only picked up the phone and called the Reverend—his *father*—once in a while.

What Davis remembers most about that night is Christopher driving them home from JFK to their apartment on Jane Street. The cold that had arrived in the city, so early, with such ferocity; he'd felt it as soon as the car door opened, but he couldn't move. Then Everett's warm, strong arms lifted him with ease, covering him—a shield guarding him from the elements. Davis remembers the hardness of Everett's chest, and the way Everett held him so close he felt his heart beating through his jacket. Everett has continued to do this, ever since. At every turn, in every moment that Davis has needed him.

To have, and to hold.

He wonders what the fuck is wrong with him that he's been pushing Everett away all this time. It's like he's been living in a fog.

He parks the car, determined to enter the house. Again he pulls out his phone, calling his husband. Again there's no answer.

HE SWINGS THE front door open, walking quickly through the foyer and main hall. It takes two tries to push open the heavy double doors of the Reverend's office, that venerable room where his father willingly held himself captive.

As a boy, Davis had thought his father a slave to the Word of God; now he understands what it is to move through the world with a purpose, to serve a calling that's higher than yourself. In the office, he's greeted by boxed-up books and a nearly empty bookshelf. Sunlight slants through the window, draping the enormous wooden desk where so many sermons were written. Davis traces a finger along the top of the giant globe that rests next to the desk. He spins it gently; the golden hue of sunlight illuminating a puff of dust as the globe turns. Davis holds a fist to his mouth, coughing slightly. He wonders how many years have passed since he's been in this room. How many times had he waited, silent and patient, on the other side of that heavy door, playing first with his wooden building blocks, then Matchbox cars, then quietly reading, wanting only a glimpse of the Reverend, a moment of his time?

When Davis had started playing the viola, he'd found something—a practice as some called it, a faith as others called it—formidable enough to ask of him a devotion that was similar to his father's. From that point on, there was no more waiting on the other side of that door.

In fact, Davis remembers, as he sits in the Reverend's chair, just how much he'd enjoyed turning the tables on his father. As the years passed, and his talent became more evident, he practiced more and more, every year, every new piece, for every statewide, and then nationwide competition. The result of all this practice was that the Reverend was sometimes left waiting on the other side of Davis's door. The room that had been his nursery, the room where he'd spent so many hours held by his mother—that became Davis's practice room.

Davis spreads his hands over the desk, running his fingers along the rim of the looseleaf pages. He traces the words, and he hears, for the first time in years, something he thought he'd forgotten: his father's voice. It's gibberish, the words following no rhyme or reason, but there it is, in his ears—his father's voice.

Not booming as it so often did from the pulpit. His tone is tender, soft, dulcet.

Davis can almost feel his father behind him, holding him as he did many a night when Davis was a boy, soothing him back to sleep after he'd violently thrashed his body all over his bed in the throes of a night terror.

It's too much. He has to get out of there. Whatever it was that was recovered from the accident, he'll ask Olivia to mail it. Davis pushes himself up, and an envelope falls to the ground. He could've easily missed it, but there it is, lying on the floor in plain view.

It's nearly bare, except: DAVIS printed in Sharpie, in his father's trademark script.

Davis kneels, picks up the envelope, and instead of rising and running, he sinks to the floor. He leans his back against the edge of the desk. He runs his fingers along the bottom edge; he taps one of the corners against the pad of his first finger. He tells himself to open the goddamned letter.

It's almost disturbing to speak, to hear his own voice in this house, in this room. Memories collage—moments when the Reverend beckoned him through the door, sat him on his lap, read to him from that giant Bible or pointed out various countries on the globe. The few times he allowed Davis to play at his feet or in the corner with his toys. The parables he loved listening to as a boy. Standing in front of that desk as the Reverend wrote a check, and then another check, and another—for violas, for sheet music, for lessons and private school tuition.

In all of this, Davis begins to realize that he's painted his father with one stroke, one color. And yet, there was so much more to him; there has to have been so much more, or else the ache that has burrowed itself so deep inside him wouldn't be so malignant. By the time he's ripped open the envelope his cheeks are wet, tears streaming down his face, blurring his vision, dripping to the page.

My boy,

I wanted to write you a sermon, but this is what came out in-stead. I've made a lot of mistakes in my life. I want to be very clear about this: You, in all of who you are, and all you will be-come, are not one of those mistakes.

In the years since you fled, I've sustained myself on memo-ries of you—memories you wouldn't share because you were too young to remember them. I traveled a lot for work in those years—before your mother died—and every time I came home, I dropped my bags on the floor, and there you were, running toward me with open arms, open heart, your warm little body mine to hold, to tickle, to pick up and spin around. I loved this, because I love you—because you are my child, you are born of me—but also because it is this running toward each other, with open arms and open hearts, that is the great project of life. One of the great tragedies of my life is that I did something that made you run from me.

But you are, right now, running toward someone else. In a few days, you will marry him. I want you to know that the run-ning doesn't stop when you settle down. We call it that— settling down—but it is anything but. The path will become more difficult, but when the harvest comes you must have faith in your goodness. My boy, you are the wheat, not the chaff, and you must keep running. It doesn't matter the distance, nor the obstacle. You must continue on—if he is the man you believe him to be. You'll always be running, that's part of it. No two people ever stop, no matter how close they get. But hear me when I tell you that they can get close. Your mother and I got very close. This is where faith comes in. I'm not talking about God; I know he's not your thing. You must have faith in each other. Each of you must have faith that perpetually running toward the other will be worth the difficulty of the running in the end. And if you love him, and I know that you do, it will be.

But you must also run toward yourself, as urgently and desperately as you run toward him. This is the other great project of life.

My boy, my son, my youngest—I am so very sorry. I was scared of who you were, and who I thought you might become. I acted out of fear, which, as your father, was not my place. It was my place to protect you, not to become the thing you needed protecting from. In this, I failed you.

You were right to run—keep going.

> *Love,*
> *Your Father*

> *P.S. I always thought your mother's middle name, Vivienne, was quite beautiful.*

Davis rolls onto his side, then onto his back, where he lies, staring at the ceiling. He takes a few moments to breathe, to gather himself. Then he sits up, looks around for a box of Kleenex to wipe his tears. He finds nothing—his fingers will have to do. He leans against the desk once more, feeling, perhaps, closer to his father than he's ever felt. He doesn't know how long he sits there like that, stretching his back, steadying his breathing, blinking his eyes until they are dry once more.

He pulls himself to his feet, suddenly feeling as if the room is closing in upon him. He grabs his tote bag, telling himself to go outside, to go back to the car, back to the city and to the hotel. His stomach growls; he realizes he hasn't yet eaten. But when he exits the office door he turns left, walking down the hallway, through the kitchen, boots clicking against the hardwood floors, prying open the sliding glass doors. He steps into the grass, picks up speed moving down the hill, wind swooping around him, blowing his locs behind him. By the time he reaches the gazebo, he's out of breath.

Davis sits on the bench that lines the gazebo. He reaches into the tote bag, pulling out his cellphone. No missed calls, no texts. He holds it up to his mouth. "Call Everett." He puts the phone on speaker and wraps his other arm around his knees, which he's pulled up to his chest, as Everett's phone goes straight to voicemail. As he wonders what to say, tears well in his eyes once more. He stands up. He glances around the yard. The gazebo, the trees, the brown grass and dead rosebushes, and when he cranes his neck, the wishing creek that lines their property. Anything but that tearstained letter.

He's prompted to leave a voicemail. "Everett, where are you? If you're angry with me, you should still talk to me. We're married. Call me." He looks down at his phone and hangs up. He starts typing out a quick text message, heart beating like it wants to break out of his chest. Then the sound of feet approaching, and Everett's voice, its deep timbre rising, brushing Davis's ear with the same softness, the same gentleness, as his lips. "I wanted to surprise you. I've been missing you all day."

By now Davis has risen; in seconds he crashes into Everett. His lips can't find Everett fast enough. He kisses him everywhere—his lips, his chin, his nose, his cheeks. After a moment he buries his face in Everett's chest. Everett tucks a finger under his chin, lifting it until their eyes meet. He smiles, his eyes as kind as ever. "Hi."

He cups Davis's cheek, stroking it with his thumb, the warmth radiating from his skin a balm. He moves to kiss Davis, but Davis pulls back, stares at him, his eyes blank for a moment, as though gazing at a stranger. So many questions, so much left unsaid.

Then Davis runs his hands up Everett's chest. His desire returns, a tidal wave rushing through him. He feels Everett's beating heart. He feels the tuft of hair curling where his shirt is unbuttoned. He feels Everett's nipples harden under his fingertips. Davis stands on his tiptoes, the letter slipping silent and unnoticed from his hand to

the floor underneath him as he tilts his head up and to the side, asking, practically begging Everett's lips to swoop down—which they
do. Davis feels Everett's hand around the back of his neck, tilting
his head farther, taking full control. Davis stumbles back—no, Everett pushes him—until his ass falls against the gazebo bench; in
one quick motion Everett lifts him onto the banister, pressing him
back against a column; he spreads Davis's legs; he grabs Davis's
face, green eyes staring into brown eyes, so much left unsaid; wet
lips meeting once more, tongues gently probing, then lashing;
breath gasping; hands clasped tight, brown and white fingers inter-
twining as Everett picks Davis up and lowers him to the floor, pushing him down onto his back. Davis moves his hands up Everett's
chest once more, over his muscular shoulders, until they rest on
Everett's neck. So much still to say; Davis studies Everett's face,
searching for home, his thumbs stroking Everett's jaw, tickled by
his stubble, until Everett buries his lips in Davis's neck once more:
Davis cries for him, then whimpers his name; Davis unbuttons Everett's shirt and yanks it down his arms, tossing it somewhere to his
right. Everett is on top of him once more, sliding one hand under
Davis's ass and lifting it inches from the floor; with the other he
unzips Davis's boots, pulling them down, and tossing them aside.
Then his jeans: pulling them over his ass, his thighs, sliding them
down his legs. Everett is rough when he shoves one hand between
Davis's legs, even rougher when the other hand pulls his hair. His
smile is devilish as he feels Davis's breath quicken. He flips Davis
onto his stomach. He bends down close to Davis, kissing his neck
and snapping the thong's waistband against Davis's skin. He licks
Davis's ear. So much waiting to be said.

"You wanted this."

Davis licks his lips. "I always want it. But now I'm ready."

By the time Davis finishes the sentence, he lies naked on the
floor of the gazebo. Everett runs a hand softly along Davis's legs.
For a moment he holds himself up, over Davis, admiring his husband's body. Then, slowly, he lowers himself onto Davis, his erec-

tion stretching well over the waistband of his trunks. He nestles it in between Davis's ass cheeks as he starts gently trailing wet kisses down his husband's back. He massages Davis, coaxing several moans from him as his lips move ever closer to his ass, as he grinds his dick into Davis, pressing harder, teasing him. When Davis whimpers, Everett knows it means he wants him to speed it up, but it only slows Everett down. The smallest part of him wants to punish Davis, wants to make him wait the same way he's been made to wait. But the bigger part of him, the better part of him, appreciates the moment he's waited so longingly for: They're together again.

With his hands, he spreads Davis's cheeks. He spits, then uses his tongue to further wet Davis. He loses himself, barely hearing as Davis moans, never coming up for air, wishing he could devour Davis from the inside out—this boy, his husband—who seems, in this moment, to be the tiniest, most fragile boy on earth. After Davis is sufficiently wet, Everett pulls himself up until he's close to Davis's ear once more. He licks it, nibbles his lobe, then moves to his neck as he presses his dick against Davis, teasing his hole. "Sure you can handle me?" He presses into Davis's hole ever so slightly. He feels Davis tense under him, then breathe, relaxing his shoulders. He kisses him. "That's right, baby, just relax." He tries to press deeper. "I've missed my husband," he whispers into Davis's ear. "I've missed you so goddamn much."

He tries to pull Davis up to his knees, but Davis turns underneath him.

"Davis?"

Davis, now on his back, smiles and wraps his legs around Everett's waist, pulling him even closer. His hands find Everett's neck, pulling him down until their lips meet. After a moment, after a few sweet, wet kisses, Davis props himself up on his left elbow. With his right hand, he caresses Everett's cheek, moving his thumb to Everett's lips. Davis strokes those lips, feeling every crease, drinking in the texture of his skin; then he pushes his thumb into Everett's mouth. He enjoys the way Everett's tongue swirls around his finger.

Then he pulls himself up, up—until his mouth is by his husband's ear. With his left hand, he braces himself against the floor.

"This is the life that I want. You are the man I want." Everett starts sucking on Davis's thumb. Davis continues, "But I am not your husband." He pulls back until they face each other once more. Green eyes staring into brown eyes, everything soon to be said. "I am your wife."

Her voice is warm, loving, steely strong. She pulls her thumb from Everett's mouth, strokes his lips once more. Then she trails her wet thumb down his chest, their eyes never altering their gaze. When she reaches his waist, she wraps her hand around his dick, and pulls herself up to his ears once more. She kisses him, her lips wet, tongue tentative. She whispers, "Tell me you love me."

Everett swallows. "I do." He kisses his wife, cups her cheek in one of his hands. "You're everything to me."

They nod in unison, nothing more unsaid; matching heads bobbing up and down. She believes him. "Show me how you love me."

Everett leans back on his heels. He pulls his wife close to him, until she rests her weight on her knees. He runs his fingers up her neck and into her hair, massaging her scalp, kissing her neck, his other arm around her waist, hand pressed against the small of her back as she slowly lowers herself onto him. He's tender when he guides himself into her, pausing with every heightened breath, until she is comfortable. Until he is all the way inside, as deep as he can possibly go.

"Are you mine?" He whispers the question into her ear, just as she moans. Brown and white fingers braid themselves together.

"Yes."

"Say it. I want him to hear you." Everett's voice is so deep it rumbles under her skin. She shudders. She kisses her husband, wraps an arm around his shoulders. Somehow, in this moment, she's never felt more safe, more protected. More loved.

She raises her volume, stares into his eyes. "I'm yours."

"That's right," Everett says. "Only mine."

They kiss like there is gold in each other's mouths. She rides him, grinding herself harder and harder against him; his arm around her waist, hips slamming against her, lips fluttering over her skin like butterfly wings.

SHE LIES ON the table in the gazebo, her husband's arm stretched under her neck, her hand pressed against his stomach. She turns toward him, closing her eyes each time he kisses her. Then she nuzzles her cheek to his chest. With her finger, she traces his belly button; her fingers dance in the hair that runs down the center of his chest.

"Call me Viv," she says. "Vivienne Freeman Caldwell. Vivienne was my mother's middle name. My father thought it was quite beautiful." She smiles as though proud of this. Then she sits up and turns to him. "Are you sure you still want me?"

Everett answers without taking a breath: "I'm sure." He pulls his wife back down, repositions her head against his chest. "Viv. Vivienne."

"She'll always be a part of me, Everett. And so will he. With Freeman, I get to keep something from my father in my name." She sits up and hops down from the table. "I have to show you something."

In the mess of their sex, clothes now coat the floor of the gazebo. Vivienne bends down onto her hands and knees, moving various items around, searching with her hands as well as her eyes.

Everett glances down at her and chuckles. "That's the position I was trying to get you in at first."

She rolls her eyes. "You've been trying to get me in that position for six months!"

Everett brings two fingers to his lips, kisses them, and salutes the air. "I'm so glad you're you again." He props himself up, his eyes filled with tenderness when he looks at her. "I've been worried."

"I know. I'm sorry." She looks at him. "I shut you out, and I shouldn't have done that." She spies the letter—upright, between two wooden slats, leaves encircling it. She grabs it, then climbs back onto the table.

"What's this?"

She hands him the letter. "Read it." She looks toward the house. "I think he knew before I did." She's radiant, even as she watches Everett read the letter. She creeps close to him, begins rereading it, her eyes dancing between the words on the page and her husband's face. She can't quite read the expression he wears.

"Wow," he says when he finishes. Then he flips it over. "Hey, did you read the back?" He pulls it closer. "It's to me."

"I didn't even think to turn it over." Vivienne sits behind her husband, crossing her legs so he can lay his head in her lap. She's silent as she holds Everett by the temples, massaging him. His face is unreadable.

"Well, it's only three sentences. But he definitely knew."

"Read it to me."

Everett turns back to the letter.

Everett,

> *You don't need my blessing, but you have it.*
> *Be good to her. I was nowhere near good enough.*
> > *With warm regards,*
> > *The Reverend*

Everett sits up, puts the letter down, and turns to his wife. "What did he do?"

She pauses, thinking about how to proceed. She uncrosses her legs, slowly rising as Everett rises, too. She turns her back to him, pulling up her underwear, gathering her clothes.

Everett grabs his trunks from the floor and pulls them up, over his legs. Then he grabs Vivienne's hand and leads her down the stairs, where they stand barefoot in the grass. Everett stands behind his wife; he wraps his arms around her, bringing his lips to her cheek, then to her ears, then her neck. "Maybe I haven't been patient or understanding enough. I love you, and that's not going to change. Tell me, please." He tightens his arms, pulling her to his chest, moving his hands down to her waist as she leans into him and begins, finally, to speak.

Six

Now Everett paces, walking in circles, hands in his pockets. He kicks the base of the gazebo, marches up the stairs, then back down. He moves like a boxer, right fist punching into left hand, picking up speed, growing his stride. He's ready to fight, until, for the first time since Vivienne started talking, he stops and looks at his wife. He takes a breath. Vivienne, having revealed herself and her past: standing there, wanting to touch him, needing to be touched by him. He rushes over but stops short, eyes filled with questions he can't escape, face frozen, unsure of what to say.

She speaks first. "I'm okay, Everett."

He's so close she can feel the hair on his arms standing erect.

"You're not. How could you be?"

She nods, averts her eyes, says nothing.

"And that was your first time?"

"Yes."

"No wonder I couldn't touch you."

She nods, looks at the grass. "When I told you he can see me now, I meant that kind of literally. My father saw me getting fucked, and then he beat me. I thought I was over it, but clearly I wasn't."

She looks at her husband, sees his love for her mingling with his hatred for her father in his eyes. "I'm not proud of it."

Everett is so scattered he's not sure what to say first. "You told me you were a virgin."

"I basically was. I'd only had sex that one time. The next time was with you." Vivienne steps toward him. "I spent those years burying all of it—that night, that memory. That version of me." She brings her palms together in front of her face as though praying. "I didn't know it would take me all this time."

Everett steps away, pacing around the yard. "What happened next?"

She gives a clipped laugh. "I grew up in sixty seconds. He passed out on the floor of his office. I grabbed my car keys, and I drove to Olivia's. Luckily she was home."

"Does she know what he did to you?"

Vivienne nods. "I told her last night."

Everett stops pacing, turns, stares at the house. "Fuck!" he bellows. He punches the air, then he walks toward the house. "How could you not tell me this?"

She follows him. "I wanted to forget it. I wanted it not to be real."

"You don't forget that kind of thing."

"I know." Her voice is small when they enter the house, Everett stepping first through the sliding glass door. "It happened here?" She shakes her head.

"Tell me," he says. But he's off, unable to wait for her to show him around. He walks quickly through the house, pointing through every doorway, asking, "Here? Was it here?"

By the time they reach the office door, she's in tears, begging him to stop. He looks at her and enters the room. Immediately, he's cloaked in the weight of the history of this room. It's almost suffocating, how powerless he is to protect his wife from the demons of her past. He throws the giant Bible down from the desk, kicking it clear across the room. He knocks a box of books to the floor. He wants to destroy this place, to incinerate any sign it ever existed. He wants to erase it completely; he wants to do that for her. He wants to free his wife from a captor he can't see and doesn't know. For the first time in his life, Everett feels truly, undeniably helpless.

He walks over to his wife, sinking to his knees on the carpet. Vivienne, no longer crying, who stands and smiles and forgives. He rests his forehead against her stomach, waits for the softness of her hands, craves her agile fingers burrowing into his hair, palming the crown of his head.

After a few minutes: "I would've killed him, you know."

"You wouldn't have."

"I swear to God I wouldn't have left you alone with him. I would've gotten you out of there."

He looks up into his wife's eyes, pleading. He needs her to believe him, to trust in his ability to keep her safe.

"He was my father."

"I know." Everett nods.

"I loved him."

IN A REVERSAL of roles, Vivienne drives them back to the inn, her hand resting on the gear shift, her husband's hand resting atop hers. At no point does Everett move his hand from hers, at no point does he want to remove himself from her in any way.

They enter the inn, her smile dancing across her face—light, free, joyous once more. Then they break, Everett letting her walk ahead of him, wanting to watch her walk—no, bask—in her fullest, most realized self. It takes a minute before she realizes he's not right next to her, and turns around, suddenly bashful, tucking a loc behind her ear.

"You go ahead," he says. "I'll be right up." He doesn't want to leave the premises, so he goes to the front desk, asks to borrow a pair of scissors. In the waning light, he steps outside and walks around the building, following the trail he'd run that morning until he comes across a rose garden he'd seen earlier. He crouches, looking for the perfect red rose to give his wife. He surveys the entire rose garden; there are many candidates, but every time he bends closer, he finds a flaw: a ripped or folded petal, a browning stem. Until he finds one, tucked away in the back of a bush of taller, more impressive roses. He's careful as he works his fingers down the stem, pressing lightly so as not to puncture himself with thorns. When he reaches the bottom of the stem, he carefully cuts it and pulls it out. He was right—exquisite.

When he enters their room a few minutes later, there she is, lying in bed on top of the sheets, hair billowing out onto the pillows. Her lips and face are newly painted, and she wears lacy white lingerie. He walks over to her, too stunned to speak.

"We never got to have a proper wedding night," she says as she sits up, as she pulls him into a kiss, then into her, the rose falling to the floor by the bed.

LATER, THE ROOM is dark, the inn quiet. Vivienne wakes, startled, but hears nothing; only the sound of Everett's chest rising and falling with each breath. Bodies exhausted, sore from a night spent making up for lost time.

She looks at the clock. Still a few more hours before sunlight. She quietly slips from under the covers, disentangling herself from her husband, and walks over to the window. She pulls the curtain aside. Out there everything is still, but she doesn't trust it. Inside, the room feels too charged for such serenity: herself, her husband, their lovemaking.

And, in a way, her father.

It comes back to her, the dream she'd been having, so real it could have been a memory. Vivienne isn't a woman who remembers her dreams once she's awake, but on the rare occasion that she does, that dream imprints itself in her memory—in her bones. It becomes an experience of sorts, almost as though she can feel him in the room, his presence like static electricity. It's almost as though she can feel him with her, embracing her.

SHE'S DRIVING, AN abundance of colors surrounding her. Leaves painted in chestnut, mahogany, amber, all of them spiraling to the ground, scattering at the approach of a car, or a strong wind. The drive is otherwise tranquil, though there must be other cars on the road. She doesn't notice them—only the setting sun, casting brilliant rays of yellow and deep, rich orange. By the time she arrives at the church, it disappears. She steps out of the car, into a world cloaked in midnight blue. The church is ethereal: a sprawling white building, only two stories tall. Suburban mansions surround it, many taller than the church, which gives it the illusion of modesty. The setting inspires a quiet elegance, particularly at night, with a dull white light beaming from the cross atop the spire.

But it's the sanctuary that most enamors Vivienne, that has long been revered throughout the city for its beauty. Slender stained glass windows, almond-shaped, stretch floor to ceiling, each window only a few feet from the next, each depicting a scene from the life of Christ.

Vivienne walks the long procession to the pulpit in the dark, boots clicking against the stone floor with every step, echoing through the darkened building. She grew up in this church, spent countless hours here every Sunday for as long as she could remember until she graduated from college, so she isn't afraid. So much history; so many Sundays and sermons, hymns and prayers.

Ahead of her are bales and baskets of flowers, mostly white, some taller than the highest podium, standing across the width of the altar. The only open space is the rectangle where, come morning, the casket will stand.

She sets her viola case on the front pew. To her right is the light switch that controls the sconces placed along the walls in between the windows. She climbs over the altar and turns on the lights, illuminating the pulpit, reveling in the majesty of the sanctuary.

She tunes her viola. She begins "Amazing Grace," the notes sounding into the rafters, making the sanctuary feel cavernous. She fills the room with her rich, warm tone, her vibrato soaring to the farthest seat. When she finishes, she takes a moment, basking in the way the sound echoes into stillness.

She's about to leave, to step down from the pulpit, when she thinks of another piece. Obscure, French, originally composed for cello and orchestra. A sweeping motif filled with mourning and drama, love and turmoil and conscience. A piece she'd learned when she was nearing the end of eighth grade. She'd been relentless in her pursuit of perfection because it was her first opportunity to perform as soloist with her school orchestra. Her father had loved this piece. She also knows it was the first piece she played that really moved him. Something an orchestra conductor told her years ago, at summer camp when they were rehearsing Mahler, would make itself known in the recesses of her memory—that music, when done right, would linger in the ether of her soul.

She places the tip of her bow delicately on the string. She takes a breath. As she begins to move, lightly sweeping the bow across the instrument, her vibrato swelling, then shrinking, she pictures herself on the side of a mountain. Standing, feet planted firmly in the snow, she doesn't feel the cold—not her fingers, nor her cheeks, nor anywhere else. And it doesn't matter that snow continues to fall around her, tiny flakes dotting the viola's fingerboard. She, and her instrument, are protected.

That she hears the orchestra underneath her—feels the vibrations of the harp's stately pavane, the cello's steady warmth, and the growing tremolo of the violins—all of this compels her to keep playing. She throws herself into the solo line. Its first gesture, a question: *Where have you gone?* In its repetition, it strengthens. With the precise planting of her feet and the exact angle of her first finger against the frog of the bow, she extracts the melody—shifting, soaring—from the belly of the instrument. She asks with more force, more speed: *Where have you gone? Will I see you again?*

The snow falls faster, in larger clumps, the orchestra's volume a slow growth, her viola singing as it reaches the upper register. She knows the trick is to move the bow more quickly, with buoyant weight, the left hand dancing a fast and narrow vibrato, if she wants her cry to reach the heavens.

Where have you gone?

There are no answers; only silence filters through her fingers, through the viola. Each question hangs in the air, adding weight, further planting her.

Do you forgive me? At the end of your life, were you ashamed of me?

She presses and lifts her fingertips with expert precision. Her right arm guides the bow fluidly from string to string, her wrist bending and leveling as necessary. She uses the weight of her arm to maximize the sound she produces, knowing that straight pressure or brute force will cause the bow to crunch against the string. A teacher once told her that the sound of a viola should fall on the ear the way semi-dark chocolate melts on the tongue.

THERE COMES A break in the solo line. Now she rests, lowering the viola from her chin. She drops her right arm, and the tip of the bow brushes the grass. Behind her, the orchestra continues; she moves her head silently as they attack, in elaborate harmonies, the melodic line she'd landed a moment ago. She lifts her head when it rises a third, tapping her foot to each pizzicato from the violins as they echo her previous line.

Where have you gone?

When the orchestra descends from its heights and comes to rest, she resumes her part. The key shifts, calling for the lowest, most mournful notes. She keeps the bow at the frog for extra weight; her vibrato is nearly dead.

She finds redemption in the return of the harp's dance, the warmth of all the strings, and the sailing of her bow. The snow stops; the sky brightens. Before her, rising with the solo line to the softest heights the instrument allows, is a lone cardinal, its wings flapping with great effort. As she reaches her final note, as her fourth finger floats up the A string until she finds the wispy harmonic, as she adds the slightest vibrato and pulls the bow, nearly weightless, the bird glances her in the eye as it, too, continues to rise. She lifts her eyes, then rises to her tiptoes following the cardinal, swaying in the direction of his flight until there is no more bird to be seen, no more sound to be made. Silence now, from her instrument, from the orchestra, but she keeps the bow where it is, quivering against the string, struggling, enduring.

THEY SPEND MOST of the week locked in their room. When Vivienne isn't rehearsing, they take short walks, never far, jaunty in their pursuit of food and fun. They feed each other, their bodies constantly brushing up against each other. One night they have dinner with Olivia.

On the day of the first concert, Everett wakes early, leaves the room in search of good coffee and pastries. He drives to the florist, orders a bouquet of blue and white irises for his wife. After so much time spent together, he better understands the gravity of this performance, what it means for her to be performing as soloist with the Cleveland Orchestra—what it will mean for her stature, her career.

During the day they take it easy—relaxing, chatting, holding each other, gentle kisses—and when it's time to head to the concert hall, he drops her off, clad in jeans and loose sweater. She carries her garment bag, her makeup bag, and her viola. He goes back to the inn, takes a shower, picks up the bouquet.

IN THE DRESSING room, Vivienne takes the soft cloth she keeps in her instrument case and wipes down her viola, gently brushing the cloth against the wood. She re-attaches her shoulder rest, then lays it on a table next to her case. She walks over to the mirror, stops, and lets her eyes wash over her body.

She loves what she sees, who she sees.

The assistant knocks on the door, sent to fetch her, to bring her to the stage. When Vivienne opens the door, the assistant gasps. Her eyes well up; she begins a round of applause. "You look amazing," she says.

Vivienne laughs quietly, then kindly asks if it's time, even though she knows it is. She walks along the corridor until they reach the backstage area. The conductor is next, wordlessly hugging her before walking onstage.

"Stunning," she says. She winks, then takes her spot by the stage door. They listen as the orchestra settles down, stops tuning, as a disembodied voice reminds everyone that flash photography isn't permitted. The lights dim; the audience is silent.

When they rise the audience begins a round of applause. The musicians applaud by stomping their feet against the floor. The door opens, and out walks the conductor. She turns to the audience, bows, then signals to the concertmaster to tune the orchestra. After a few moments, the stage door opens, the lights momentarily blinding Vivienne. The applause overwhelms her; it feels as though the stage rumbles beneath her. She blinks, standing at that door.

SHE WILL ENTER from stage right, walking quickly, gripping her instrument in her left hand, the seam of her gown gathered in her right. She will be determined not to trip in the heels she's chosen for her Severance Hall debut.

She will feel cast among the highest of angels, the spotlight like a divine halo. She will walk across the stage, through the orchestra with authority. She will bow with a flourish, her smile the epitome of feminine grace. Everett, sitting in a reserved seat in the second row, applauding her entrance, will love her even more when he sees her. Regal. He will recognize her gown—the wedding gown, the one she loves, in the picture he loves of the woman he loves. He will hear the word *wife*, his ears and tongue exploring anew—listening, enunciating—excavating the newness of something that is not really so new.

"That's my wife," he will say almost audibly to Olivia who sits next to him, but not quite, because this is not something they are naming for people. Not just yet.

To Everett's eyes, Vivienne will always be without flaw, whomever she is, whatever form she takes. But for that night: The gown has been dyed midnight blue and dusted in Swarovski crystals from the hemline about halfway up the skirt. They will shrink in size from the bottom to their apex, looking more like a shimmering mist than actual gems. Her hands will glimmer, her nails coated in clear polish and a single gemstone placed delicately in the center of each. Vivienne will look out over the audience, waiting for the applause to die down, her eyes skimming everyone, recognizing a few faces. She will smile briefly at Olivia. She will linger when she meets Everett's eyes. *I am your wife,* she will think.

Moments from several nights ago will swirl around in her head. Everett's face when, after months of her silence, she chose to stand in her truth and pulled him into it, too. Glancing into his eyes, she thinks of how they looked—the way they watered until he blinked back tears, expansive in a way she'd never before noticed. In the days since, in the quiet of their makeshift honeymoon, his reactions in the moments when she revealed herself have returned to her: She thinks of how he gasped, still hears it in her ears. She thinks of how he didn't interrupt her, the way he listened with complete rapture. The way he held her hand as they drove back to the inn. The way he brought her that rose. The way he tucked her in, safe and sound, and then climbed in next to her. The gentle way he held her. The way he asked her why she'd chosen now, this moment—just days before her solo debut in a city she'd vowed to never return to—to say the things she had to say.

"I don't know," she'd said. "But I had to."

She thinks of how he touched her. How his hands caressed her body, knowing it would soon begin to change. He had never before been so loving, so gentle, and yet his lips so urgent. She thinks of how he kissed her with a different kind of ferocity, and the way she kissed him back, and for the first time in seven months, didn't stop.

Vivienne will feel all of that again, in an instant, and then she will return to the moment at hand. She will be desperate to make sure her viola remains in tune, but she'll refuse to tune it onstage, having tuned it moments before in the dressing room. She will remember the Reverend; she will think of how hard they both worked for this moment. She will feel the kind of intense, swift sadness a person thinks will topple them. She will think of all the things he feared, and she will let her fears go because they are his fears, and he is gone. She need not carry them forward any longer.

She will take a deep breath, assuming her stance, for a split second stepping backward, unsure of her footing. Everett will see the microscopic stumble, the only break in Vivienne's perfection, the kind of thing only a lover would notice. Everett will hold his breath for a moment, his legs coursing with enough energy to propel him onto the stage to catch his wife, should she fall.

Of course, she doesn't fall. Barely loses any balance. She doesn't need him up there. She holds mastery over her body, over her instrument. Over the stage, which, for the next ninety minutes, belongs to her.

She will place the bow just above the D string, ready for the orchestra to begin. Their notes must come from stillness, from silence. When she begins, her left hand will be static, the pitch slow and pure, like a thin beam of light soaring into the night. Only when she nears the end of the note will she give a few slight finger vibrations. Her minimal vibrato will rise through the stillness of the recital hall as she launches into the melodic solo line.

An opening like the earliest embers of sunlight bursting across a colorful sky. A piece she's been playing since high school, but never really understood, never really felt until recent years. This is what it is, she knows, to be a musician, to sit with the composer's genius for years and years and years—over the course of a life. This concerto is love. This concerto is death. When she lands, booming, on the open C string—the lowest note the viola produces—she will feel as though the instrument has exploded, that her insides are plastered all over the walls of the recital hall. Three C's, sounding at once.

Carried, carried, carried, away.

She is a vessel now, sound vibrating through the instrument—an extension of her heart, mind, and soul. She feels her father's warmth, rare though it was, and for the rest of her life, she will swear that she smelled her mother's perfume, permeating everything, coating the molecules moving between herself and the audience.

She will know—in that moment—that everything is okay, that she, her, Vivienne is okay.

"I got tired of running away from what I should've been running toward," she'd said as they drifted into slumber. She'd put her cheek against Everett's chest, brushed her lips against his nipple.

Carried, carried, carried, away.

In death they are fleeting, but for now they remain nearby, ever close. Watching, listening, praising. Her entire life: past, present, and future—husband, sister, father, mother—together, in the same room.

Seeing her. Loving she.

She will understand that no one is alone, that she was never alone, and that she never will be. Someone has come. Someone has found her.

ACKNOWLEDGMENTS

The process of writing is often solitary, but the act of bringing a book into the world is not. I was fortunate to work with two spectacular editors, Noa Shapiro, who kept her promise to stay by my side in the editorial trenches, and Caitlin McKenna, who led me across the finish line. I'm also enormously indebted to the rest of my Random House team: Carrie Neill, Windy Dorrestyn, Jaylen Lopez, Alison Rich, Erica Gonzalez, Dennis Ambrose, Samuel Wetzler, Michael Morris, Caroline Cunningham, and Madeline Hopkins, as well as Andy Ward, Maria Braeckel, and so many others. Special shoutout to Naomi Goodheart, Peter Dyer, and Will Lyman, because assistants truly do make the world go round. From the bottom of my heart, thank you all for ushering this book into the world.

To my agent and tireless champion, Robert Guinsler, and the entire team at Sterling Lord Literistic, thank you. To Leslie Shipman, Katie McDonough, and the entire team at The Shipman Agency, I'm grateful to be one of yours.

Hilary Leichter and Emma Copley Eisenberg, thank you for listening to my twenty-minute voice memos, for responding in kind, and for two decades of holding space for each other and sharing work. May our great art wheel forever spin. Sara Cappell Thomason for your reading, cheerleading, and hours-long phone conversations— I could not have finished this novel without your friendship. To Deesha Philyaw, Khaliah Williams, Esmé-Michelle Watkins, and George Kevin Jordan—my literary aunties—for all the advice and late-night phone calls. To Jennifer Baker and Jon Reyes for reminding me to hydrate, to rest, and for the delicious trips to KAL. To Isle McElroy and A. L. Major for the freedom to vent. To Morgan Jerkins, Cleyvis Natera, Karissa Chen, Nafissa Thompson-Spires, Marisa Seigel, Alejandro Varela, Jeffrey Masters, Vanessa Chan, Marcela Fuentes, Qian Julie Wang, Greg Mania, Matt Ortile, Catherine LaSota, Bethany Ball, Jonathan Vatner, Brian Lin, Alexandra Watson, John Manuel Arias, Robert Jones Jr., Peter Kispert, Michele Ferrari, Joss Lake, Melissa Rivero, Genevieve Hudson, Celia Laskey, Tracey Rose Peyton, Dianca London, Tope Folarin (where my bag at?), Rion Amilcar Scott, Jackson Howard, Molly McGhee, Minda Honey, Edgar Gomez, Harron Walker, Tommy Pico, Joseph Osmundson, Fran Tirado, Alexandra DiPalma, and Kenya Anderson, for your advice, hugs, and always keeping it fun. To my dearest, darlingest thotties far and wide, thank you for listening, reading, and *reading*! And to my beloved QuAC: Meredith Talusan, Austen Osworth, Michelle Hart, Nick White, Torrey Peters, and Garrard Conley: all of you have stolen my heart. Frankly, I would like it back.

I was fortunate to have several teachers in high school who nurtured my interest in writing, and who made me feel safe and seen in a violently racist and homophobic institution: Jim Quinn, Janice Fazio, Marty Kessler, Meg DeGulis, Margaret Mason, Karen Axelrod, Scott Lax, Carol Pribble, James Reeder, Jim Garrett, Paul Gibbs, Marilyn Doerr, Susan Carle, and Mayuri Reddy Wynn. To Janice Kalman for giving me a safe space to stuff envelopes. To Haverford College and Theresa Tensuan, for seeing a sad little political science major and welcoming me into the English Department, where my ambition to write a novel was born. To the graduate writing program at Sarah Lawrence College, for seeing me through two of the darkest years of my life: Kathleen Hill, Mary Morris, Joan Silber, Brian Morton, Stephen O'Connor, Lucy Rosenthal, and Carolyn Ferrell, and to the residence life and student affairs team: Paige Crandall, Carolyn O'Laughlin, Genevieve Knapp, Joshua Luce, Joan Reilly, and Natalie Gross, for helping me keep it even a little bit cute, and for giving me a job.

Thank you to the team at Juilliard: Sabrina Tanbara, Eddie Buggie, Melissa Hoodlet, Rebecca Kopec, and Nichole Knight, for helping me gain my city legs. To my HCZ fam: Rickey Laurentiis, Fred McKindra, Erica Buddington, Talia Saxe, Safia Elhillo, Camonghne Felix, Candice Iloh, Natali Rivers, Laura Vural, and Writing Corps writ large, thank you for being the smartest people I've ever worked alongside, and being luminaries in your own right. While working at Figure Skating in Harlem, I was granted significant time away to work on this novel at several residencies. That generosity can be credited to Amy Abbott, Darline Lalanne, Sharon Cohen, Mary-Lou Ibadlit, Tifané Williams, Wendy Tinkoff, Andrew Ford, Serena Aquino, Laura Hushion, Raquea Hemingway, Lisa Blue, Lisa Blair, LaJuné McMillian, Clarissa Minchew, Lindsay Wilkinson, Melissa Czarnik, and Andy Lane. Thank you for your camaraderie. To Included Health and Colin Quinn for giving me a job when I badly needed it, and for modeling a healthy, happy workplace. To Electric Literature: Halimah Marcus, Wynter Miller, Jo Lou, Kelly Luce, Katie Robinson, Preety Sidhu, and our many staff and interns, past and present, thank you for everything you do every single day.

Several institutions dedicated to art, music, and literature have supported me in writing this novel: Kinhaven Music School, VONA, the New York State Summer Writers Institute, Kimbilio for Black Fiction, Tin House, MacDowell, the New Orleans Writers Residency, VCCA, and Cloudhill (IYKYK). Each of these places left an imprint on me, and this novel. Thank you to M. Evelina Galang (forever #teamgalang), Amy Hempel, Mary Gaitskill, David Haynes, Angela Flournoy, Dolen Perkins-Valdez, Jeffrey Renard Allen, Lance

Cleland, Alexander Chee (and the inimitable #teamchee), for your sustained encouragement and support over the years. To Sarba Aguda and Chris Aguda, thank you for the cottage, the wine, and the fancy espresso maker.

It is, at this point in time, a well-known truth that queer people have the privilege of forming intimate bonds apart from our given family. I'm grateful to call these folks my chosen family. From childhood: Kelli Liverpool Bledsoe, Daniel Dittrick, John Hickman, and Amy McConnell, thank you for loving me exactly as I am. From college: Sonia Williams-Joseph, Jessica Joseph, Anna Krieger, Rosie Guerin, Jenny Rabinowich, Tovah Tripp, Shashi Neerukonda, Jimmy Meagher, Joanna Benjamin, Stephanie Rudolph, Katie Crisona, Meredith Zackey, Margalit Monroe, and Halley Cody, I love each of you to the moon and back. From my time in Philly: Ragina Arrington, Dave Weinstein, and Ashley Gunn. From graduate school: Jennifer Chelebi, Alexandra Ford, Sarah Kuhn, Leah Schnelbach, Kate Schmier, Kelly Devine, Nicole Dennis-Benn, Ursula Villarreal-Moura, Anna Qu, and T Kira Madden, look where we are now! From my time in New York City: Patrick Carter, Sean Davis, Thatcher, and Roosevelt; DJ Pimm and Mike O'Neill; Jaydan Heather Malsky and Mr. Sheffield; Pamela Matuszewski, Zero, Callie and Dulce; Tim McGeever, Heidi Denman Wade, Terence Degnan, Melanie Degnan, Stacie Evans, H'Rina DeTroy, and Grace Jahng Lee.

Music is the lifeblood of this novel, and I would be remiss not to thank the composers whose work inspired specific sections of this book: Johann Sebastian Bach, Bela Bartok, York Bowen, Johannes Brahms, Max Bruch, Gabriel Fauré, Paul Hindemith, Dmitri Shostakovich, Georg Philip Telemann, William Walton, John Williams, and Rebecca Clarke. To the teachers who taught me to play many of these pieces: Adrienne Elisha, Nancy Cooke, Marcia Ferritto, Aundrey Mitchell, Kenneth Kwo, Heidi Jacob, and Charles Parker, thank you for teaching me, even when I refused to practice.

To Andrea Gates Sanford and Darin Collins: thank you for always believing in me.

To Harriett Cody and Harvey Sadis: thank you for providing a place to stay.

To Libby and Don Sobota: thank you for being second parents.

To the Norrises, the Medleys, the McIntoshes, and my many, many cousins across generations: I stan each and every one of you.

To my mom, Joan M. Norris, and my siblings, Natalie, Jean, Marcus, and Rowan, and to my canine child—light of my life—Hughes Pondexter: quite simply, thank you for everything, always.

To my dad, Reverend Doctor Dennis Earl Norris, I miss you every day.

To anyone I may have forgotten, I'm sorry, I love you, but also I am les tired.

And finally, to the ancestors, specifically Black trans femmes: I am because you were.

ABOUT THE AUTHOR

DENNE MICHELE NORRIS is the editor-in-chief of *Electric Literature,* winner of the Whiting Literary Magazine Prize. She is the first Black, openly trans woman to helm a major literary publication. An Out100 Honoree, she has been supported by MacDowell, Tin House, and Kimbilio for Black Fiction, and appears in *McSweeney's, American Short Fiction,* and *Zora.* She is co-host of the critically acclaimed podcast *Food 4 Thot* and holds an MFA from Sarah Lawrence College.

ABOUT THE TYPE

This book was set in Caledonia, a typeface designed in 1939 by W. A. Dwiggins (1880–1956) for the Merganthaler Linotype Company. Its name is the ancient Roman term for Scotland, because the face was intended to have a Scottish-Roman flavor. Caledonia is considered to be a well-proportioned, businesslike face with little contrast between its thick and thin lines.